THE WOMAN UPSTAIRS

An unputdownable psychological thriller
with a breathtaking twist

MCGARVEY BLACK

Originally published as *A Text Before Dying*

JOFFE BOOKS

Revised edition 2023
Joffe Books, London
www.joffebooks.com

First published in Great Britain in 2021
as *A Text Before Dying*

This paperback edition first published in
Great Britain in 2023

Cover art by Nick Castle

ISBN: 978-1-80405-912-8

This book is dedicated to Marlene Scoville Pedersen — my partner in crime on many capers over the years. A constant supporter of my writing and one of my trusted readers, it's amazing we never ended up in jail. There's still time.

CHAPTER ONE

Monday — June 1, 2020

She told her husband she bought the high-powered black-and-gray binoculars to watch birds in Central Park. The truth was, thirty-one-year-old Zoe Brandt watched people — every single day.

Athletic and cute rather than conventionally pretty, Zoe tamed her overzealous, shoulder-length, wavy brown hair using numerous products, a round brush and a professional blow dryer. With warm hazel eyes and an infectious laugh, she was charming and approachable. A yet-to-be published mystery writer of short stories, she earned her living as a shift manager at Villa d'Luna, an upscale Italian restaurant on the Upper West Side of Manhattan.

When not at work, she'd spend hours reading mystery and conspiracy theory books or watching pedestrians stroll along Central Park West. From the third-floor picture window of her unusually gigantic New York City apartment, she scrutinized the clothing of passers-by, the produce stuffed in their grocery bags or the type of leash on their dog.

"There's a man walking by who has a choke collar on his chihuahua," Zoe screeched while peering through her binoculars during her daily FaceTime session with her best friend and partner in crime, Sean McAllister. "Choke collars are inhumane in any capacity but why would you put one on a dog that weighs less than four pounds? It makes no sense. Unless that man is running some kind of illegal dog fight? That's a huge business, you know. They hold them in basements of abandoned warehouses." Zoe adjusted the magnification on her binoculars. "The chihuahua man has dark, evil-looking eyes. I should call animal protection and report him."

"Didn't animal protection tell you to stop calling the last time you called?" said Sean softly.

"It's my moral and civic duty. I see so many people not treating their pets properly. Somebody has got to stop this travesty."

With her new high-powered binoculars Zoe's world had expanded significantly, and she regularly reported to Sean on which women needed root touch-ups in their hair or a refresher on their pedicure. She might identify a possible carcinoma on someone's face or comment on a particularly obvious comb-over. "I don't understand it," she would often say. "Don't balding men know everyone else can see that their part is halfway down their head and the hair that's left is being hijacked to drape over their hairless dome?" Observing a person's walk, physical appearance or the company they kept, she'd concoct intricate and detailed stories about their lives. When she saw someone particularly interesting, she'd jump in the elevator, race out of her building and follow them for blocks. Sean often joined her on the "investigations". If Zoe took things too far, which she often did, he was there to reel her in. His best friend made the ordinary exciting and Sean enjoyed the ride, even if it sometimes got them both into hot water.

Because her husband Conner was in law enforcement, Zoe hid her voyeurism from him, convincing herself she only watched people as research for her writing. When the Covid-19 virus forced everyone in New York into masks, it nearly ruined everything. Now unable to see faces, everyone looked the same. For that reason alone, Zoe Brandt couldn't wait for the pandemic to be over.

"It's no fun with everyone covered up," she said to Sean. "You can't see what anyone looks like anymore. It's just a sea of masks. If I can't see people's facial expressions, how will I know if they're up to something?"

"Let's go out on the street and resume our investigations on foot today," Sean replied. "We can cover a lot more territory together."

"I want to get a look in the back of the Metropolitan Museum of Art," said Zoe, squinting her eyes as she looked at Sean on her screen. "Something strange is going on over there. When I walked around behind the building yesterday, there were a bunch of men in blue jumpsuits loading wooden crates into unmarked white vans. I think they were possibly stealing antiquities."

"Maybe they were moving some art into storage," said Sean. "You might be jumping to conclusions."

"You sound just like Conner. All I know is, something looked funny. You know I have a sixth sense about these things; it's like I have radar."

"You must have had your radar turned off the day you called US immigration and blew the whistle on that Peruvian girl."

"She didn't know anything about Lima. How could you be Peruvian and know nothing about the largest city in the country? It was an honest mistake."

"Tell that to the FBI," said Sean.

"They already knew. Do you think I'm on a federal watchlist?" said Zoe. "Conner went completely ballistic that day, remember? I really thought my marriage might be over. How was I supposed to know she was the niece of the Peruvian ambassador? She said she didn't eat ceviche. Ceviche is practically the national dish of Peru."

"There was no way you could have known she was a legitimate exchange student," Sean said in solidarity.

The incident with the Peruvian ambassador had gotten pretty sticky until her FBI special agent husband stepped in to smooth ruffled political feathers. After a solemn promise by Zoe that she would never ever visit Peru under any circumstances, and a formal apology in writing from the Mayor of the City of New York, the Peruvian debacle had been put to bed.

While chatting with Sean in her kitchen, Zoe heard someone struggling to open the front door of her apartment. The door's lock hadn't been working properly for months.

"Sean, I gotta go," said Zoe in a half-whisper. "Conner's back from the store. We'll FaceTime later."

"Zoe? Where did these come from?" said Conner Brandt from their palatial though extremely cluttered living room. Holding up her pair of obviously powerful binoculars in his right hand and an overstuffed canvas weekend bag in his left, he stared at his wife through the opening between the dining room and kitchen. "These look like something we'd use down at the bureau for long-range surveillance of a drug cartel."

Standing with her back to him at the sink, Zoe spun around. *Damn. I didn't put the binoculars away.* "Oh, those . . . I bought them a while ago. Didn't I show them to you? I thought I had."

"And you have these because . . . ?"

"I've taken up . . . bird-watching . . . in the park."

"Bird-watching?" said Conner, staring at his wife, a dubious expression on his face. "You've never mentioned anything about birds before. You don't even like birds. You regularly scream at pigeons on the street."

"Are you kidding? I adore birds, especially pigeons with their cute warbling sounds."

"You call them flying rats. When did all this bird-watching start?" asked Conner, narrowing his eyes.

Shit. "So . . . I saw this documentary . . . on PBS . . . about bird-watching and got completely hooked. Turns out, birds are really interesting . . . and loads of fun too," said

Zoe, a forced smile plastered across her face. "We should go together sometime. There are so many different species in the park. You'll love it."

"Okay," said Conner warily, putting the binoculars back on the table. "Sure. We can do that. It's just that you've never mentioned this new-found hobby before."

"Great," said Zoe, still smiling a little too much. "We'll go on Saturday morning."

"Hello?" said Conner, holding up his weekend bag. "I'm leaving today for five days for in-service training at Quantico, remember? I won't be home until Saturday early evening. I've told you five times."

"Right, I forgot."

"We can go bird-watching on Sunday morning," said Conner with a gotcha smile. "I can't wait to hear all your new bird knowledge."

"It's a date. You'll be really impressed with how much Audubon stuff I know."

"What's going on, Zoe?" said Conner, squinting and tilting his head.

"Nothing," said Zoe, widening her eyes. "You insisted I stop all my, as you call it, 'conspiracy theory stuff,' so I took up bird-watching. I thought you'd be happy about that."

"Why is my bullshit meter going off?" said Conner. "Remember our deal, no more crazy, deep-state plot stuff. You get way too obsessed and then that little narrative in your head takes over your world, and ultimately takes over mine. Even your therapist said, and I quote, your 'morbid curiosity and convoluted conclusions affect our marriage in an unhealthy way.'"

"I told you, I'm bird-watching. Robins, blue jays, cardinals, bald eagles."

"There are no bald eagles in Central Park."

"There have been sightings."

"Zoe, if you're starting in again with the whacky stuff, I'm telling you right now, I've got a huge problem with it," said Conner, tucking a few more items into his travel bag.

"Sometimes, I think you married me only because I was in the FBI. You're always pumping me for information which, by the way, I will never reveal. I don't want to go down that crazy path with you again. When you get like that you become obsessive and impossible to live with. Let's not forget how you've put my career in jeopardy."

Zoe flew across the room to her husband and put her arms around him. "Now you're the one with the conspiracy theory. Nothing's going on. I'm just watching little woodpeckers peck."

Conner gave her a look, kissed his wife on the forehead and let out a sigh. "Make sure if you go over to the park you wear your mask and gloves," he said before he went into their bedroom to finish packing. "And, could you pick up all your crap that's strewn from one end of this place to the other. Don't you ever put anything away?"

Zoe let out a sigh of relief when her husband left the room. *That was close. How could I have been so careless to leave those binoculars out? Bald eagles? Even I think that sounds stupid.*

CHAPTER TWO

When Conner finally left for his five-day FBI training in Virginia, Zoe grabbed her binoculars and sat in her favorite surveillance spot; a navy-blue upholstered chair next to the picture window in the living room. Taking her good binoculars out of their case, she was about to start her long-range viewing when a FaceTime call from Sean interrupted her.

The two worked together at Villa d'Luna where Sean did a little bit of everything and the restaurant's owner, Miranda, was totally dependent upon him. Part-time sommelier, purchasing agent, bookkeeper, and wait-staff psychologist, Sean even subbed in if one of the wait staff called out sick. He and Zoe had met three years earlier when she started on the night shift. From their first shift together, they had been hopelessly devoted to each other. When not working, they talked, texted or FaceTimed dozens of times each day.

"Hey," said Sean as his freckled face surrounded by red hair and a closely-cropped ginger beard, popped up on her iPhone, "just finished watching *The Golden Girls*, the one where they get arrested for prostitution."

"I love that episode," said Zoe, still holding the binoculars up to her eyes, homing in on a family of three walking on the street below.

"Oh. My. God," screamed Sean, looking down at the palm of his hand.

"What?" said Zoe, glancing over at her phone screen.

"There's a brown spot on my palm. I've never seen it before. Do you think it's a melanoma?"

"Show me."

Sean held the palm of his hand up to the screen. Zoe picked up her phone and zoomed in so she could better look at Sean's spot. "How long have you had this?"

"I don't know, I just noticed it," he said, touching it. "What if it already spread?"

"You're jumping to conclusions."

"Said the queen of conclusion-jumping."

"Don't pick at it," said Zoe, watching him scratch.

"Oh my God, do you think I'll need chemo?" said Sean as he licked his finger and vigorously rubbed the lethal spot on his hand. A moment later he let out a yelp of relief. "It came off," he said as he put his finger in his mouth. "Soy sauce. I had sushi last night."

"You're an idiot."

"Thank you. Want to do something tonight since Conner's out of town?" said Sean. "We could spy on that florist on 99th Street. Or what about the guy who owns the dry cleaners on 101st? You always say his Greek accent sounds fake and that he's weird."

"He strokes the clothes and rubs his fingers over the fabric when I drop stuff off," said Zoe, narrowing her eyes. "He's totally creepy. I could see him being someone who exposes himself. Not only that, when I went to the post office last week, I could swear his photo was in the 'most wanted' pictures posted on the wall."

Since becoming best of friends, Sean had indulged Zoe's obsession with sleuthing and solving crimes. While he knew it was all a game, he always had a good time whenever they went off on "assignment." She was Sherlock Holmes and he, Dr. Watson.

Sean defended Zoe when his other friends questioned his relationship. "I know she's a little out there," he'd say, "but we have such a good time. What's the harm?" While he considered their activities just for fun, she took much of what they investigated seriously, making their excursions even more fun and exciting for him.

"Let's go over the West Side Strangler case again," said Zoe. "Six women have been murdered so far, always on the fifteenth of the month and always on the Upper West Side of Manhattan. It must mean the killer lives or works on the West Side."

"How do we know it's a he?"

"A female murderer might have gotten it over on one or two of the victims, but some of those women who died were really fit. Rosie Florio was a professional dancer and took kick-boxing. She would have been strong enough to fight off a woman. Plus, they were all strangled, which takes a tremendous amount of upper body strength. I definitely think it has to be a man. From what I can tell from the news reports, the police have nothing. They need our help, don't you think?"

"Definitely. Let's go over the facts," said Sean, suddenly serious. "The first murder was on December 15th — Lisa Eng, mid-twenties, inside her apartment on West 95th Street."

"Right," said Zoe, still looking out the window.

"Next, Carly Faircloth, mid-thirties, on 104th Street in January, also strangled. Then, Nicole Barrett in February on West 96th Street, followed by Rosie Florio on West 97th in March."

"Don't you think it's interesting that the pandemic and the lockdown hasn't slowed our killer down. He stays right on schedule — the fifteenth of the month."

"Good point," said Sean. "Okay, the fifth killing in April was slightly different. Michelle Rothberg, was a little older than the others, in her thirties, and according to the police reports, she was temporarily disabled, having recently had foot surgery."

"Right. They said on the news that she wasn't supposed to be walking around. But, witnesses in the neighborhood said they saw her limping down her street the day she was killed," said Zoe, still scanning the street below.

"Last but not least, victim number six, Katie Tierney on May 15th on West 100th," said Sean. "The police believe all six women let the killer into their apartment because there was no forced entry. Why would a woman let anyone into their apartment when they know there's a serial killer loose?"

"Maybe they all knew him?"

"Let's walk around to all the West Side Strangler kill locations today? Maybe we can talk to a few locals. We might uncover something the police missed."

"I can't go sleuthing for a while," said Zoe, sighing but still pointing her magnification glasses on the street below. "Before he left today, Conner found my new binoculars and gave me the third degree. He made me promise not to investigate anything. He gets so worked up over this stuff."

"Things did get a little bit out of hand last year," said Sean.

"Are you taking his side? I thought you were *my* friend," said Zoe, still looking out the window while playing with the focus controls on the binoculars. "These new binocs are incredible, so much better than my old ones. I see a man reading a newspaper across the street in the park and I can read the headline. There's an old lady walking down Central Park West with a stroller. She's coming towards me. Bet you a million dollars she's got a dog in the carriage. Let me see." Zoe played with her focus controls again. "Well, it's either a beagle or a very hairy baby." She put the glasses down and looked over at Sean's face. "Why do people walk dogs in strollers? Aren't dogs supposed to get exercise? Isn't that the point of 'walking a dog?'"

Zoe turned back to the window and looked through her binoculars again. "I'll tell you one thing; all these masks are ruining everything. I can't see anyone's face. Six months ago, most people had never tried one on. Now, they color-coordinate their masks with their outfits." Zoe shook her head in disgust.

"I bedazzled mine," said a smiling Sean, holding up a royal-blue mask decorated with faux diamonds in neat rows. Zoe glanced down at her phone.

"Nice, Sean. Make me one?" she said, turning back to her binoculars and screwing around with the focus controls again. "I'm still getting used to these but I think if I get it just right I can see even more detail. There. Oh my God! Wow!"

"What?" said Sean.

"Across the street on the edge of the park, there's a man and a woman sitting on opposite ends of a bench with their backs to me. It looks like they're talking to each other," said Zoe, her voice getting higher. "I can't tell if they're together. The man's wearing a NYC Fire Department hat, a red T-shirt, and gray sweats. He's got on a NY Rangers mask and I think, Ray-Ban Wayfarer sunglasses. The woman has on dark-blue leggings, a long-sleeved white T-shirt and a white baseball hat. She's wearing a navy-blue mask with some kind of emblem on the side that looks like a white dress shirt with a red tie. She's also wearing a pair of oversized blue aviator sunglasses. Those are seriously nice shades. Between her glasses, mask and hat, I can't see her face at all. This masking thing totally cramps my spy style."

"What brand of sunglasses is she wearing?"

"Wait a second, they're both playing with their phones and . . . oh my God, I can see their phone screens. Sean, I can read what's on their phone. I can see what they're doing, what they're saying."

"Get out!"

"No seriously," said Zoe, leaning closer to the glass in the window. "The man is bidding on a used lamp on eBay. His username is SlyDog303 and he just bid twenty-eight dollars for this incredibly hideous lamp. Why would anyone want that lamp?"

"You can really see all that from your window? Holy shit," said Sean, laughing. "What's the item number on the lamp, I'll go to that page on eBay and bid up his auction."

Zoe giggled. "Let me see what the woman is up to," she said, shifting her gaze to the far end of the same bench.

"What's she doing?"

"Hold on a minute. I think she's texting. Yes, she's texting."

"Can you read it?" said Sean.

"Oh my God. I think so."

"This is fantastic. It takes stalking to a whole new level."

"Sean, I can read her texts," said Zoe, squealing. "She's typing." Zoe read the first text to Sean. "'When I got furloughed from T and C, I thought it would only be a few weeks. Now, they're closing some stores. Rumor is they're going to file for bankruptcy. Great! What am I supposed to do now?'"

"What do you think T and C is?" said Zoe, her eyes remaining on the woman's phone.

"Town and Country?" said Sean.

"That's a magazine, not a store," she said, looking over at Sean's face and giving him a disapproving look.

"Sorry. If it's a store, it's got to be Thayer and Company, the high-end clothing store."

"Good one, Seanie," said Zoe, turning back to her glasses. "Okay, wait a minute, she just got a text back. It says . . . 'Relax. Everything is under control. Forget about T and C. You're too good for that place. It will all be over Thursday, my love.'"

"What will all be over Thursday?" said Sean, his eyes widening. "This is getting good. Keep watching."

"Holy moley," said Zoe, her binoculars laser-focused on the woman's phone. "What do you think that means?"

"Maybe she's getting a new job?"

"Hold on, she's texting again," said Zoe. "'My husband is driving me crazy. I want it done now and I hate using this stupid phone you gave me.'"

"What does she want done?" said Sean.

"Wait, she just got another text," said Zoe, glued to the window. "The name of the person she's texting with is 'Sr.

Bello'." As the texts went back and forth, Zoe read each one to Sean.

SR. BELLO: Where's your husband right now?
WOMAN IN THE MASK: Where he always is, attached to my hip bidding on junk on eBay. I can barely breathe when I'm with him. He deserves whatever he gets.

"What does that mean?" said Zoe, turning away from her binoculars for a second to look at Sean's equally puzzled face.

"Don't look at me. Keep watching them," Sean commanded.

Zoe lifted the binoculars to her eyes again and read the texts to Sean as they appeared.

SR. BELLO: Trust me, it will get done and then we'll be together.
WOMAN IN THE MASK: You promise, Thursday is a go? We'll be together after that?
SR. BELLO: Not right away, have to give it some time. But soon. A few months.
WOMAN IN THE MASK: By October?
SR. BELLO: Yes.
WOMAN IN THE MASK: What's going to happen?
SR. BELLO: Better you don't know anything. I've got everything arranged. I'll be in touch when it's all over. Always remember, I love you. Very soon, we'll be together in our own place.
WOMAN IN THE MASK: Then I'll never let you out of bed. Ugh. Going home now with him, unfortunately. XXX.

Zoe looked over at Sean's face. His mouth was wide open. "Are you thinking what I'm thinking?" he said.

"That the woman in the mask is planning to kill her husband and this Sr. Bello is going to do it," said an agitated Zoe, her binoculars refocused and zoomed in on the couple on the bench. She looked at the man wearing the NY Rangers mask.

"Now the husband is bidding on a bunch of green glass bowls on eBay and the woman is shopping for thong bathing suits on Amazon," said Zoe, watching her for a few more moments.

"What is she doing now?"

"Hold on, she's texting someone about a hair appointment. Wait a second, something's different. Before, she was using an Android phone and now she's got an iPhone."

"What do you think that means?" said Sean.

Zoe picked up her phone from the table and looked directly at her friend's face. "She's obviously got a burner phone. Sean, we've got to call the police right now. That woman is obviously planning to murder her husband."

"We don't know for sure that's what's happening."

"What else could it be?" said Zoe, getting excited. "It seems pretty clear to me. The woman in the mask and Sr. Bello are going to kill her husband on Thursday."

"Maybe her husband committed a heinous crime or maybe he beats her and they're going to expose him, not actually kill him. Maybe it's a happy thing? Maybe they're the good guys?"

"Seriously Sean?" said Zoe, scrunching up her forehead while staring him down. "They're totally plotting to murder her husband. We've got to follow them. Are you with me?"

Sean reluctantly nodded. "I guess."

CHAPTER THREE

"You've got to come over here right now," shouted Zoe to Sean as she got up from the chair, her eyes still fixed on the couple in the park. "No, no, no. Shit. The woman's getting up. We're going to lose them. Wait . . . she's walking over to the man and standing in front of him. I can't see her face because of her damn mask. She must be talking because her head and hands are moving. If she's not talking, she's got a really bad tic."

"She's probably talking," said Sean, rolling his eyes. "What's happening now?"

"Nothing. She's just standing there, staring at him. She's turning around and facing me. She's wearing a gold chain necklace with a charm of the letters GG. Those must be her initials."

"Who wears both of their initials on a necklace," said Sean. "It's either the first initial or the whole first name spelled out. Nobody wears both."

"Maybe her name is Gigi and she spells it GG?" said Zoe.

"No one does that either. I'm walking out the door right now," said Sean. "Keep your eyes on them. I'll be there in eight minutes."

"I'll meet you downstairs in front of my building," said Zoe, grabbing her bag, mask and a pair of plastic gloves.

With her adrenaline pumping, Zoe adjusted her mask as she got in the elevator. When the doors opened in the lobby, an older, gray-haired doorman sporting a red-white-and-blue striped mask waved to her. "That you, Mrs. Brandt? Hard to tell who anyone is these days."

"It's me, Don," said Zoe as she tore out the front door of the building praying the masked couple on the bench hadn't left. Looking across the street, she saw they were still there but were now both standing. Waiting for the traffic to pass so she could cross the street, she FaceTimed Sean again.

"How far away are you now?" she yelled into the phone, her eyes fixed on the masked couple.

"Three blocks," said Sean, breathing hard as he ran.

"Hurry, Sean!"

"Hey, dial it down, Miss Marple, I'm running as fast as I can."

"They're moving southeast now," shouted Zoe as she sprinted across Central Park West. "They're heading into the middle of the park. I'm going to follow them. When you get to my building, walk directly across the street into the park and head southeast. Call me and I'll direct you to wherever I am."

As Zoe got closer to the couple, she slowed down. The man and woman appeared to be walking leisurely, almost strolling which allowed time for Sean to catch up. Ten minutes later, with Zoe directing him, Sean caught up to her.

"I thought my lungs were going to burst," he said, bending over, trying to catch his breath. "It's not easy running in a mask. Where are they?"

Zoe tipped her chin up to the right. "Over there where the path splits?"

Sean followed her gaze. "The guy with the green mask and the woman with the brown hair in a ponytail and pink mask?"

"Not them, further to the right. The man has on a New York Rangers mask."

Sean looked at her in total deadpan. "Why would you think I know what the NY Rangers' colors are?"

"Blue, white and red, you're welcome. Do you see the masked man standing next to the woman in the navy mask?"

"I see them. How do you want to play this?"

"Let's tail them. The woman said in her text that she was going home," said Zoe. "We'll follow them to their building, find out their address, copy down their name from the mailbox and go right to the police. We'll be heroes. We might even get our pictures in the newspaper or be interviewed on CNN. Wouldn't that be so cool? Except I have not had a haircut in months. Isn't that just my luck. I finally get on prime time and my hair is a total disaster. I wonder if I could get a hair appointment?"

"What the hell are you talking about?" said Sean, making a face. "Someone is going to be murdered and you're worried about your hair?"

"I haven't had a haircut in months."

"Neither has anyone else. Can we get back to our case?"

Zoe nodded as they followed the masked couple walking east through the park. Careful to keep a safe distance behind, they hung back while the couple wandered up hills and around a pond and then finally exited the park on 96th Street and Fifth Avenue. Taking cover behind a tree, Zoe and Sean watched the couple look uptown and step off the curb into the street.

"Shit, they're looking for a taxi," Zoe gasped. "We're going to lose them."

"No we won't, I'm getting us an Uber," said Sean looking down at his phone.

"Good one, Sean."

"I'm not just a pretty face."

Minutes later a yellow cab stopped in front of the masked couple. As they climbed in, Sean and Zoe's Uber drove up right behind the cab as it pulled away from the curb. The two sleuths jumped into the blue Honda Civic and told the driver to follow the yellow cab in front of them.

"I get it," said the young Uber driver with a big smile, "This is like in one of those action movies. I can do this for you."

The blue Honda Civic stayed right behind the yellow cab as the two vehicles moved swiftly down Fifth Avenue passing the Metropolitan Museum of Art and the Plaza Hotel. At East 55th Street, the masked couple's cab pulled over.

"We'll get out here," Sean shouted from the back seat.

"We've got to be careful they don't see us," said Zoe as they got out of the car. "Maybe we should walk on the other side of the street. That way we'll be able to watch them from a distance without attracting attention."

The masked couple walked slowly down Fifth Avenue looking in the windows of various shops, many of which were closed.

"Look at her," said Zoe, her eyes never leaving the couple on the other side of the street. "She just conspired with her lover to kill her husband and now she's window shopping with the man she's going to have murdered. She's quite the cool cucumber."

"We don't know for sure she's planning a murder. Maybe they meant something else," said Sean.

"Like what?"

"I don't know," he said, shaking his head. "Look, now they're turning right and walking towards Rockefeller Center."

Sean and Zoe darted across Fifth Avenue through the sparse city traffic pretending to window shop whenever they got too close to the couple. They followed them into the famous Rockefeller Plaza, home to an ice-skating rink in winter that turned into a restaurant in spring and summer. This year the plaza was empty, like everywhere else in New York City.

The amateur detectives stayed a fair distance behind the couple, who were soon on the move again, walking south on Fifth Avenue unaware they had company. At 42nd Street, the couple turned left and walked towards Grand Central

Station with Zoe and Sean right behind. The masked man opened the big brass door to the train station allowing his wife to pass through.

"Oh my God, do you think they're taking a train somewhere far away? What if they live in Connecticut?" said Sean. "I don't have any money."

"I've got my debit card," said Zoe. "C'mon, we have to keep going. We can't stop now."

They followed the couple through the huge train station to the entrance of the Lexington Avenue subway line.

"They're not going on a commuter train, they're going for the subway," said Zoe, pulling out her wallet. "I have my MetroCard. I'll swipe us both through."

The masked couple went through the turnstiles and walked down the stairs leading to the downtown trains. Moments later, all four stood on the platform. There were few people around so Zoe and Sean tried to hide behind a large pillar. Soon, a practically empty 6 Lexington Avenue Local pulled into the station with a screech and a hiss.

The sleuths got on at the opposite end of the same subway car as the masked couple. The car sat in the station without moving for nearly two minutes, when the bells sounded. Just as the doors were about to close, the 4 Express pulled in across the platform. Before Zoe and Sean could react, the masked couple jumped up and ran out to the express train. Zoe and Sean tried to follow but the doors of their car shut before they could get off. Seconds later their train pulled out of the station.

"Damn it," Zoe shouted. "How did we let that happen?"

"Stay calm. We'll get out at the next express stop. Maybe they'll be there," said Sean. "That will be 14th Street. That's where we'll get off."

Their local train moved slowly and soon the express train carrying the masked couple blew right by them in the dark tunnel.

"Shit," said Zoe, biting her lip. "We're going to lose them. If they get away, that man is as good as dead."

CHAPTER FOUR

When the number 6 local pulled into 14th Street station, Zoe and Sean bolted off the train onto a deserted platform while looking in both directions.

"No. No. No," shouted Zoe, stamping her feet. "Shit." Frantically looking around, they spotted the nearest staircase and raced up the steps hoping the masked couple had gotten off at that station and were somewhere in the vicinity.

Zoe was the first to reach the top but there was no sign of the masked woman or man on the street. "You go right, I'll go left," she commanded. Several minutes later they both returned to the subway entrance out of breath.

"We lost them," said Zoe throwing her head back and looking up at the sky. "Now, we have no idea where they live. They could be anywhere. They could be going all the way to Lower Manhattan to the City Hall stop."

"Wait a second," said Sean, "Let's think about this a minute. If you lived near City Hall, would you *ever* take the local?"

Zoe thought for a moment. "Probably not, it would take forever. I'd only take the local if the train board said the express was down or delayed."

"How about if you were going to Canal Street?" said Sean, his eyebrows raised.

"No way, would take too long," said Zoe, following his reasoning. "But, I would take the local from 42nd to 14th Street or maybe even to Bleecker, but no further."

"Exactly. It stands to reason that our masked couple got off at either 14th or Bleecker," said Sean. "That means they must live somewhere on the east side between those two stops."

The two friends stared at each other for a long while without speaking. "That's a really big area," said Zoe, breaking the silence, looking defeated. "We're never going to find them, are we? That poor man is going to die. We've *got* to do something."

"Why don't you call Conner and ask him to help us," said Sean.

"I can't do that," said Zoe, agitation visible on her face. "He'd freak out. Remember what happened last year when I thought the woman at the nail salon on 101st Street was a Ukrainian spy?"

"Turned out she was from Sweden," said Sean nodding in solidarity. "She'd never even been to the Ukraine. Then there was that Brazilian au pair who worked in your building that you thought was part of an international slave-trade ring."

Zoe nodded slowly.

"You called the Brazilian embassy. Poor girl almost got deported," said Sean.

"I thought she was recruiting other au pairs," said Zoe, rolling her eyes. "I couldn't let that happen, could I?"

"Maybe you should have waited until you knew for sure before you alerted the authorities."

"I guess. When Conner had to leave work and intervene with the consulate and the Brazilians threatened to call the State Department, that's when the shit really hit the fan."

"I remember," said Sean, grimacing. "Wasn't a good day for you."

"That's when Conner made me start to see Dr. Eisdorfer."

"I remember that too," said Sean. "I never thought therapy was necessary. That was overkill if you ask me."

"I had to go, or my marriage was going to implode," said Zoe. "Conner insisted. It wasn't so bad. Dr. Eisdorfer was pretty nice and she always kept Jolly Rancher candy in a bowl on her coffee table."

"I love the watermelon flavor," said Sean, his eyes lighting up.

"I like the sour apple. Anyway, Dr. Eisdorfer said I had an extremely creative imagination but made me promise Conner that I was finished with all the conspiracy stuff. I don't consider what you and I investigate to be 'conspiracy stuff'. We make educated opinions based on hard evidence."

"That Brazilian au pair *was* acting very strange," said Sean supportively. "She didn't know a thing about caipirinhas when you asked her, remember? That's the official drink of Brazil. You can't be from Brazil and not know about caipirinhas."

"That's exactly what I thought," said Zoe, taking one last look around for the masked couple. "I still think that au pair was involved with an international madam or drug smuggler. She could have been a drug mule."

Half a block down on the opposite side of the street, the masked man and woman emerged from a Jewish deli. "Look, it's them," said Zoe, pointing as Sean's eyes followed her finger.

"Where?"

"Over there, across the street, halfway down the block, walking past that red SUV. See them?"

"Yes," said Sean. "It's definitely them."

"C'mon, let's go," said Zoe as she ran across the street with her partner in crime by her side. "We're back in business."

Hanging back, they carefully followed the masked couple down East 13th Street.

"She's quite the ice princess," said Zoe, "strolling leisurely with the man she's planning to murder like she doesn't have a care in the world. You'd never guess from her demeanor that she was going to have her husband bumped off in a few days. She's even holding his arm. If I didn't know the truth, I'd swear she likes him."

"No kidding," said Sean walking alongside her. "Slow down. There's hardly anyone else on this street. We don't want to draw attention to ourselves. Once we follow them to their home address, we go to the police, right? Then, we're done."

"Wait, what's the man doing?" Zoe gasped. "Shit, he's hailing another cab." When a yellow taxi pulled up next to the masked couple, the man opened the car door for his wife and they both climbed in.

"We've got to get a car fast," said Zoe. "They're stopped at that light. We've only got a minute."

Frantically, Sean looked up and down the streets. There were hardly any cars on the roads and not a taxi in sight. "I'll get us an Uber?" Sean shouted as he opened his app.

"We're going to lose them," Zoe wailed, her eyes still on the couple's car. "How far away is the Uber?"

"There are none around here. The nearest one is in Midtown," said Sean shaking his head. The light at the intersection turned green and the yellow taxi containing the masked couple turned left and disappeared.

Defeated, the two sleuths turned around and walked silently over to Fifth Avenue heading towards Midtown when Zoe abruptly stopped and faced Sean. "We have to go to the police. If that man in the NY Rangers mask turns up dead and we do nothing, it'll be on us."

They googled police stations on the West Side and got an Uber to the 24th Precinct on West 100th Street.

A police officer wearing a face mask took their temperatures at the entrance and asked them a few questions about their general health. They were then directed to the front desk to speak to another masked policeman sitting behind a Plexiglas divider.

"Can I help you?" said the uniformed officer looking down at some papers on his desk.

"Yes," said Zoe, swallowing. "We want to report a murder."

The cop's head jerked up and he sat back straight, his brows knitting together. "Excuse me, with the masks and the Plexiglas, it's extremely hard to hear these days. Can you say that again?"

"We're here to report a murder," said Sean loudly.

"Where did this murder happen?" said the cop, slightly flustered, preparing to take notes.

Zoe looked at Sean and then back at the police officer. "It didn't exactly happen yet, but it's going to."

"When?" said the cop.

"Thursday, a man is going to be murdered this Thursday," said Zoe confidently.

"What's the man's name and where is this murder taking place?" said the cop writing notes.

"We don't exactly know his name," said Zoe, "or where it's going to happen, but it *is* going to happen on Thursday."

"Do you know *how* this murder is going to happen?" said the cop, a leery expression creeping into his eyes above his NYPD mask.

"We don't know that either," said Sean, jumping in.

"Do you know who the perpetrator is?" said the cop, now relaxing and fiddling with the mask loop over his right ear.

"We think his name is Sr. Bello. He's the boyfriend of the wife of the man who is going to be killed," said Zoe matter-of-factly.

"We don't know for sure that he's her boyfriend," Sean said, looking at Zoe.

"He talked about being in bed with her," she said. "Who else would he be?"

"Excuse me," said the cop, rapping on the Plexiglas to get their attention. "Let me get this straight. You're here to report a murder that didn't happen yet. You don't know who the victim or the perpetrator is or how, where or why."

"We know why," said Zoe with absolute confidence. "The woman wants to get rid of the husband so she can be with the boyfriend. It happens every day, officer."

"I'm going to call the duty detective and let him do a more thorough interview with you," said the policeman. "Because of Covid, we're not using our conference rooms so Detective Williams and Detective Kim will meet you down here in the lobby. Take a seat."

CHAPTER FIVE

Six months earlier on December 17, 2019, the police had found Lisa Eng's half-naked body in a pool of melted chocolate-chip ice cream. Ironically, they later learned from her family chocolate chip was her favorite flavor. She was the first. By June of 2020, five more women would be found strangled to death on the Upper West Side of Manhattan.

> *THE NEW YORK ECHO — December 26, 2019*
> *WOMAN FOUND MURDERED ON WEST 95TH ST.*
> *by Tommy Devlin*
>
> *Breaking News: According to police, Lisa Eng, 27, was found murdered in her apartment on West 95th Street. After attending a company holiday party at a loft in Soho on December 15, Ms. Eng and a female co-worker walked to the subway. Several bystanders on the subway platform in Soho remembered seeing the young woman while she waited for the uptown train. They reported she had been shouting to another woman waiting across the tracks on the downtown side. Both women appeared to be intoxicated. When Ms. Eng's uptown train pulled into the station, witnesses saw her step onto the train, trip and nearly fall. Several reports say*

a stocky man with dark curly hair, hat, scarf and glasses caught her by the elbow, stopping her fall. He then settled her onto an empty seat and sat directly across from her as the train pulled out of the station.

At midnight, cameras at the 86th Street station captured Ms. Eng getting off the train onto an empty platform. It was unclear from the footage if anyone was with her.

The police found Ms. Eng's body two days later on December 17th. Preliminary reports from the medical examiner determined that Ms. Eng had been strangled.

Detective Daryl Williams and Detective Heather Kim from the 24th Precinct whose jurisdiction covers most of the Upper West Side of Manhattan are the lead detectives on the case.

"There don't appear to be any signs of forced entry," said Detective Heather Kim. "It's possible the person who did this was known to Ms. Eng. We're following up on a number of leads."

There is no indication that the man seen with Ms. Eng on the train had anything to do with her murder. Police are asking him to come forward to provide any information he may have about that night.

With unrelenting headlines, Lisa Eng's murder was front-page news. Her death would be the start of a string of killings that would soon terrorize women across the Upper West Side of Manhattan. That investigation would remain a major headline until March of 2020 when a deadly virus hit New York and bumped the murders right off the front page.

CHAPTER SIX

Monday — June 1, 2020

The Covid-19 pandemic had turned the 24th Police Precinct into a beehive of activity that had taken its toll on police resources. With an uptick in violent crime, increased homelessness along with numerous protest marches, New York City was nearly at its breaking point. Add to that, a serial killer had strangled six young women on the West Side of Manhattan. Stretched thin, the NYPD on permanent high alert had no time to humor people touting wild conspiracy theories about murder plots hatched in Central Park.

Partners for more than two years, Detectives Daryl Williams and Heather Kim headed up the now five-month-old West Side Strangler task force. Williams, a six-foot tall former US Marine with dark hair and brown eyes instantly conveyed tough and smart. Gruff but kind at his core, Williams had been an NYPD police officer for nearly twenty years. Immigrating to New York from Jamaica with his family when he was ten, he had long ago lost the gentle island lilt in his speech and now sounded like a born New Yorker. Petite but tough, Heather Kim, eight years his junior, wore her shiny shoulder-length black hair pulled back in a no-nonsense ponytail to 'keep it out of my freakin' eyes'. Before joining homicide, Heather had worked in the NYPD cyber division. A serious technology geek who missed nothing, she was all business and got straight to the point. Both highly decorated, Williams and Kim were considered the gold standard by NYPD brass.

The first Strangler killing occurred at the end of 2019, months before an unknown virus would change everyone's lives. With a city-wide lockdown, adding a serial killer into the mix pushed the city resources to the brink and the mayor wanted the murders stopped — yesterday.

On the third floor of the 24th Precinct, every inch of wall space in the "Strangler War Room" as it had been dubbed, was filled with intelligence and notes about the case. A large white-board with lists of locations and possible suspects was written in blue, red and green and fixed at one end of the room. Pictures of victims, the buildings where the crimes took place along with timelines were pinned on a battered corkboard wall. Stacks of folders and photos were piled in every corner.

Seated at the beat-up rectangular wooden table with more coffee cup stains on it than clean surface, five police officers combed through witness interviews and other data related to the case.

A large map of the Upper West Side of Manhattan hung prominently on a long wall. Each of the six murder locations were marked with a large red X. A duplicate copy of that map was also pinned to the bulletin board in the bullpen next to the detectives' desks.

"There's a pattern here. We just don't know what it is yet," said Daryl looking up at the map for what he figured was the millionth time.

Walking over to the whiteboard Heather grabbed a blue marker and pointed at the map. "Let's give the crime-scene locations another look," she said. "December, Lisa Eng on West 95th Street and Tenth Avenue."

Marking the location on a clean whiteboard, she continued. "Next, Carly Faircloth on 104th and Columbus, then Nicole Barrett on West 96th between Columbus and Amsterdam."

"We've been over this a million times," chirped one of the younger cops sitting at the table. "Ain't gonna change."

"And, we'll keep going over it until we catch him," said Heather glaring at the young man. "You want to work on a different team, officer? Because I think they need help on the coronavirus response team bringing bodies to the morgue."

The young officer shook his head and buried his face in a file.

"Moving along," said Heather as she continued to write in blue, "On the Ides of March, it was Rosie Florio on 97th and Columbus."

She drew a red line from one address to the other.

"Then Michelle Rothberg on April 15th," said Daryl.

"What we're grappling with here," said Heather while she worked it out in her own head, "is whether these crimes were murders of chance or were they carefully planned? Did the killer identify his victims in advance? Some of them seem like they could have been a random encounter, like Lisa Eng leaving her Christmas party. Did the killer accidentally bump into her or did he plan it?"

"Eng's co-workers reported she had a lot to drink that night and the autopsy showed her blood alcohol level to be three times the legal limit," said Daryl. "It's possible our perp ran into her on the street and decided to go for it. We still don't know who the man was who she met on the train."

"What we do know is that Michelle Rothberg had a bum foot the night she was killed. She and our sixth victim, Katie Tierney, who was found inside her apartment on West 100th near Central Park West, definitely let the killer in." Heather completed the red lines joining all six murders in a lopsided hexagon. "This is our playground, people," she said as she pointed to the red geometric shape she had created with her location points. "Whether it was by chance or not, we believe all six women allowed the killer to enter their homes."

"After doing background checks, canvassing friends and relatives," said Daryl taking over, "we have not found any personal or professional overlap between the victims. If the killer did know each of them, it wasn't through any activity or person the women had in common. The only thing that links them is that they are all young, female, single and lived on the Upper West Side."

"If they didn't know him, why did they let him in?" said a young officer.

"Anyone can come up with a believable ruse to gain entrance to an apartment," said Daryl. "What we can't figure out is how the killer knows the women are alone. How does he know they don't have a room-mate, a husband or a boyfriend?"

"Or a girlfriend," said Heather.

"Or a girlfriend," said Daryl, nodding.

"If he gets into their apartments with a lie, does he abandon his plan if someone else is there and move on to another victim?" said Heather looking out at the roomful of young officers, thinking they looked like teenagers. "We don't think so."

"Our killer appears to be enamored with rules and patterns," said Darryl pacing in front of the map, "He works the same neighborhood, never veering further east than Central Park West and stays within a fifteen-block radius. He kills the same way, by strangulation, and always on the same day — the fifteenth of the month. Nothing is left to chance. We don't believe he would waste time getting into an apartment, only to have his moment ruined by a room-mate or friend. If he had attempted a few kills and aborted, with all the publicity surrounding the case, someone would have reported it and we've heard nothing to that effect."

"That's right. Not a single woman has come forward and reported an attempted attack or a suspicious person coming into their apartment and then leaving on those specific days," said Heather. "For some reason, this maniac is compelled to kill on the fifteenth of the month and somehow knows for sure the victim will be alone. But how? That's what's keeping me up at night."

"If we can figure out how he selects his victims and how he knows they'll be alone," said Daryl, "we can catch him."

CHAPTER SEVEN

Waiting for nearly twenty-five minutes in the lobby of the 24th Precinct, Zoe and Sean prepped each other for the talk with a detective.

"Remember, stay calm and tell the story slowly," said Sean. "Don't embellish. No extra stuff, none of your hypotheses, no tangential stories. Just the facts."

"I know. I've done this before."

"Exactly, that's why I'm telling you to stay on message," said Sean. "Sometimes you add personal opinion as if it were fact."

Zoe gave him an incredulous look over the top of her mask.

At the end of the institutional beige hallway, a metal fire door swung open, hitting the concrete wall with a bang causing an echo. Detective Daryl Williams in a gray suit and matching gray mask strutted into the main lobby. Even with his face half covered, it was clear to Sean and Zoe that the man was someone who didn't enjoy bullshit.

After making introductions, the detective took a seat several feet away from them, placed a writing pad on his lap, and pulled out a pen. "I understand you two came in to report a murder. Why don't you start from the beginning," said Daryl.

Zoe leaned slightly forward. "I live across from Central Park on the north end and I recently took up bird-watching. You'd be amazed by how many species of birds are in the park, detective. It's a virtual bird wonderland. You can see blue jays and woodpeckers and I bought this amazing pair of super-powerful binoculars so I could better watch the birds and—"

"Can we get to the crime?" said the detective, already losing his patience. Sean kicked Zoe in the ankle.

"Like I said, I bought these really great binoculars to look at birds but sometimes I look out my window and watch people," said Zoe.

"You do know about Peeping Tom laws, right?" said Detective Williams.

"I don't look into people's windows, detective. I only watch people outside on the street or in the park. I'm a short story mystery writer and watching people helps me absorb the collective humanity."

Sean looked over at his friend with one eyebrow askew, and cleared his throat.

"You still haven't told me what you know about a murder," said the weary detective, suspecting the woman in front of him was a kook and he looked around for someone to relieve him.

Aware she was losing her audience, Zoe clearly explained exactly what had happened and how she had read the murder-plot texts from her window. When she finished, the detective excused himself to find his partner, leaving Sean and Zoe sitting on the straight-backed wooden chairs that lined the precinct hallway. "That went well," said Sean once the detective was out of earshot.

"You think?" said Zoe, optimism in her voice. "I tried to stay with the facts and not veer off."

Sean covered his eyes with his hands. "Are you kidding me? He thought you were a whacko. Did you see the look in his eyes?" said Sean. "'Virtual bird wonderland?' Seriously, Zoe?"

"I wanted to give him some context. I didn't want him to think I spend my days peering out my window at people. That sounds so weird."

"That *is* what you do."

Just then, Detective Williams reappeared through the fire door with Heather Kim. "I've brought my partner up to speed," said Daryl. "Ms. Brandt, you were saying you could read every word on the woman's phone from your third-floor window. Is that correct?"

"Every single word," said Zoe, nodding.

"And, the woman's husband — the one we think she's going to have killed — he was sitting right next to her bidding on a profoundly ugly lamp on eBay," said Sean.

"Ms. Brandt, before, you told me you were alone," said the detective, cocking his head to one side and staring at her.

"I was alone. Sean and I were FaceTiming when I saw the couple in the park," said Zoe. "We FaceTime every day. We usually do our first session right after we wake up in the morning, sometimes even before I brush my teeth. The next time is usually before nine—"

"I've got it," said Daryl, pinching the space between his eyes with his thumb and forefinger. "I'm going to assume for a moment that everything you've reported is true. Can you describe this mystery masked woman to me?"

Zoe and Sean looked at each other.

"That's a little hard," said Zoe, "because like everyone else in the world in 2020, she was wearing a face mask."

"Hair color? Eye Color? Height? Ethnicity?" said Detective Kim tapping her foot.

"She had on a baseball cap and a long, dark-brown ponytail was sticking out the back," said Zoe. "I couldn't see her eyes because she had on oversized aviator sunglasses with blue tinted lenses."

"Skin color?" said Heather.

Zoe squinted as she thought. "Medium-ish? She might be olive-skinned, maybe Italian or someone with a tan. She could also have been a light-skinned African American. Or, I guess she could have been Indian or Southeast Asian too."

"That narrows it down," said Heather, looking at her partner and rolling her eyes. "Age?"

"Her face was covered up but based on her body . . ." said Zoe staring up at the ceiling, "It looked young. She was very fit. I'd say she was in her twenties or early thirties tops and she had fairly large breasts."

"Height?" said Detective Williams.

"She was petite, maybe five foot three-ish," said Sean.

"I thought you weren't there," said Detective Williams, "Didn't Ms. Brandt just say you were FaceTiming?"

"I wasn't there in the beginning but later I met up with Zoe," said Sean. "We followed the couple through the park and over to the Lexington Avenue subway."

"If those people are killers, like you say they are," said Detective Williams, "that was a very dangerous thing to do."

"They didn't see us," said Zoe. "We followed them but then we lost them, twice. We think they live somewhere on the Lower East Side."

"Right after we lost them the second time, we came directly here," said Sean.

The two sleuths described the masked man on the bench, and mentioned his blue, red and white NY Rangers face mask and his fire department hat. They provided additional details including the woman's gold "GG" necklace, employment at "T and C," and the funny shirt and tie emblem embroidered on the side of the woman's navy-blue face mask.

"Shirt and tie?" said Heather, wrinkling her forehead. "A bow tie or a long one?"

"The image was from the neck to mid-chest," said Zoe using her hands. "No head, just the top half of a button-downed white shirt. The tie was long and red."

"Maybe her mask came from some sort of haberdashery or men's clothing store," said Heather.

"That's exactly what I thought," said Zoe getting excited. "We think T and C stands for Thayer and Company. Maybe the store made up masks for their employees, so everyone looks the same. A lot of companies are making their own masks now with their logos on them."

Detective Williams nodded as he made a note.

"The woman wore a white baseball cap that had three blocks of color on the front, kind of like a flag," said Zoe.

"What were the colors?" said Daryl.

"I think they were green, white and then red in that order from left to right," said Zoe, scrunching up her face.

"Did *you* see the hat," said Detective Williams to Sean.

"I didn't get close enough when we were tailing them," said Sean, "but Zoe got a good look at the hat and mask with her binoculars."

Detective Williams played with his phone for a moment, searching for something. "Is this what you saw?" he asked, holding up his phone.

"It could be. Yes, I think so," said Zoe.

"It's an Italian flag," said Daryl.

"Do you think that means she's Italian?" said Zoe.

"Who knows? She could have borrowed the hat or received it as a gift from an Italian friend," said Heather. "Or she could have gone to the Feast of San Gennaro in Little Italy last fall and bought it as a souvenir."

"I guess," said Zoe, "but it's still a clue, isn't it?"

"I've been doing this a long time, Ms. Brandt. The key to successful police work is staying focused on the right information and not getting distracted by extraneous data," said Detective Williams. "Sometimes irrelevant information can send an investigation in the wrong direction. Not everything means something."

"I almost forgot," said Zoe, "the masked woman also had a navy leather bag. I think it was a Gucci because she was also carrying a Gucci shopping bag. Maybe she had just bought the bag? You should check out the Gucci store on Fifth Avenue. A salesperson there might remember her. Then we can get her name from a receipt and the whole case will be solved."

"Thanks for the tutorial. I think that's all we need right now," said Daryl, standing up.

"Do you think you can find her?" said Zoe. "Before Thursday?"

"Ms. Brandt," said Heather, giving her partner a look, "we'll do what we can, but we can't investigate something if we don't know who or what we're investigating."

"But—" said Zoe.

"We'll follow up on the information you provided," said Daryl, observing how anxious the young woman had become. "I promise." He handed Zoe and Sean his card. "Keep watching out your window. If the masked woman comes back, please don't follow her. Call me instead."

CHAPTER EIGHT

THE NEW YORK ECHO — January 17, 2020
SECOND WOMAN FOUND DEAD: IS THERE A WEST SIDE STRANGLER?
by Tommy Devlin

Yesterday, the body of Carly Faircloth, 34, a single, petite, brunette investment banker originally from Minnesota was found dead from strangulation. Her body was discovered in her Upper West Side apartment on 104th Street. The medical examiner estimates her time of death to be sometime on the evening of January 15th. Ms. Faircloth's colleagues told police that Carly had worked late the night she was killed and mentioned she planned to stop at a market to pick up something for dinner. Witnesses at a supermarket on 102nd Street remembered seeing the young woman trying to navigate the icy sidewalk with a half-dozen grocery bags.

The market's cashier noticed Ms. Faircloth struggled with her bags as she left. Police recovered two unopened cans of tuna fish from the gutter a half block from the store and not far from the victim's apartment. According to the market's computer system, Ms. Faircloth had purchased those cans of tuna that night.

"It's possible she had an accident with her groceries on her way home," said Detective Daryl Williams, lead detective on the case. "We're canvassing the neighborhood to see if anyone saw her drop her bags and if she did, did anyone help her."

When Ms. Faircloth didn't show up for work the next day, her company called her emergency contact number, a cousin in Brooklyn. Late yesterday, the police were summoned to her apartment. Her body was found on the kitchen floor surrounded by several cans of tuna. Her face was smeared with some spoiled vanilla yogurt. The medical examiner determined she'd been dead for eighteen hours.

CHAPTER NINE

By the time Zoe got home that night it was nearly seven. Exhausted and too tired to cook, she opened a can and zapped a cup of chicken soup in the microwave. With her hot bowl of broth, she settled in on the living-room couch to watch the news and wait for her husband's nightly call. Whenever Conner was away on assignment, he always called at the same time, eight o'clock — like clockwork.

Her attention drifted from the TV news when she heard a ping. It was a text from her handsome husband with the piercing blue eyes. She smiled. Did she marry him because of his all-American good looks and unwavering moral compass or because he was a bona-fide FBI agent who packed a gun. She suspected it was a little of both.

Her little crush on the dashing lawman began the first time she laid eyes on Conner Brandt. He had been sitting next to another agent in her living room wearing a crisp navy-blue jacket. That's when she noticed he had a single dimple on his right cheek. Something about the asymmetry of that dimple intrigued her. Special Agents Brandt and Wallace had come to her Upper West Side Manhattan apartment to ask some questions about a bank robbery she had witnessed.

"Ms. Ferreira," said Agent Brandt sitting across from her on a gray living-room couch, "is there anything else you remember about the assailant?"

Zoe shook her head. "Like I said, I went into the bank with my co-worker, Juliet Pasternak. We're co-captains on the night shift at Villa d'Luna. It's an Italian restaurant."

"Co-captains?" asked Agent Wallace.

"Sorry, restaurant speak. We're the evening shift co-managers. We're responsible for all the servers and anything else that comes up during our shift."

"Got it," said Conner Brandt making a note.

"On the day of the bank robbery, Miranda — she's Villa d'Luna's owner — asked me to take a large amount of cash to deposit at the local bank before my shift started," said Zoe. "I was a little nervous because it was a lot of money so she asked Juliet to go with me. Juliet and I aren't really friends but she was the only one who was free. Anyway, we went into the bank together and were waiting in line when there was this loud bang and the front doors slammed open. I started to turn when I heard somebody scream 'gun'. You don't have to tell me twice if there's a gun involved. I hit that floor, closed my eyes and prayed."

"It must have been scary," said Agent Brandt.

"I couldn't move," said Zoe. "The man with the gun was shouting commands. I opened my eyes for a second and saw Juliet next to me on the floor trembling and crying. That's when I realized I was crying too."

"I met with Ms. Pasternak yesterday and she told a similar story," said Agent Brandt. "Do you think you could identify the gunman?"

"I didn't see his face, but I'd recognize his voice if I heard it again," said Zoe. "If you do a line-up, can you make them talk so I could hear them speak?"

"That's possible," said Conner.

"The whole time I was on the floor, I kept wondering if he was a crazy shooter whose sole purpose was to hurt people or if he was just a poor man who needed money to feed his family. I would have given him whatever I had. Did he clean out the bank? Was this his first offense, because he didn't seem very good at bank robbing. He kept changing his instructions."

"He got away with a fair amount of money," said Agent Brandt.

Zoe's eyes widened. "You think organized crime was involved? Or, could he have been part of a gang?"

"Unlikely," said Conner, glancing over at his partner. "We believe he may be the same person responsible for a string of bank robberies across several north-eastern states."

"After you called, I wondered if it was mob-related because the FBI was involved as opposed to the NYPD," said Zoe, her eyes growing round. "You don't think the robbery had anything to do with terrorism, do you?"

"No," said Agent Wallace, "no terrorism."

"The FBI gets involved when a local police department asks for our help," said Conner Brandt, but otherwise we don't typically investigate robberies. However, since banks are federally guaranteed, when a bank gets robbed it is our jurisdiction. You can rest easy, we don't believe there's any gang, terrorist or organized crime connection to this crime. Just some bad guys who wanted to find an easy way to make a buck."

Zoe shifted in her seat and leaned forward. "Is it cool being in the FBI?" she said in a knowing way, leaning further towards the two men. "It must be fascinating. I'd love to be a fly on the wall in your office. Have there been any near misses of major terrorist attacks that the FBI stopped but the public never found out about?"

"I'm afraid we can't discuss confidential information like that," said Conner. "But, let me assure you, we do our jobs and we take our role in protecting Americans very seriously."

"Did you ever shoot anyone?" asked Zoe, eyes widening again.

Conner smiled and gave his partner another look. "I'm afraid we can't disclose that kind of information either," said

Conner, glancing around Zoe's huge third-floor apartment. "You have an extraordinarily beautiful and large home here. The view of the park through that window is spectacular. Is this a three-bedroom?"

"Four, if you count the maid's room," said Zoe, "I don't have a maid, although it would be nice, right? When this building went up, I think live-in help was pretty common. On what I make, that ain't gonna happen. The apartment is about thirty-eight hundred square feet."

Agent Wallace let out a loud whistle. "You could put an ice-skating rink in here."

"My grandfather was the live-in super in this building for nearly fifty years," said Zoe, walking over to the large window that framed the park below. She picked up a black-and-white photo of a dark, handsome man with a mustache on a nearby table. "This was my grandfather when he was a young man. I really miss him."

Agents Wallace and Brandt nodded.

"When the building went co-op in the late 1970s, this neighborhood wasn't quite as fancy as it is now. My grandfather took out a loan and was somehow able to buy this place at a significantly reduced insider price. My father always suspected the other tenants chipped in to thank him for all his years of service. Everyone loved my grandfather. When I was thirteen, my mom died and my dad and I moved in here with him. I've lived here ever since."

Zoe didn't mention that shortly after her mother died she started to suffer from bulimia that lasted for most of her teen years. It was around then that she started embellishing stories and turning little things into bigger ones. Therapists had told her father his daughter's illness was probably caused by grief and the loss of control after losing her mother so young.

"Why do you think you invent stories?" asked her therapist at the time.

"I don't invent them," Zoe had replied. "I have a more acute sense of things than most other people."

"This is your time, Zoe, so if you're not going to be honest, you won't make any progress," said her therapist. "I'm here to help, not to judge."

Zoe's sad teenaged eyes had filled with tears as she swallowed several times to keep herself from crying. After a long silence, she spoke. "I guess I enhance certain things to make my life feel more exciting, so I can be more like other people. When my mom died, the world went gray. Dad and I moved in with my grandfather but nothing was ever the same. To everyone, I'm the girl with the dead mother. I wasn't like all the other kids anymore with a mom and a dad. I think a piece of my dad died when my mother passed away. When I exaggerate or make up stories, it makes the world full of color." Zoe had only been fourteen then, and could still recall the sad look on that therapist's face.

"You've got quite the place here," said Agent Brandt, standing up and walking over to the window to look out at the park.

"When my grandfather died," Zoe said, "the apartment went to my dad. My father died last year, so now it's all mine and here I am."

"It's really something," said Agent Wallace, pacing the four corners of the living room.

"I think you've answered all of our questions," said Conner, walking towards her while taking one last look at the massive room. "We'll be in touch if we need anything else."

"You can always count on me to support law and order," said Zoe, smiling at Conner as she walked the two agents down the long hallway through the octagonal-shaped foyer to the front door. "I write mystery and crime stories. Would it be okay if I occasionally called you with questions about FBI protocols so I can get my facts straight?"

Conner smiled and nodded. "Sure."

"If you find the bank robber, will I have to testify?" asked Zoe. "Because I think I'd be great on the stand. I pay very close attention to details. I probably should have joined the FBI myself."

Conner stifled a laugh by turning it into a smile. "It's never too late. The age cut-off for an FBI agent is thirty-seven. You look like you've got a few years to go before you'd be disqualified."

Zoe blushed and grinned as she let the two agents out. With her head still buzzing from the fabulousness of being interviewed by the FBI, she lay down on the living-room couch and examined Conner Brandt's business card. *Special Agent Conner Brandt. He was so cute and he carries a gun, too. I love that. Did I say "You can always count on me to support law and order"? Ugh. Why did I say that?*

A week later, Zoe's doorman buzzed her apartment. There was an FBI agent in the lobby who wanted to speak to her. Zoe's heart beat faster while she waited for the knock on her front door, hoping it would be Conner Brandt.

"Agent Brandt," said Zoe, her eyes wild and fluttery as she opened the door. "Was there another robbery? Because I've been thinking, I didn't see that bank robber, but the more I played the scene over in my head, it occurred to me that his voice sounded a lot like this man who works in the fruit market I go to on Columbus Avenue and 93rd Street. Same exact accent. I think he's Moroccan."

Conner tried to respond but Zoe kept going. "You're probably wondering why I go so far out of my way when there are much closer produce markets," said Zoe, shifting her voice to a loud whisper. "Don't tell anyone, it's a little-known secret but that market has the best mangos and melons on the West Side. It's totally worth the trip. And, their prices are insanely low. Do you want me to describe the man at the fruit market to you?"

"Actually, I came to tell you we've closed the bank robbery case. We caught the shooter. He was in another robbery in the Bronx and was shot and killed two days ago."

Zoe's eyes got large. "Wow. So, it wasn't the fruit man? I thought for sure it might be him. That's good, because if it was, I would have had to find a whole new place to get my grapes and kale. Still, in my opinion, the fruit man has the face of a killer. You should check him out. He's got weird eyebrows."

"You have an extremely active imagination," said Conner, laughing. "Our bank robbery perp was not so exotic, just a run-of-the-mill bad guy and now he's off the street for good."

It was during that second encounter with Conner Brandt that Zoe's minor fascination with the lawman turned into a gigantic crush.

CHAPTER TEN

The day after her second meeting with Agent Brandt, Zoe pulled a double shift at the restaurant, filling in for the day manager who was off sick. She then stayed on for her regular night hours. When Juliet, her co-captain showed up for work in the late afternoon, Zoe briefed her on everything that had happened that day and what needed to be done to get ready for the night shift.

Juliet listened to the litany of tasks, a look of irritation on her face. "You could have done some of this stuff before I got in?" said Juliet. "I'm not your assistant. You should have taken care of some of those things during the afternoon."

Maybe it was because the restaurant owner favored Zoe and the staff liked her more that soured Juliet on her co-captain. After working together for a couple of years, Juliet had zero patience for Zoe and her constant stream of crazy theories and rambling chatter. Every day she had to listen to Zoe's outrageous conspiracy theories and convoluted sightings of criminal masterminds. Whenever a party of men came into the restaurant who looked Italian, which was often because it was an Italian restaurant, Zoe had half the staff terrified that they were waiting on gangsters. The fact that Zoe lived in an eight-million-dollar apartment on Central Park West while

Juliet shared a cramped studio with a room-mate on a seedy block on the Upper East Side only furthered Juliet's contempt.

"Any other little jobs you need me to take care of, Your Majesty?" said Juliet as if she smelled something foul.

"Nope. That's about it," said Zoe with clenched teeth and a forced smile, not understanding Juliet's wrath. "I almost forgot, I heard from Agent Brandt again yesterday. They got the shooter from the bank job we were in. He was killed in a robbery in the Bronx so it looks like you and I are off the hook. We won't have to testify."

"When was Agent Brandt going to let *me* know?" said Juliet.

"He told me to tell you," said Zoe, smiling to herself as she turned and walked away.

Seven weeks after the armed robbery case was officially closed, Conner Brandt called Zoe and invited her to lunch. Sitting in a small Greek restaurant in Midtown not sure if it was business or a date, Zoe was uncharacteristically at a loss for words.

"You're awfully quiet today," said Conner as the waiter handed them menus.

"Do you usually take your witnesses out to lunch?" said Zoe, hoping the answer was no.

"Not usually," said Conner sheepishly. "I don't mix business with my personal life. But, since your case was closed due to the perp being deceased and there were no other loose ends, I figured it was okay. Are you uncomfortable with us having lunch?"

"I was surprised when you called."

"Good surprised?" said Conner, smiling.

Zoe smiled back, lost in the intensity of his light-blue eyes. "Very good surprised. It's not every day I get to have lunch with a man who carries a gun. You *are* carrying a gun now, right?" said Zoe, her eyes flashing, making Conner laugh.

Weeks later, when news got back to Juliet that Zoe was dating Special Agent Conner Brandt, Juliet's knives came out. From then on, she only spoke to her shift partner when it was absolutely necessary. After weeks of icy silence that made it difficult for Zoe to do her job, she confronted Juliet.

"Do you have a problem with me?" she whispered to Juliet in the back of the restaurant on a slow night.

"What gave you that idea?" said Juliet, turning to walk away.

"You've always been bitchy to me but ever since I started dating Conner, it's become more pronounced. Even the staff have noticed. What's your problem?"

"No problem," said Juliet with a haughty smirk. "You think I care that you're dating some FBI agent? He's cute but that's about it. If you want to date a civil servant, go right ahead. I'm waiting for a hedge-fund manager or a technology entrepreneur so I can live in style. Go knock yourself out with your cop."

Four months later, after a whirlwind courtship that took Zoe's breath away, Conner Brandt asked Zoe Ferreira to marry him.

Sitting on the couch in Zoe's living room watching TV one night, Conner got down on one knee.

"What are you doing?" said a confused Zoe.

Conner cleared his throat. "Zoe, the past sixteen weeks have been the happiest time of my life. While I know it's only been a short time—"

Zoe's eyes widened as it dawned on her what was happening. "Are you saying what I think you're going to say? Because if you are maybe you should—"

"Zoe, can you be quiet. I'm trying to ask you to marry me."

"For real?"

Conner smiled. "Can I finish?" Zoe nodded.

"Things have moved along so fast but I know I want you in my life. Will you marry me?"

Zoe smiled and nodded enthusiastically. "Yes, yes. Oh my God. Wait until Sean hears about this. I'm going to marry a real FBI agent. How cool is that? Do they have an FBI family Christmas party because I'd love to go to that?"

Conner laughed and shook his head. "What am I getting myself into?"

Not wanting a long engagement, Conner suggested they do something simple. A month later, with Sean managing the entire event catered from Villa d'Luna, they got married in Zoe's living room surrounded by a half-dozen of Conner's FBI colleagues, about twenty of Zoe's friends from the restaurant and a few old friends from high school.

Filled with baskets full of white flowers, candles and ivy, Zoe's cavernous living room had been transformed into a magical wedding venue. Wearing a cream-colored silk chemise gown that hugged her sinewy body in all the right places, fresh flowers had been woven into a headpiece and fastened into her thick dark-brown hair. Large South Sea pearl earring drops, borrowed from her boss Miranda, dangled from her ears. Beside her stood a smiling six-foot tall Conner, his tuxedo fitting him like a second skin. When she looked over at her handsome groom Zoe thought he looked like a poster boy for a wedding cake topper.

After the ceremony, Zoe introduced her new husband to all her friends. For most of them, the wedding was the first time they had laid eyes on Conner.

"He's totally cute," whispered a high school friend, "and you met him at a bank robbery?"

"No," said Zoe, laughing. "I was in a bank during a robbery and Conner was the FBI agent assigned to the case. I met him afterwards."

"Lucky you. He's hot," said the school friend, "and obviously totally into you. Nice work."

Conner's mother and brother had flown in from out west for the wedding and met Zoe for the first time that week.

"You've got quite the place," said Conner's mother, while Conner showed her and his younger brother around his new home. "Looks like one of them New York apartments you see on TV. Ain't got nothing like this where we live, do we, Jeremy?"

Conner's brother Jeremy shook his head. "No, Ma, ain't got nothing like this. Your place is real nice, Zoe."

"As of today, it's *our* place," said Zoe, looking up at her groom. "*Mi casa es su casa.*"

Conner leaned over and kissed the top of his wife's head.

After the festive wedding celebration, the newlyweds left for a short honeymoon in Key West, Florida. Conner was in the middle of a complicated undercover investigation, and could only take five days off. Longer time away would have raised suspicion with the players in his case. His unit director promised he could take another week off once the investigation wrapped up. When that would be, he didn't know.

With only a few days to enjoy, the newlyweds flew to Miami, rented a car and drove south, stopping in Key Largo to go snorkeling and then continued on to Key West. The Florida beach town was at the southernmost tip of the state and the former home of one of Zoe's literary idols, Ernest Hemingway. Arriving on Duval Street, Key West's main drag, they found it filled with partying tourists literally spilling out of the many bars and restaurants.

"This place is crazy," shouted Zoe over all the music and noise while laughing at all the characters and antics going on around them. "Reminds me of New Orleans, anything goes."

"That's about the size of it," said Conner, trying to steer his new wife out of the way of a group of obviously drunk college students.

For the next four days, the newlyweds slept in, rented kayaks, had long boozy lunches followed by longer boozy dinners, holding hands the entire time. For Zoe, the days flew and soon it was the morning they were to leave for home. Conner looked at the time as he watched Zoe dawdle with her packing.

"Can you pick up the pace a little?" he said. "We have to get in the car soon or we'll miss our flight to New York."

"I know," said Zoe, sitting on the bed looking glum. "We had so much fun here. This trip was too short. In a few hours I'll be back in my apartment and it will be like it all never happened."

"*Our* apartment," said Conner, sitting down on the bed and putting his arm around her. "What never happened, that you married me? We'll take another trip as soon as I finish my assignment. It will give us something to look forward to. Okay?"

Zoe looked up into her new husband's clear blue eyes and told herself that she must be the luckiest girl in the world.

The first year of their marriage was like a storybook romance. Zoe was the princess and Conner her prince. They lived in their castle off Central Park. The park soon became an integral part of their lives. In the fall, they wandered along the walking trails arm in arm, singing favorite rock songs while enjoying the changing colors of the leaves and the cooler New York weather. Months later when it snowed, they grabbed sleds and raced over to the park. Many weekend afternoons were spent sliding down icy park hills along with hundreds of city kids. They'd even built a few snowmen, some lasting a few days or even a week while others melted by the next morning. In spring, when it was warm enough, they picnicked in the park and tried to remember the names of the new flowers struggling to push their way out of the earth. A least once a week Zoe pinched herself, grateful for such a wonderful life.

CHAPTER ELEVEN

The elusive serial killer, nicknamed the West Side Strangler by the media in January after the second body had been found, appeared to have both a pattern and a purpose. After months, the method to his madness still continued to mystify the police.

They knew the very personal act of slow strangulation, the Upper West Side locations and even the choice of women selected were part of the killer's pattern. The police suspected that nothing was random and that each monthly event had been carefully choreographed, each victim specifically chosen.

THE NEW YORK ECHO — February 15, 2020
WS STRANGLER STRIKES AGAIN — THIRD VICTIM FOUND
by Tommy Devlin

A third woman has been found dead on the Upper West Side of Manhattan. The latest victim has been identified as Nicole Barrett, 30. Ms. Barrett's body was found inside her apartment on West 96th Street next to an open can of fancy mixed nuts. Police believe this is the third in a series of heinous crimes by the killer now known as the West Side Strangler. Police say the perpetrator may live or work in the neighborhood, and a clear pattern is emerging. All three of the female victims were young, single and lived alone. They were also strangled in their own homes on the fifteenth of the month.

"We're still in the early stages of this investigation," said Detective Daryl Williams, head of the West Side Strangler task force. "With this third unfortunate death we can no longer assume the killings on the fifteenth of the month are unrelated or the date a coincidence. We believe it is the same killer and we suspect there is some significance to that date. We urge women on the west side of Manhattan to be vigilant. Don't walk around alone, especially not at night and don't let anyone into your apartment."

According to police, Ms. Barrett did tell a friend that a heavyset man had approached her at the Barnes and Noble on Broadway and 83rd Street two weeks before her death. She told the friend the man was flipping through books about serial killers when she walked down the aisle. They spoke for a few minutes and traded some book recommendations. Apparently, the conversation unnerved Ms. Barrett enough that she mentioned it to a friend, Audrey Gibson.

"Nicole was super friendly to everyone," Ms. Gibson reported. "She called me on her way home from the bookstore. We were making plans for that night when she mentioned this weird guy at Barnes and Noble. She wasn't afraid or anything. She said he was kind of sad and nerdy but he gave her the creeps. She didn't describe him physically other than to say he was heavy with dark hair." Police have stated that this man is not a suspect but they would like to speak to him and ask that he contact the 24th Precinct.

The medical examiner estimates Ms. Barrett's time of death sometime in the early morning hours of February 15th. The weather that night was a mix of sleet and rain. Ms. Barrett, a promotions assistant for a corporate event planning company, lived in an old brick walk-up on West 96th Street between Columbus and Amsterdam. According to co-workers, Ms. Barrett had worked late that night and took a subway home. A cashier at a food market near her house reported Ms. Barrett stopped in earlier that night. Cash register receipts show she purchased cheese, a can of mixed nuts, ham, olives and bread and then made a second stop at a local wine merchant where she bought a couple of bottles of red wine. Police are trying to find out if Ms. Barrett was expecting a guest that night. According to Ms. Gibson, Nicole had recently ended a relationship over the Christmas holidays with a long-term boyfriend. Police are questioning the ex-boyfriend but have said he is not a person of interest. When her body was found, Ms. Barrett was wearing yoga clothes and didn't appear to be dressed for receiving guests. A bottle of wine had been opened and only one glass was found. The cheese and bread were out on a board on her coffee table, and the TV tuned to Netflix.

According to the police, a neighbor remembers seeing a man with a wheeled luggage bag standing outside of her building. At the time of this publication, the police would not confirm if this person had any connection to the murder.

Perhaps the most chilling aspect of the crime scene was the message left behind by the killer. Ms. Barrett's shirt had been pulled up and "I LOVE YOU" was spelled out on her naked stomach using eleven almonds to form the straight letters and five large cashews to form the O's and U.

"We're dealing with a sick and extremely dangerous individual here," said Detective Williams. "I urge all women living on the Upper West Side to exercise the utmost caution."

CHAPTER TWELVE

Sitting on her living-room couch that Monday night waiting for her husband's call from Quantico, Zoe replayed happy-mind videos of their Key West honeymoon. When the theme music from *Law and Order* blasted out of her phone, she lunged for it. The popular TV show's music was her special ringtone for Conner.

"Hey, babe, I miss you," she cooed. "How's everything going in Quantico? Learn anything cool?"

"It's been hot as hell here. Doesn't get much stickier than DC in the summer," said Conner. "Thank God we're inside most of the time. It's brutal enough here in June. I don't know how people live here in August. Stupid place to put our capital."

A year earlier, Conner had put in for a promotion and transfer that moved him from the organized crime division into the white-collar crime unit. His previous job arresting members of organized crime families could get an agent killed and he had had enough. White-collar crime didn't typically involve guns or murder and was considered to be a less hazardous job at the bureau. Though he never told his wife anything about his current assignment, she knew it was a long-term undercover operation. The FBI had even set him up with a fake apartment on Park Avenue to maintain his cover as a successful banker.

"So, how's your in-service training going?" asked an always curious Zoe. Dying to tell him about the masked woman and the texts she had seen but convinced he'd jump to the wrong conclusions, she remained quiet.

"Dull stuff," said Conner. "Just a bunch of new protocols and intelligence that wouldn't mean anything to you. New tricks the fat cats use to hide money and new technologies for scamming. That kind of stuff."

"Sounds pretty interesting to me," said Zoe. "Now that you mentioned hiding money, I think one of the office staff at Villa d'Luna might be cooking the books. I've seen her taking certain ledgers home. When she leaves, she gets picked up by this old bald guy with a pencil-thin mustache who drives a small black truck with Pennsylvania plates and—"

"Zoe, where are you going with this? You're manufacturing drama where there isn't any," said Conner. "It never leads to a good place."

Her husband's visceral reaction to what she had thought had been an innocuous comment, convinced her not to mention the masked woman in the park or the murder plot. "Don't bite my head off. It's just that this bookkeeper has a weird forehead and eats her sandwiches cut into exactly nine pieces. Who does that? When I noticed she took the ledger books home I thought—"

"Zoe," said Conner, "let's not go there tonight. I've had a long day. I think you should make an appointment with Dr. Eisdorfer like we talked about. It feels like you're slipping back into some not so good old habits."

After their less than happy call ended, tears filled Zoe's eyes and her lips quivered. *I was looking forward to his call tonight but he was grumpy from the minute we started talking.*

Walking into one of her four bathrooms, she splashed cold water on her face and looked in the mirror. *You look horrible.* Going into the kitchen, she poured herself a small glass of bourbon and headed down the hallway to her large blue-and-beige master bedroom. Placing the bourbon on her nightstand, she opened her big brown leather bag and plucked out a brand-new prescription container of Ambien that she had picked up that afternoon. She looked at the label. *Count: 60. That should last for a while.* Going into the bathroom, she opened the medicine cabinet over the sink and placed the bottle of pills inside.

From the bathroom, she heard her phone beep and raced to the bedroom to get it. It was Sean trying to FaceTime. When his face popped up on the screen, it made her smile.

"Hey girl," said Sean. "Quite a day we had today."

"Tell me about it," said Zoe crossing her eyes, making him laugh.

"After our meeting at the restaurant tomorrow morning, we'll go through every piece of information from today and try to figure it all out."

"I bought a notebook on my way home to keep all of our thoughts and facts in one place," said Zoe, holding up a medium-sized, hot-pink spiral binder. "Was it me or were the cops not very interested in our case?"

"We didn't give them much to go on," said Sean as Zoe took another sip of her drink. "I think it's up to us to bring the police something real and tangible that they can investigate."

"That poor eBay man has only four more days to live if we don't do something," said Zoe. "Maybe we should hire a private investigator?"

"I don't have the money for that, and neither do you. Besides, there's not enough time."

Zoe nodded as she looked at her surroundings. The irony was staggering. She owned a seven- or eight-million-dollar New York City apartment and could barely pay the maintenance and taxes. With what she earned at the restaurant and Conner's salary they made it work, but had little left over.

When her father died, she had inherited the lavish apartment as well as his savings account containing about $200,000. After she paid the funeral expenses and settled some of her father's other bills there had been $145,000 left. Since then, she had used the remainder of that money to cover her monthly expenses but it was running out.

When Conner asked her to marry him after only a few months, she had accepted, believing they would live a charmed New York City life. She was madly in love with him and for Conner, marrying the beautiful Portuguese-American girl with the over-the-top Central Park West four-bedroom-four bath co-op was like marrying a queen with a castle.

"Tomorrow, we have one mission," said Zoe, taking another sip of her bourbon and looking directly into Sean's eyes. "Stop that murder. We can't let that woman get away with it. If the police won't help, it's up to us."

"Again, we don't know for sure that it's definitely a murder," said Sean, trying to reel in his entertaining but highly imaginative friend.

"How can you say that? We totally know it's a murder," said Zoe, a little drunk and getting animated. "What else could it possibly be?"

While they chatted and argued amiably, Zoe opened her nightstand drawer and dug around for an old Ambien container that still had a few tablets left inside. Pouring one tiny pill into her hand, she broke it in half with her teeth. She put one half back in the bottle and downed the other half with bourbon.

"Did you just take an Ambien and wash it down with bourbon again?" said Sean.

"Only a half, you know I have trouble sleeping," said Zoe rolling her eyes.

"That is *so* not a good idea. Either have a drink or take the pill but don't mix them."

"I'm only having one drink and I only took half a pill. Relax. I've got this."

Sean shook his head.

The two friends kicked the murder can down the road for a few more minutes before saying goodnight. When she placed her phone on the nightstand, Zoe noticed the nearly empty Ambien bottle still sitting there. She took out another half pill and popped it into her mouth. *At least I'll get some sleep after that not happy call with Conner.* Switching off the bedroom lamp, she closed her eyes.

* * *

At nearly the same moment, a young woman high on meth entered Central Park from the north entrance on West 110th Street. They wouldn't find her body until six thirty the following morning when a cleaning crew came through the park to empty garbage cans.

CHAPTER THIRTEEN

Ten minutes after the contentious call with his wife had ended, Conner walked through the hotel bar to an outdoor lounge. Several other FBI agents also attending the in-service training had planned to meet there that night. Looking around the open space, he spotted his group at the far end of the patio. Required to take Covid tests before they traveled to the training in Quantico, they were also given rapid tests each morning before the daily sessions began. As long as they stayed outside together and maintained their viral-free bubble, there was a low risk of catching anything. One of his colleagues saw Conner and waved him over.

"We thought you bagged out on us, Brandt," said Peter Haywood.

"Had to call my wife," said Conner.

"Shit, I forgot to call mine," said one of the other agents as he pulled out his phone and walked out onto the street to call home.

"Don't forget the all-important spousal call," said Peter, "if you do, you'll never hear the end of it."

A murmur of agreement went through the group from everyone except the lone female agent who had her mask down around her neck.

"You guys are throwbacks," said the tall, leggy blonde woman with a cocky smile. "You think your wives are sitting at home waiting for your phone calls? She's probably banging your next-door neighbor."

There was a round of chuckling and some catcalls between the agents. "My next-door neighbor is ninety-six, good for him," shouted one of the men.

Peter and Conner grabbed two open seats at a distant table and ordered a beer.

"Let me ask you something," said Conner. "Does your wife ask you questions about work all the time?"

"Constantly," said Peter shaking his head. "Every night when I walk in the house, I kiss the kids and then my wife asks how my day was. I say 'Fine' and she says, 'So what are you working on?' And I say, 'You know I can't tell you that.' Then she says, 'But I'm your wife.'"

Conner laughed and nodded. "My wife does the same thing. It's like they think they're junior G-Men. Do you ever get the feeling they only married us because we were in the FBI?"

"I would think that if I had been at the bureau when I met her, but we got married before I signed up," said Peter. "I was in banking. Kind of ironic, isn't it? I went from banking to the FBI white-collar crime unit and now I arrest dirty bankers."

The two men laughed again. "My wife is completely obsessed with my job," said Conner. "I've caught her looking through my work stuff under the guise of cleaning. Trouble with her cover story, she doesn't clean — ever. My apartment is in a permanent state of chaos. When I bring my bag home from the office, suddenly she wants to clean. I can't take anything home that's confidential."

"I hear you. It ain't easy."

"You don't understand, my wife takes things to a whole other level," said Conner, glad to have someone to talk to. "She goes to the hairdresser and comes home convinced the owner of the salon is running an international gambling operation out of the back room. In our apartment building, she got it in her head that this nice old man in a wheelchair who lives on the fifth floor can actually walk. She thinks the wheelchair is a cover."

"Did she see him walking?"

"No. She just *thinks* he can," said Conner.

"She's a little like a conspiracy nut—" said Peter who then stopped himself. "I'm sorry, I didn't mean to say nut."

"Hey, don't worry about it, some of her behavior is way out there," said Conner. "It got so bad last year that we couldn't go anywhere without her suspecting somebody of something. The Uber driver looked like a terrorist, the woman on the bus was spying on us and recording our conversation. She thought our dentist who is Swiss, didn't sound Swiss. She decided he sounded Russian and that he might be a double agent."

"Did he sound Russian?"

"Not even a little."

"Your wife sounds challenging."

"Tell me about it. Last year, I made her go to a therapist after an unfortunate incident with the Peruvian embassy. I even went to therapy with her a few times to make sure she didn't downplay things," said Conner as he waved to the waiter to bring them each another beer.

"What did the therapist say?" said Peter as he took a sip of his drink.

"She said my wife had a very active imagination and her fantasies sometimes register as fact. She told Zoe to take a deep breath when she had one of those thoughts and to ask herself if it made logical sense."

"Did the therapy work?"

"For a while. Don't get me wrong," said Conner, "My wife is a really sweet person but sometimes her imagination runs wild. It gets us both into trouble. I can't have that while I'm working for the bureau."

"Did something happen recently?" said Peter, reaching for his personal bowl of peanuts on the table and popping a few into his mouth.

"Our call tonight," said Conner, "started out as a normal conversation until she told me she thinks the bookkeeper where she works might be embezzling money — because the woman cuts her sandwiches into nine pieces."

"Is it possible there's something to it?" said Peter, a skeptical look on his face.

Conner stared at his colleague and pointed to his head. "Trust me, it's all in her noggin. I've been down this bumpy road before."

CHAPTER FOURTEEN

With each passing month of 2020, the murders piled up and the NYPD was no closer to identifying the killer. A tremendous amount of police resources had been dedicated to the manhunt and the West Side Strangler had everyone in the city on edge.

> *THE NEW YORK ECHO — March 16, 2020*
> *UPPER WEST SIDE ON HIGH ALERT*
> *by Tommy Devlin*
>
> *With three young women already dead, the West Side Strangler has established a discernible pattern. According to the police, he kills on the fifteenth of each month and yesterday was no exception. For several weeks, increased chatter about the Strangler and "Beware the Ides of March" was all over social media warning young women to be careful on that day. When the City of New York recently put initial coronavirus restrictions in place, everything changed. The new virus usurped the "Strangler" story as the top headline — until today.*
>
> *For months, police had warned young women to be extra careful as each fateful date approached but most people's attention was focused on politics and the emerging*

pandemic. Despite numerous public service announcements and all the precautions women have been taking, a new victim, Rosie Florio, 31, was found early this morning on her bathroom floor. Her shirt had been pulled up and "Thanks" was written on her stomach in toothpaste.

Ms. Florio was a dancer with the West Side Funk Dance Corp, a modern jazz ensemble. Another dancer in Ms. Florio's company said the victim left the rehearsal studio on West 72nd Street and Broadway at 9 p.m. on March 15 with plans to walk home to her apartment on West 97th Street. After changing into her street clothes despite protests from several other dancers about walking alone at night on that date, Ms. Florio began her trek home.

"I told her not to walk," said another dancer, Jamie Holt. "She said, 'Stop worrying, Granny. I'll be fine.' Rosie was always joking around and stayed away from the serious stuff. I remember she stood up and did one last back-bend stretch and said, 'Between the virus and this Strangler, everyone's acting like it's doomsday. I don't pay attention to any of this stuff. I'm more worried about our dance company being shut down because of this damn plague than running into the West Side Strangler.'"

"'He's killed three women already,' I told her," said Ms. Holt. 'Today's the fifteenth. You should take a car home, it's late.' She said she didn't have the money so I offered to pay for an Uber but she wouldn't let me, said she wanted to walk and clear her head."

According to Ms. Holt, Rosie Florio left the rehearsal hall alone with two fully loaded dance gear bags slung over each shoulder. The police have said a man whose name is being withheld remembered seeing a woman fitting Ms. Florio's description walking on 74th Street last night. He remembered her because he witnessed her collide with a man, knocking him over as her bags went flying. He heard the woman apologize to the man as he passed them.

Later, a woman leaving Ms. Florio's building passed the victim and a man wearing a face mask walking up the steps to the front door. The man was carrying one of Ms. Florio's large duffel bags and the neighbor overheard the man ask if he could use Ms. Florio's bathroom.

The investigation into Ms. Florio's death is still in the preliminary stages. Detectives Heather Kim and Daryl Williams, who head the West Side Strangler task force, suspect this new murder is the work of the same killer they've been pursuing. The police strongly advise women to be vigilant and aware of their surroundings. New theories on how the killer gains the trust of his victims have emerged. "It may be that he looks for women in distress and offers a helpful hand," said Detective Williams. Police say women should be on the lookout for those types of offers and stay away. "Bottom line," said the detective, "don't let anyone into your apartment who you don't know well."

* * *

THE NEW YORK ECHO — *April 17, 2020*
WEST SIDE STRANGLER STRIKES AGAIN
by Tommy Devlin

It was a chilly Wednesday evening in April, when according to neighbors, Michelle Rothberg, 36, limped slowly down 103rd Street with a cane. Ms. Rothberg, a paralegal for a Midtown law firm, was an outgoing young woman with freckles and strawberry-blonde hair. Friends reported that she had surgery on her foot in March, right before the hospitals stopped all elective procedures to make room for Covid-19 patients.

Friends said that after her operation, Ms. Rothberg wasn't supposed to put any weight on her foot and had planned to have everything delivered. Not anticipating a global pandemic, she could not have known food deliveries would become nearly impossible. Laura Davidson, Ms. Rothberg's college room-mate, said that she had called Michelle, worried about how her friend was going to get food.

"She told me she didn't have much left to eat and was down to a few boxes of crackers," said Laura Davidson. "I

live in Chicago so there wasn't anything I could do for her. If I had been in New York, I would have brought her some food myself but that wasn't doable. I sent her a food care package through Amazon, but I don't think it arrived yet." When Ms. Rothberg couldn't get through to any delivery services she apparently called several friends to see if they could help. A few had the virus and the others were afraid to go out shopping. "Michelle told me on our last call yesterday that if she couldn't get a delivery that day, she was going to go out herself to the corner store. I reminded her that she wasn't supposed to put any weight on her foot, but she said she didn't have a choice," said Ms. Davidson.

According to police, a neighbor in her building spotted Ms. Rothberg using a cane as she inched her way down two flights of stairs and out the front door. Based on the conversation with her friend, police believe that Ms. Rothberg's destination was the corner market at the end of her block. What the victim didn't know was that the store on her street had closed down nearly three days before because the owner and his wife had both contracted the coronavirus.

An elderly woman living across the street told police she remembers seeing Ms. Rothberg standing out in front of her building around 6 p.m. on April 15 talking to a deliveryman. "I didn't get a good look at him," said the woman. Police say she reported that the unknown man appeared to be stocky and wore a dark-gray face mask with dark glasses. According to the woman, he had been standing by the front door of Ms. Rothberg's building holding what appeared to be bags of Chinese food when Ms. Rothberg slowly hobbled up.

"I couldn't hear what they were talking about," said the neighbor, "but I saw the deliveryman start to walk away with all his bags. Then the woman who was killed said something to him and he turned around and came back. She could barely get up the front steps and the next thing you know the deliveryman followed her into the building."

After repeated attempts to reach their daughter, Michelle Rothberg's parents, who live in Oak Brook IL, contacted the NYPD and asked them to do a wellness check on Michelle. When the police arrived at the woman's apartment, they found Ms. Rothberg's body slumped in a chair at her kitchen table, a pair of chopsticks in her left hand. Open cartons of moo shu pork, wonton soup, two egg rolls and shrimp lo mein were neatly placed on the table. White paper fortunes from the inside of two broken fortune cookies were found in her closed right hand. One said "A beautiful, smart, and loving person will be coming into your life" and the other "A dubious friend may be an enemy in camouflage." Truer words could not have been spoken.

CHAPTER FIFTEEN

In spring 2020, New York City looked like a ghost town. Thousands of office buildings stood empty, a range of hollow mountains. Sirens echoed endlessly through the streets while the governor and the mayor told people to stay home. Emergency field hospitals had been set up in Central Park to handle the overflow of coronavirus patients. Healthcare workers were stretched to the limit and the general feeling in the city was dire. Infection levels had hit a new high and a vaccine was still off in the future. No one knew if or when it would be available.

Shuttered stores and restaurants were evident on every block. Restaurants that remained open ramped up their take-out service for deliveries and pickups in order to stay in business. The city streets were mainly deserted with few cars or people daring to venture outside.

Terrified citizens hoarded crazy things like toilet paper, paper towels and hand sanitizer. Most people wore face masks though some refused, believing the virus wasn't real. The last thing New Yorkers needed was a murderous predator on the west side of Manhattan but that's exactly what they had.

By May, a prolific serial killer on the Upper West Side had claimed his sixth victim. With thousands of new

Covid-19 cases, people sick and dying and hospitals overflowing, it was unimaginable that New Yorkers had to shoulder one more thing. Eager to write about anything besides the virus, the press was all over the serial killer story.

> *THE NEW YORK ECHO — May 17, 2020*
> *SIXTH STRANGLER VICTIM FOUND THIS MORNING*
> *by Tommy Devlin*
>
> *When the governor of New York State essentially closed down the city, thirty-six-year-old Katie Tierney found herself furloughed from her public relations firm, a job she loved. Yesterday afternoon, Ms. Tierney's body was found in her apartment. She had been strangled and police believe that this is likely the work of the West Side Strangler, making her victim number six.*
>
> *Like so many other young women, Ms. Tierney had come to the Big Apple from Pennsylvania to begin her career. Joining Wilner PR nearly seven years ago, she was considered a key member of their executive team. Wilner PR specializes in high-end restaurants and when the pandemic hit, almost all restaurant dining stopped. With no one eating out or taking clients out for expensive dinners, Wilner PR's clients, which consisted of an assortment of four- and five-star restaurants across the United States, had put a hold on all public relations efforts. While their clients didn't sever ties with the company, all promotional plans had been delayed — indefinitely.*
>
> *Like so many other small business owners, with no money coming in, founder Nancy Wilner valiantly tried to keep her team of forty on the payroll. As weeks wore on she had to let some employees go and kept only a skeleton crew at fifty percent of their original salary. Like so many other Americans, Katie Tierney lost her job in the first round of cuts at the end of March 2020 through no fault of her own.*
>
> *According to friends, Ms. Tierney's job loss caused her significant financial difficulty. With no hiring going on due to*

the pandemic, her bills were overdue and piling up. "She told me she was willing to take anything, but there were simply no jobs," said her former room-mate who moved back in with her parents in Colorado when the pandemic started. "I know Katie reached out to her parents for help, and they gave her what they could but I don't think they had a lot of extra cash."

According to former Wilner colleague Anne Fitzpatrick, Ms. Tierney only left her apartment on West 100th Street to get food or go for a walk. "Katie spent every waking hour applying for jobs online. She never went anywhere and was so afraid of getting sick because she had lost her health insurance. She mostly job-hunted online and watched movies on Netflix, that's about it." Friends reiterated that Ms. Tierney had recently been optimistic about a few job prospects. During the last two weeks of April she interviewed via Zoom for a public relations position with the City of New York where she was one of two final candidates. "She was desperate to get that job. I had my fingers crossed for her every day," said Ms. Fitzpatrick. "Katie wasn't stupid. She knew about the Strangler. We talked about it. She wouldn't have let a stranger into her apartment."

May 15 was damp and chilly and Katie Tierney had closed all the windows in her third-floor walk-up which may have accounted for no one hearing any noise during the attack. "An examination of the crime scene showed there had been a significant struggle in her apartment," said Detective Daryl Williams, head of the NYPD task force. "It appears Ms. Tierney fought back and held her own for a while. From the looks of the apartment, she put up a good fight." A letter was found on the floor next to her body and according to the victim's parents who flew in from Pittsburgh, it was a job offer. Katie was to start on June 1 as a new public relations manager for the City of New York.

CHAPTER SIXTEEN

Tuesday — June 2, 2020

At exactly 7:30am, the alarm on Zoe's phone went off. Groggy from the bourbon and Ambien mix the night before, she groaned twice before forcing herself out of bed. Heading directly to the kitchen, she made a cup of coffee and checked the news headlines on her phone. She spilled her coffee when she read the lead story — there had been a murder in Central Park the previous night.

> *THE NEW YORK ECHO — Tuesday June 2, 2020*
> *WEST SIDE STRANGLER OR NEW MENACE?*
> *by Tommy Devlin*
> *During the day, Central Park is filled with New Yorkers — men, women, children, dogs. It's one of the few places city residents can still go to get some fresh air and leave the Covid-imposed solitude of their apartments for a few hours of sunshine. Late at night, Central Park becomes a gathering place for only a few intrepid souls and people who are up to no good. Central Park after dark is not a place you typically find a middle school teacher.*

On Monday night, a clear sky and a bright moon likely made Karina Kubiak's path into the park visible. Perhaps it was the combination of bright moonlight and the various drugs that were found in her system that emboldened the young woman to enter the park so late. According to a friend who asked to remain anonymous, Ms. Kubiak may have been looking for a drug connection. "I know Karina had gone to the park at night once before," said the friend. "I told her I didn't think it was safe but she blew me off."

A couple walking by the park near 110th Street around 11:30 p.m. on June 1st, remembered seeing a young woman who fitted Karina Kubiak's description.

"I normally don't look at people, especially not at night," said Fran Crane, an Upper West Side resident. "But my husband Harold and I were out at a dinner party and it was so nice out we decided to walk home. I only noticed the woman because she looked so out of place. Even in the dark I could see she was pretty and kind of preppy-looking, not dressed like someone you'd see hanging around Central Park late at night. What caught my eye was that she was swaying. I said to my husband, 'Harold, that woman is totally trashed.' As we got closer, I called out and asked if she was all right. She said she was fine and waved us away. If I'd known what was going to happen I would have been more forceful. I would have insisted we get her an Uber or something. She looked like a kid. When we walked away, I looked back and saw her stagger into the park. I should have stopped her."

Karina Kubiak's bruised body was found next to a boulder off a walking path in the northern part of Central Park near 110th Street. A can of pepper spray was found clenched in her hand, still capped. Police are trying to determine if Ms. Kubiak's murder is the work of the West Side Strangler or if there's a new killer in our midst.

After finishing the article, Zoe glanced out the window at her beloved park. With the morning sun shining, it was hard to believe anything bad could happen there. She checked the time and reached for her watering can. Two slightly parched ficus trees stood tall on either side of the window. "Which one of you is thirsty?" she said to her plants while dousing them with water. When she emptied the can she headed back into the kitchen. The original wood floors and kitchen cabinets had recently been painted a pale gray and new handles put on all the drawers and doors. Conner had insisted they replace the old painted wooden countertops with white-and-gray-streaked marble to modernize the room. That home improvement had gone way over budget but Conner convinced her that giving their ancient kitchen a facelift was money well spent. They had used up almost all of the remaining inheritance Zoe's father had left her for the renovation.

"Trust me, babe, this apartment is our biggest asset," said Conner. "We've got to keep it up-to-date or it will lose value. You'll love it when we finish. You'll see."

She watered the two purple-and-white orchids sitting proudly on the windowsill in her kitchen. Moving into the dining room that seated sixteen, she sprinkled water into the ivy planter at the center of the long, dark wooden table that had been her grandfather's.

Watering complete, she put on her running clothes and left the apartment. When the elevator doors opened in the lobby, Don the doorman was by the front door peering onto the street through the glass. Red and white police lights flashed outside.

"What's going on?" said Zoe, walking over to him and looking out through the glass.

"Not sure," said Don. "All I know is, there are cops everywhere. Must be ten squad cars lined up and down Central Park West. Heard on the radio a few minutes ago that some woman got killed in the park late last night. Must be that."

"I just read about it. You think it was the West Side Strangler?"

"I heard they're closing all the entrances on the north and west sides of the park to keep people out," said Don. "At least that's what the doorman next door told me."

"Why would any woman go into Central Park late at night? That's crazy. Everyone knows the only people in there then are criminals, pervs and drug addicts."

"It could be the West Side Strangler. How many has he killed now? Six women since December, I think. Guess this makes number seven."

"This is a depressing way to start the day," said Zoe, adjusting her KN95 mask loops around her ears.

"If you're going for a run, Ms. Brandt, you'll want to go west over by the river and stay clear of all this messy business in the park."

"Good idea," said Zoe as she pushed the front door open. *Stay clear of all the business in the park? Ha! Not a chance.*

The city streets were visibly empty, the pandemic forcing millions to stay inside. That June as the weather got warmer, the infection rate went down and a few more intrepid Manhattanites ventured out. Despite the virus, Zoe's daily morning runs had become a ritual. Running cleared her head, forced some of the endless chatter out of her brain. Ignoring her doorman's advice, she turned left as she stepped out of the building and like a heat-seeking missile, ran uptown directly towards the crime scene. Cruising at a good clip while watching the police activity across the street in the park, she followed the flashing lights to what appeared to be the hub of police activity. Turning right on 110th Street, she stumbled upon a mass of police and emergency vehicles.

Slowing down her pace to take it all in, Zoe counted twenty-three police cars, a couple dozen officers on foot, two ambulances, a fire truck and four police officers on horseback. A lone patrolman stood out in the center of 110th Street directing foot traffic away from the park.

"What happened here, officer?" said Zoe approaching the policeman.

"Looks like a homicide," said the masked cop, barely looking at her and waving to other pedestrians.

"Was it the West Side Strangler?" said Zoe, her eyes now like saucers. "It was, wasn't it?"

"We don't know anything yet. Sanitation crew found a woman this morning about 200 yards from the north-west entrance," said the cop. "That's all I know."

"It would certainly make sense if it was the Strangler," said Zoe bouncing around the officer, her hands moving for emphasis. "I mean, he's already killed six women. This one makes seven. Was she young too?"

"I don't know anything. I'm only here to keep people out of the park. I really can't comment," said the officer. "And, you need to keep moving along."

"But the funny thing is, officer, all of the Strangler's victims were attacked inside their apartments," said Zoe, still fishing for info. "I've been following this case very closely. If this *was* the Strangler, she would be his first victim attacked outside. Maybe he's changing his MO. Or, maybe this is the work of a copycat, because I've read that a lot of murderers have copycats and—"

"Like I said, I don't know anything," said the cop. "You need to keep moving."

"There must be Argus cameras in this section of the park," said Zoe, looking across the street at all the trees. "Although, it would be difficult to get a picture with all the leaves at this time of year."

"No comment," said the officer, tired of the conversation with the persistent woman.

Lingering on the edge of the crowd, a stocky, olive-skinned man with dark-brown curly hair, wearing dark sunglasses and a blue surgical face mask watched the police operation across the street. Clenching and unclenching his fists, he noticed Zoe making inquiries with the police officer.

"If it *was* the West Side Strangler," Zoe continued, "that would mean he's moving east because all the other murders happened further west. The first one was on West 95th Street and the second was on—"

"You really need to move along now," said the cop, losing his patience.

Zoe let out an audible sigh for effect and moved over towards a small crowd of masked onlookers by the curb. The mob of looky-loos craned their necks to see what was happening while at the same time trying to stay socially distant from one another. Next to them, a slew of reporters lined up, all hoping to get their scoop for the evening news. Zoe stood on the outskirts of the crowd for a few minutes asking questions of fellow onlookers. Learning nothing significant, she walked over near the news crews. *They'll know something.*

"You guys reporters?" she called out as she approached two men. One had a camera.

"That's what it says on my paycheck," said the young, handsome man without the camera, barely glancing at her as he focused on the police activity across the street.

"What's happening here?" said Zoe casually. "I heard there was another murder."

"Looks that way," said the handsome man.

"I live around the corner and when I walked out of my building this morning I—"

"You live around here?" said the reporter turning towards her, now more interested.

"I live right over there on Central Park West," said Zoe, pointing. "I can see the whole park from my living-room window."

"Yeah?" The reporter reached into his pocket, pulled out a business card and handed it to Zoe. "I'm Tommy Devlin with *The New York Echo*. You hear any intel about this murder? Any of your neighbors talking? The cops aren't saying jack. I've been reaching out to some of the locals. Got a tip this morning that it might be the work of the West Side Strangler."

"Tommy Devlin? I read your article this morning right before I left my house. I was thinking the exact same thing about the Strangler," said Zoe, studying the reporter's face as he took his mask off for a second to adjust it.

"You read my piece today?" said Devlin, cracking a smile. "Like it?"

"Absolutely," said Zoe. "I think you're dead right on the West Side Strangler angle. I've been following the whole case very closely."

"Yeah, well, that's my theory," said Devlin, "I gotta cover all the angles though."

"Wait a second, I've seen you before," said Zoe, squinting while examining his facial features more closely as he put his mask back on. "Do I know you?"

Devlin's photographer snorted as the reporter squirmed and shot him a look.

"You look so familiar," Zoe continued. "I can't seem to place you but I'm sure I've seen you—"

"We've never met," said Devlin without emotion.

"People say I have a photographic memory. I never forget a face," said Zoe as she scrutinized him further. Devlin looked away at the police activity going on across the street.

"Wait a minute," said Zoe, a smile spreading across her face. "I know who you are. You're that CNN reporter from Alaska who was chased into a lake by a moose."

Devlin's cameraman doubled over with laughter as Tommy gritted his teeth.

"Am I right?" said Zoe, smiling, oblivious that Devlin was not enjoying the conversation. "That video of you went totally viral. It was on TikTok and Instagram and YouTube. They played it on the morning TV shows and all the late-night shows for weeks, maybe months. You're totally famous."

"See, Devlin, isn't that nice? You're a regular celebrity," said the photographer, smothering his laughter as Devlin glared.

"You're not with CNN anymore?" said Zoe.

"I did the Alaska gig for a year but I wanted to come back to my roots. I'm a New York City boy," said Tommy. "Talked it over with my buddy Anderson Cooper. We're really tight and Anderson told me I should go for *The Echo* job. CNN offered me an anchor spot in Atlanta but New York is where it's all happening so I turned it down. I already did the CNN thing. Been there, done that. *The Echo* was begging me to take the position here, so it was a no-brainer."

"Did you get hurt by that moose? Because it looked like it mauled you a few times before you ran away and jumped into the lake," said Zoe. "The expression on your face was priceless. You looked terrified. When you let out that high-pitched scream after you went into the icy water — that was social-media gold. Twitter totally lit up."

The photographer stifled another snort that was met by a death stare from Devlin.

"It's a little-known fact, but moose are extremely dangerous animals," said Tommy. "They're brutal killers. Speaking of, can we get back to the murder? You hear anything from any of your neighbors?"

"Well," said Zoe, moving closer but not too close and speaking in a half-whisper, "I'm a bit of a sleuth hobbyist myself and as it turns out, I happen to be working on a murder investigation with the NYPD right now."

"You're working on the Strangler case?" said Tommy, a surprised look in his eyes.

"Not that case, a different murder," said Zoe, "but it's a real case too."

"No kidding?" said Tommy Devlin, writing in his notebook. "What's it all about? Why are the police working with you?"

"It's top secret. I really can't say," said Zoe, now fully whispering so the two men had to lean in closer to hear her. "I chalk it up to karma because a few years ago, I was in a bank during a robbery. Crazy, right? Afterwards, I worked very closely with the FBI on that case. I even wound up marrying the FBI agent who was assigned to it. And just this week, I witnessed someone conspiring to a murder for hire. I don't know why but somehow, crime always follows me."

"Or you follow crime," muttered the photographer as he gave Devlin a sideways glance and raised his eyebrows. The two newsmen exchanged a look.

"I've got your card, Mr. Devlin," Zoe continued, "I'd be happy to keep you informed as I learn things about any of these cases and am always available for interviews. Of course, it would have to be strictly confidential. My name has to be kept out of it. I'm Zoe Brandt, by the way."

"Naturally, we never divulge our sources," said the reporter looking over at his cameraman as the photographer rolled his eyes. "We appreciate your time, Ms. Brandt, but we've got to get going. We'll be in touch if anything comes up."

"But you don't have my number," shouted Zoe as the two men disappeared into the crowd. "Don't worry, I know how to reach you. I'll call you."

Learning nothing about the new murder, Zoe turned around and slowly ran west. The stocky man with the olive complexion still standing in the crowd had watched her full exchange with the reporters. His eyes followed her as she ran west on 110th Street before she turned left and went south down Central Park West.

By the time she got back to her building, it was nearly 9am. The police cars that had been parked in front earlier were gone. With just enough time to shower and change before the all-hands staff meeting at Villa d'Luna at 10am, Zoe breezed by the doorman and jumped on the elevator.

"I think Miranda is going to announce lay-offs tomorrow," Sean had said the night before while they FaceTimed. "Why else would she be calling us in when the café is closed. Let's face it, a restaurant doesn't need a sommelier or a waitress if there are no customers."

Zoe put on a pair of black yoga pants and an oversized baby-blue T-shirt and grabbed her white high tops from her walk-in closet. Like practically every other New Yorker, thanks to the virus, she hadn't had a haircut in months and combed her now long, thick dark-brown hair into a ponytail. Putting on a white baseball cap with a shamrock embroidered on the front she looked at her reflection in the hall mirror. The St. Patrick's Day parade the previous March had been cancelled, but she had gone to a party anyway and worn the hat. Days later, everything in New York shut down. *St. Patrick's Day was my last normal night before we all went underground like moles.*

After a quick coat of mascara, a brush of blush, and some tinted lip gloss, she grabbed her large, brown leather bag and her mask and walked out the door.

The doorman was again standing looking out when Zoe stepped into the lobby. "I read on my news feed that the woman they found in the park was a school teacher," said Don. "What the hell was a teacher doing in Central Park in the middle of the night? I'll tell you one thing, she wasn't selling Girl Scout cookies."

CHAPTER SEVENTEEN

A popular mid-sized Northern Italian bistro on West 98th Street between Columbus and Amsterdam, Villa d'Luna had been owned by Miranda d'Luna, a larger-than-life redhead and former chef, for nearly sixteen years. With a big heart and equally big boobs, Miranda was loved by her employees and considered each of them part of her extended family.

Since the shutdown, Miranda had kept all of her employees on the payroll but the virus had taken its economic toll and her money was running out. Having to make some big and painful decisions she had summoned her restaurant "family" for a meeting to be held in front of Villa d'Luna that morning.

By 9:45, twenty-five masked members of the Villa d'Luna staff waited in front of the shuttered bistro. Chairs from the restaurant had been placed outside on the sidewalk to provide some seating. It had been over two months since most of the employees had seen each other and the joy of being together was palpable. Even with no hugging and faces covered by masks, they joyfully greeted each other from six feet apart shouting questions and answers and bumping elbows instead of the usual hug. Eventually, Miranda emerged from inside the café making a grand entrance, arms high in the air like a queen holding court.

Her long red hair was pulled up into a topknot and she wore a dark-green mask that said *Villa d'Luna Rocks*. The crinkle around her bright green eyes told the crew she was smiling underneath.

Standing in the middle of her team while keeping a safe distance, Miranda, who enjoyed the limelight, blew kisses to the staff and then raised her hands high above her head again. "Welcome back, everyone! I've missed you all so much," she said. "It's been a difficult time for all New Yorkers, for the whole world. One thing I know for sure, we'll get through this if we all stick together and help each other out."

Everyone nodded and applauded. "As you know, we just got word that the city is going to start 'on-the-street dining' and I'd like Villa d'Luna to give it a try. If we stay closed much longer, I don't know if we'll ever open again and that would be heartbreaking. When the mayor gave New York City the go-ahead, I thought, 'All right, Miranda, we can do this.'"

After more applause and nodding Miranda continued. "I'm still working out the logistics. It's going to be a very different business, this new outdoor Villa d'Luna. Shorter hours, fewer customers and meals served. The good news is that our restaurant will be open again in another week. The bad news is that while I've been able to keep all of you on the payroll thus far, I'm afraid I'm going to have to make some staff cuts to stay afloat. I just haven't figured it all out yet."

A murmur went through the crowd.

"Even with the outdoor seating, we'll only be earning a fraction of what we did before," said Miranda. "I'm working with my accountant all day today on my Covid-19 emergency plan. If we could all meet here again tomorrow morning, I'll announce how Villa d'Luna will be restructured and which members of the staff will move forward with us in this crazy new world."

Fifteen minutes later when the meeting broke up, Zoe waited outside for Sean. He had gone inside the empty restaurant to retrieve some personal items left behind when the restaurant abruptly closed in March. Carrying a large, overstuffed oatmeal-colored canvas tote bag with *Justice Valley Vineyards* emblazoned across the side, Sean signaled for Zoe to follow him.

"What's all that?" she asked, eyeing the giant bag.

"Swag from all the different vineyards and liquor distributors I work with," said Sean as he pulled out a few items from the bag and held them up. Each one had a company name or logo printed on it. "They give me glasses, coasters, corkscrews, stirrers, fancy-shaped ice cube trays . . . you name it. I must have fifty corkscrews at home which is a joke because half the wine today has screw tops. Take whatever you want."

Zoe plucked out a set of fancy drink stirrers, a corkscrew and an ice cube tray that made cubes in the shape of hearts.

"Love these," she said, holding up the ice cube tray. "I can put little ice hearts in my bourbon." She tucked her new toys into her large leather cross-body bag as she and Sean started back to her apartment frequently stepping over piles of debris. Garbage had become commonplace on the city streets. Since the city went on lockdown, government services had been seriously strained and most people who could remember agreed New York hadn't looked this bad since the early 1980s.

"I can't take this much longer," said Zoe, sidestepping around another bag of garbage in the middle of the sidewalk. "Have you been over to the Broadway theater district? With all the shows closed, the streets in the West 40s are abandoned. What's left is a whole neighborhood filled with drugs and crime. I know someone who got mugged on West 45th in the middle of a work day. It's amazing how fast the changes happened."

"Don't complain, you've got a thirty-eight hundred square foot apartment to wallow in," said Sean with a slightly snarky tone. "I, on the other hand, live in a one-room studio."

Zoe let out a breath. "You're right, I have it easier than most. I may have a big apartment, but no cash flow," said

Zoe. "That means a big tax bill, expensive insurance and huge, eye-popping monthly maintenance costs. If Miranda cuts me from the staff tomorrow, Conner and I will be in big trouble. I'm practically down to nothing from the money my father left for me."

"Miranda might cut me too," said Sean, "and then what do I do? I'm a restaurant person. No restaurants are hiring."

"She won't cut you. You're her right hand. Miranda would chop her leg off before she'd let you go. You do all the ordering and purchasing and you double as bartender and waiter. She relies on you for everything. Me, I'm expendable. Miranda's got two shift managers. With the restaurant operating at twenty percent, she doesn't need both of us and Juliet has seniority."

"Yeah, but Juliet is a total bitch."

"That's true."

"Let's not worry about the restaurant or Juliet right now," said Sean. "We've got something much more pressing to deal with."

"You're right," said Zoe snapping to attention. "We have to find that masked woman. It's already Tuesday, which means we've only got two more days to save a life."

CHAPTER EIGHTEEN

Gabriela García-Harmen paced around the tiny living room of the small one-bedroom apartment on East 10th Street that she shared with her husband, Greg. The dark fifth-floor walk-up's only windows faced another building which meant they had to keep the lights on during the day.

Sitting in front of his computer in the overcrowded bedroom, Greg whooped and hollered over a successful eBay bid he had just scored while Gabriela rolled her eyes. When her husband wasn't doing online math tutoring to high school and college students on Zoom, he was bidding for items on eBay that he would supposedly resell at a profit. Most of his free time was spent on his get-rich-quick, buy low, sell high eBay schemes. His "wins" were piled up in various corners of their kitchen, living room and bedroom. From Gabriela's perspective, her husband had turned their small apartment into a junkyard, and his frequent purchases had also depleted their bank account. She was not happy.

Twenty-five-year-old Gabriela had higher aspirations than a crappy apartment on East 10th Street. When she had met Greg five years earlier, he had told her he was a teacher at a private New York City high school and a part-time import-export entrepreneur. More importantly, he had a small inheritance from his parents, and owned his apartment in the trendy Lower East Side. New to America, Gabriela was in a bit of a jam and needed to quickly vacate her current home where she worked as a nanny for a well-to-do family. When the father had lost his job, the family could no longer afford her and terminated the young woman's living arrangement. Always the survivor, Gabriela took a fast fly on Greg Harmen and deftly orchestrated a marriage proposal from him that he thought was his idea. It wasn't.

Determined to stay in New York forever, Gabriela had entered the United States from Mexico on a temporary travel visa. From the day she arrived, the Big Apple felt like home. A woman that men seldom forgot, she was petite and lean but curvy in all the right places. Her flawless sun-kissed complexion made her look like she had spent the weekend at the beach. With huge dark-brown eyes rimmed by thick rows of curly lashes, her perfectly manicured, almost black eyebrows made a statement and framed her face.

Growing up in a relatively poor town an hour south of Mexico City, Gabriela decided by the age of fourteen that she wanted to live in New York. Throughout her teens, she worked at a high-end store in downtown Mexico City saving every penny she earned for her future life in America. She also supplemented her savings by doing small favors for men — for cash.

One older gentleman became her main benefactor. Their arrangement lasted nearly four years until Senor Rodriguez expired in his bathtub. By then, Gabriela had saved almost $22,000 and accumulated a closet full of designer clothes, bags and an expensive collection of fine jewelry. Before she left for America, she sold some of the jewelry but could not part with all of it. She kept one necklace that had a charm of two connected G's dangling from a substantial fourteen-karat gold chain. *I need to look good in New York, don't I?*

Once she arrived in Manhattan, she found work as a live-in nanny for a well-to-do family, which was ironic because she didn't like children unless they were sleeping.

Regardless, she needed a place to live and moved into the Carmichael's large Manhattan apartment as their babysitter. Mr. Carmichael was an investment banker with the large banking conglomerate, Blue Crest Financial. In time, she took on other duties beyond childcare, doing small private favors for him — for cash. Six months after their arrangement began, Mr. Carmichael lost his job, the money grew tight and stopped trickling down to Gabriela.

During her time as their nanny, Gabriela had gotten to know a math tutor who came to the house once a week to help the Carmichael's oldest son. It didn't take long for the bookish and introverted Greg Harmen to develop a crush on the Mexican beauty. When she learned he owned his own apartment, had a degree from Columbia and his own business, he became more interesting. After the Carmichaels regretfully told Gabriela their finances could no longer support a nanny, she quickly set her sights on an easy target, Greg Harmen. With her travel visa already expired and nowhere to live, she had to act fast or risk being deported.

When Greg showed up for the last tutoring session before Gabriela's departure, she went into action. Offering to walk Greg out when he left, she suggested they go for a coffee. Coffee turned into dinner and dinner into a wild sleepover. That night, Gabriela García took Greg Harmen on the best ride of his life. What he didn't know that night was that he'd soon marry her but they'd never grow old together.

CHAPTER NINETEEN

When Sean and Zoe arrived at her building after the Villa d'Luna meeting, Sean opened the heavy glass and gold-plated front door before the doorman could get to it.

"Hey, Ms. Brandt," said Don looking up, "I've got a delivery for you. Looks like it might be another plant. Mr. Brandt never forgets about you when he goes away, does he?"

Zoe blushed, looking over at an obviously confused Sean. "Whenever Conner goes away on business, he always sends me a little something to remind me he loves me and he's thinking about me," she said.

"Once he sent a Vermont teddy bear with chocolates, and the last time he went away you got pastries from that 96th Street bakery that you like so much," said Don. "It's very romantic."

Zoe took the large plant box from the doorman and she and Sean got on the elevator.

"I wish I could find a guy who did that for me," said Sean, eyeing the package covered in green tissue paper as the elevator doors closed.

"You will, but you have to stop going out with anyone who asks," she said, handing him the plant so she could unlock her front door. "You need to be more selective and only go out with the best, because that's what you deserve. That's how I found Conner."

Sean nodded as the two entered Zoe's place and shut the door behind them.

Unwrapping the plant, Zoe texted her husband. When their brief text exchange concluded, she gave Sean a pump of hand sanitizer and one for herself and they moved into the dining room, sitting at opposite ends of the large mahogany table.

"Can I take my mask off now?" said Sean.

"This is a fourteen-foot table. We should be good," said Zoe removing hers as she got up to open another window and then went into the kitchen to get glasses of ice tea for them both.

"Ahhh, that's better," said Sean, letting out a breath as he took off his mask. "I don't know how doctors and nurses wear these things all day. I feel like I'm suffocating all the time."

"Let's focus on our case now. We both agree, the police aren't going to do anything about our murder plot, right?" said Zoe, sitting down at the table and tapping her pen several times. "The detectives said they would 'look into it', but I don't think they meant it. It's up to us to save that man from being killed."

"To be fair, we gave the police rather vague and not terribly useful information," said Sean.

"Don't defend them," said Zoe, aghast. "We're taxpayers, not lunatics. We did our civic duty. We went into that police station like good citizens to report a potential murder and they blew us off."

"We *are* in the middle of a pandemic," said Sean. "But you're right, they're probably not going to do anything."

"Exactly."

"Let's go over what we know for sure," said Sean. "You're absolutely certain you saw a murder-for-hire exchange on the masked woman's phone?"

"You don't believe me now?"

"I believe you, it's just that sometimes you get carried away and you had been drinking and taking sleeping pills the night before and—"

"I was a hundred percent cold sober when I read that woman's texts."

"Okay, I'm sorry," said Sean. "I'm on board. What have we got so far?"

"We've got a masked woman in her twenties or thirties. We don't know what she looks like or what nationality she is but we know she has long, dark-brown hair," said Zoe, making a note on her paper.

"That narrows it down."

Zoe made a face and continued. "She was wearing a mask and so was her husband. That means they follow safety protocols which also means . . . they're probably law-abiding citizens in every other respect."

"I hate to tell you, but with this virus, Jack the Ripper would probably wear a mask."

"Okay, so they could also be career criminals. Happy now?" said Zoe, squinting at him as Sean sighed. "The woman had on a white baseball hat that Detective Williams said looked like an Italian flag. Which means she could be Italian . . . or not." Zoe wrote in her notebook.

"We've got nothing," said Sean shaking his head.

"Don't *be* that boy. Nobody likes a quitter. We're just getting started," said Zoe, sitting up straight in her chair. "That woman was wearing a navy-blue mask that had a white dress shirt and red tie logo on it. In her text messages, she talked about working at T and C which in my mind has to be Thayer and Company."

"It's possible but . . ."

"Hear me out," said Zoe, holding up her left hand. "What if the mask was issued by Thayer and Company for their employees. Lots of companies are doing that now. Thayer and Co sells high-end men's dress clothing. I'll bet a lot of the top stores have their own company masks for employees now."

"That does make sense," said Sean, impressed by her thinking.

"Exactly," said Zoe, pointing at Sean's notebook. "Write that down. We need to find out if Thayer and Company has their own masks." Sean made a note. "Other than the mask, the woman was dressed in ordinary navy-blue leggings and a white, long-sleeved T-shirt. She had a small navy-blue leather cross-body bag and a canvas tote that said Blue Crest Financial on it. Maybe her husband, the person she's trying to kill, works for Blue Crest Financial?"

"But she said her husband was buying crap on eBay and complained in her text to her boyfriend about all the junk piled up in their apartment," said Sean, making a few more notes. "I don't see an executive from Blue Crest bidding on junk on eBay."

"Maybe her husband used to work at Blue Crest but got furloughed because of the pandemic?"

"What if she's got a friend who works at Blue Crest and they gave her the bag," said Sean. "Don't forget, she also had a Gucci shopping bag. That means, she either has money or she spends what little she has on luxury goods."

"Good one, Sean, psych profile, nice."

"Could the navy cross-body leather bag be a Gucci? What if she bought it yesterday and the shopping bag was empty?" said Sean. "Maybe she had just purchased it at the Gucci store?"

Zoe took a big gulp of her ice tea and wiped her mouth. "You might be onto something. Let's go to the Gucci store on Fifth Avenue and see if anyone remembers them," said Zoe. Sean gave her the thumbs-up sign while nodding enthusiastically.

"Now, let's do a profile on the husband," Zoe continued. "He had a slight limp."

"I didn't notice that."

"I write mysteries," said Zoe. "I'm trained to notice everything. Write that down." Sean made another note. "He had on a navy New York City firefighter's hat and was wearing a NY Rangers face mask. He could be a fireman who likes hockey?"

"Or, someone who just supports the FDNY," said Sean, "or has a neighbor who's a firefighter who gave him the hat."

Zoe made a face, finished her drink and went into the kitchen to refill her glass.

"The husband looked like he was in his late thirties or early forties. He was wearing beige shorts and a light-green T-shirt that said "Eat Mo' Pie", Sean shouted loud enough for Zoe to hear from the kitchen. "What does that mean?"

"He likes pie," she yelled back.

Sean shook his head. "I like pie, too, but I don't wear T-shirts broadcasting it. And, pie isn't particularly healthy. Why would someone wear a shirt that extols the virtues of something that's bad for you? Do you know how many people in this country have hypertension?"

"Okay, you're getting way off track now," said Zoe as she sat down at the table.

"Fine. What else?"

Zoe looked off into space and narrowed her eyes. "I believe that woman is a very sophisticated killer. Don't forget, when she texted her homicidal boyfriend she had the good sense to use a different untraceable phone."

"How do you know it's untraceable?"

"What else could it be? When she was texting someone about a hair appointment, she definitely used an iPhone. The Android is definitely the burner phone she'll toss right after she bumps off her husband."

"And don't forget what her boyfriend's name is," said Sean, writing a note on a piece of paper.

Zoe scrunched up her face and then smiled. "Sr. Bello."

"Exactly," said Sean. "Bello means beautiful in Italian. Mr. Beautiful. She *must* be Italian then. Zoe, we have our first definite clue."

CHAPTER TWENTY

Foot traffic in Manhattan that day was extremely light. Times Square, once a crowded tourist mecca, was empty. Residents around the city ventured out of their apartments only to get food or medicine and returned quickly to their homes. This June day was warm and the late spring sun drew scores of New Yorkers into Central Park. When the weather was really nice, the park got a little crowded.

"I can't believe how many people are in the park today," said Zoe as she and Sean cut east on a trail heading over to Fifth Avenue. Exiting in the 90s, they summoned an Uber to take them straight down Fifth Avenue to the Gucci flagship store on 56th Street.

"You do know there's more than one Gucci store in the city, right?" said Sean. "There are two others, one on Wooster and another all the way downtown by the World Financial Center. If the masked woman had gone shopping at Gucci the day we saw her, how do we know she went to the Gucci store on 56th?"

"We don't," said Zoe as their car sped south. "But, if she lives somewhere around 14th Street, she'd never go all the way downtown to shop, that's too far south. She might go to Wooster but since she had the shopping bag with her uptown it probably means she went to the store in Midtown. I looked at the Gucci website. I'm pretty sure the leather bag she had on was a GG Marmont Matelassé shoulder bag in navy. Price tag — almost $1,400."

When they pulled open the door of the empty Gucci store, a wafer-thin blonde saleswoman wearing a black mask waved to them. "Welcome to Gucci," she said as she approached them, maintaining her distance.

"She looks pretty eager, like she hasn't had a customer all day," whispered Zoe through her mask as the woman got closer.

"May I help you with something in particular?" the saleswoman said.

"Actually, yes," said Zoe. "I wanted to see the Marmont Matelassé shoulder bag in navy."

"Excellent choice. It's very popular, follow me," said the saleswoman as she led them over to a counter and put a small navy leather bag in front of them.

"You sell a lot of these?" said Zoe as nonchalantly as possible.

"As you can imagine," said the clerk, "since we've been in lockdown, there haven't been as many shoppers as usual. Before the virus, this bag literally sprouted wings and flew out of here on its own."

"That's impressive considering the price tag," said Zoe.

"This *is* Gucci. Chic is expensive," said the clerk dismissively as she opened the bag for Zoe to inspect the inside.

"Is this particular bag still selling? Even with the pandemic, are people still shopping?" asked Sean.

"The Gucci brand is indelible," said the clerk. "Just yesterday, I sold a woman this very same bag."

Zoe kicked Sean in the shin.

"Ow," said Sean, giving Zoe a look.

"Yesterday?" said Zoe. "What a coincidence. A friend of mine purchased this same navy bag yesterday too. She's so *au courant*, that's why I thought I might buy the same one. I wonder if the person you helped could be my friend.

Wouldn't that be funny? What did the woman you met look like?"

"Normally, I wouldn't remember because we're usually so busy, but lately we've only had a handful of customers," said the clerk coolly. "I do remember her because she had a very definite sense of style. She knew exactly what she wanted. She also had a beautiful accent with a gravelly voice."

Zoe picked up the navy bag on the counter and pretended to examine it. "What kind of accent did she have?" she said, attempting to convey only mild interest as she looked through the inside of the bag.

"She could have been Italian or Spanish, or maybe even Portuguese. She might have been from Brazil, I suppose. The Brazilians are very stylish and discerning customers. I'll tell you one thing, she knew her Gucci. The customer I worked with had a long, dark-brown ponytail and was wearing a pair of *our* aviator sunglasses in gold metal with blue lenses. Sound like your friend?"

"Gucci sunglasses? Are you sure?" said Zoe.

"I'd know our accessories with my eyes closed," said the woman reaching for a pair of aviator sunglasses in a display case and holding them up. "Does your friend have these?"

"Yes, I think so," said Zoe. "Maybe you could look in the receipts from yesterday and then we'd know for sure. I'd really like to buy the exact same bag as my friend."

The saleswoman's back straightened. "I'm sorry, but I'm not permitted to divulge any customer information. I've already shared more than I should have."

"I don't want you to *divulge* anything, I just want to make sure this was the bag my friend bought," said Zoe.

"Why don't you call her and ask her?" said the clerk suspiciously.

"Some people are funny about friends copying their clothing," said Zoe, starting to sputter. "Everyone admires and emulates my friend's style. Sometimes, she gets a little prickly about that."

The saleswoman let out a breath. "I'm sorry but it's against company rules to give out customer information of any kind."

Defeated, the two friends turned to leave when Sean spotted a jewelry display case. "Look over there," he whispered as he nudged Zoe.

Scattered along the far wall, a half-dozen necklace display stands showcased gold and silver chains each with a dangling double G charm.

"Holy shit," said Zoe. "We got it totally wrong. The woman's initials aren't GG. The masked woman was wearing a Gucci necklace. She dresses from head to toe in Gucci."

"That's so tacky and matchy-matchy," said Sean.

"I know, right?" said Zoe as she pushed the front door of the store open. "Who does that?"

"We were so close," said Sean once they were out on the sidewalk. "I thought that saleswoman was going to give up her name. This turned out to be a big waste of time."

"Are you kidding?" said Zoe bouncing on the balls of her feet. "We learned a ton. Her name isn't GG at all, but she's obviously some kind of Gucci freak — Gucci sunglasses, Gucci necklace, Gucci bag. And, she has an accent, that means she's not American. We didn't know that before. That's a huge piece of intelligence."

"Wait a second. We don't know for sure if she's the same woman we saw in the park," said Sean. "This could be a completely different person."

"It's her," said Zoe, nodding. "I know it was her. I feel it."

"Whatever you say. Where to next?"

"Madison and 53rd, the Thayer and Company flagship store."

CHAPTER TWENTY-ONE

Walking down Madison Avenue discussing "their case," the amateur sleuths devised a plan of attack for Thayer and Company — Sean would pretend to be a customer in search of dress shirts. When they arrived at the iconic clothing store, the scene inside was eerily like Gucci. With no other customers in the store, several masked salespeople rushed towards them.

"We've started a stampede. They must all work on commission," whispered Zoe as the first salesman approached.

"Good afternoon," said a middle-aged man. "May I help you with something today?"

"We're just browsing," said Sean with an air of confidence. "Give us a few minutes to look around, won't you? Can you direct me towards the men's dress shirts?"

Disappointed, the salesman pointed to the men's shirt department and the two friends moved slowly through the aisles pretending to examine the merchandise. "What are we supposed to do now?" whispered Sean. "We've been in here for nearly fifteen minutes. They're all staring at us."

Another salesperson, a younger man, approached. "Is there anything I can help you find?"

With a sudden burst of inspiration Sean spoke up, employing an affected British accent. "I've shopped here numerous times in the past and I remember there was a lovely young woman here who helped me. She had long dark hair, a delightful foreign accent and a keen sense of style. I'd like to work with her again, please. Might she be available for a consult?"

"No one here fits that description. All of our stores are on skeleton crew these days," said the salesman rather coldly. "The only salespeople in the store today are those two men standing by the front door, me, and that woman over there behind the tie counter in the beige dress." Zoe and Sean's heads snapped around to look at the woman.

"She's a blonde," said Sean, frowning.

"I didn't realize you had hair color requirements for your salesperson," said the annoyed man.

"I don't," snapped Sean. "A saleswoman who helped me before, someone I liked was a brunette. She was possibly Italian or maybe Brazilian. Do you know who I'm referring to?"

"I'm afraid I don't," said the salesman. "I've been working at this store for two years. None of the women who work here fit that description. There's Aija, she's got an accent but she's a blonde and from Latvia. We have nine stores in Manhattan. Sometimes floaters from other stores spend a few weeks here in our flagship store. Maybe she was one of those? You can try one of our other stores if you're that *committed* to only working with that woman. I assure you, I'm very good at what I do and I'd be happy to help you."

After disentangling from the persistent salesman, Zoe and Sean were out on the street again.

"Damn. We didn't make any progress and the clock is ticking," said Zoe shaking her head. "Let's go see Detective Williams and tell him what we found out at Gucci."

They grabbed an Uber up to West 100th Street to the 24th Precinct. Like before, everyone inside was masked and an officer stationed at the front door took their temperatures. For a second time, they walked over to the policeman behind the Plexiglas screen. He was the same officer from their previous visit.

"We'd like to speak with Detective Williams," said Zoe, smiling with her eyes.

"Weren't you here yesterday?" said the officer, his brow furrowed.

"Yes," said Zoe, "and it's imperative that we speak to Detective Williams immediately."

A minute later, Detectives Williams and Kim walked into the building and passed through the lobby.

"Ms. Brandt," said Daryl Williams, stopping, surprised to see Zoe waiting there as Heather continued to the elevator.

"We wanted to find out if you've made any progress on our case?" said Zoe looking directly into his warm brown eyes. "Since there are only two days left before the murder is supposed to happen, we did some reconnaissance work for you. We think that—"

"Look, Ms. Brandt, I know your heart's in the right place but we've got a lot going on," said Daryl. "In case you haven't heard, there's a serial killer on the Upper West Side of Manhattan. I'm sorry but with what you told us, we don't have enough information to go on with your *case*."

Put soundly in her place, Zoe backed down. "I understand," she said solemnly. "It's just that time is running out. Can I at least tell you what we found out today about the masked woman."

Daryl nodded.

"She speaks with a foreign accent, probably Italian or Spanish," said Zoe.

"She could be Brazilian too," said Sean. "We also learned she likes expensive things. She has a Gucci bag, necklace and sunglasses."

"Also," said Zoe, "we remembered that the masked man wore an FDNY hat and a NY Rangers mask."

"Do you know how many hockey fans wear Rangers gear?" said Daryl. "My next-door neighbor has NY Rangers sweatshirts, socks, hats, beer glasses and probably a mask, knowing him."

"We believe the husband might work for Blue Crest Financial," said Sean, trying to rescue his friend.

"Look," said Daryl, "We are following up on a few things, but I'm not going to lie, it's a long shot. In the meantime, stay out of it and let us do our job."

Sean and Zoe looked at each other, defeated. They had asked the police to search for a needle in a haystack without telling them what kind of needle or which haystack. Dejected, they left the 24th Precinct and stepped out into the sunshine onto a practically deserted West 100th Street.

"What do we do now?" said Sean, squinting from the sun in his eyes.

"I've got an idea," Zoe said, looking at her phone. "There are only two hundred and fifty-four fire stations in New York City. We could try going to the ones in Manhattan and see if—"

"Only two hundred and fifty-four? Are you kidding me? Even I think that's ridiculous. We don't even know if he *is* a fireman," said Sean. "Going to fire stations makes no sense."

"Are you saying you want to give up?" Zoe demanded.

"No, but we're chasing our tails."

CHAPTER TWENTY-TWO

Gabriela García's cleverly orchestrated romance with Greg Harmen took off like a bottle rocket. Never having considered himself terribly attractive to women, a month of the Mexican knockout's undivided attention and her ecstatic vocal approval of his lovemaking, Greg started to think he had underestimated himself.

For starters, she laughed at his terrible jokes. He was fond of a pun and she hated puns, partly because English was her second language but more because she thought puns were stupid, even in Spanish. The little quirks and idiosyncrasies other women had found annoying, Gabriela declared adorable. She also did physical things to him that he didn't know could be done. Soon Greg was sure he couldn't live without her, which was exactly what she was going for.

With the deliberateness of a shark that spotted a school of fish, Gabriela circled her prey decisively and without remorse. Greg was simply a necessary stepping stone, a means to an end. Marrying him would ensure her a green card and allow her to legally stay in the United States. He was single, which meant she didn't have to dispose of a girlfriend or wife and she'd have a home in Manhattan. Given her larger long-term goals, Greg seemed like her best option — for the moment.

For six intense weeks, Gabriela used every trick in the book to convince Greg that he was the only man for her and that she was the only one who could ever make him happy. On the seventh week of their whirlwind courtship, Greg asked Gabriela to marry him and presented her with a two-carat diamond ring. Having cleverly played all the angles, she feigned surprise when Greg got down on one knee. Her annoying little fish had taken the bait. She smiled as she slipped the diamond ring onto her finger knowing that one day she'd sell it after she gutted him like a trout.

After exhausting him in bed on their wedding night, he fell asleep and she smiled as she reviewed her situation. Everything was going exactly to plan. *I've moved to New York, found a home and will soon become a legal resident of the United States. Now, I need to find a job where I can meet some very wealthy men and set myself up for my next chapter.*

Several months later, after receiving her new green card, Gabriela applied to every high-end menswear retail store in Manhattan. Responses were few because all her past work experience had been in Mexico. After weeks of job hunting, Thayer and Company, the iconic clothing store, sent Gabriela an email requesting she come in for an interview. Putting on her best outfit, she finished her ensemble with a pair of small 14K gold-hoop earrings, her signature gold GG necklace and two thick, 14K gold bangles, compliments of her dearly departed Mexican gentleman.

Entering the venerable department store, she took a deep breath and looked around. The main room of the large store was loaded with crown molding, brass accents and shiny dark-wood finishes. Everything gleamed. The vast emporium was arranged with orchestrated rows of color. The place smelled rich — a combination of fine leather, musk and money. Several well-dressed, obviously successful men were scattered throughout the store, browsing. She smiled. This was exactly the right place to move her life plan to the next level. A handsome young salesman around Gabriela's age spotted her by the front door and crossed the main room to wait on her.

"May I help you find something?" he asked, taking in every inch of her.

"I'm here for a job interview," she said, smiling, displaying all of her sparkly, pearly teeth like a great white shark. Minutes later, Gabriela sat in front of gray-haired sixty-year-old Robert Franklin, Thayer and Co's regional VP of human resources. Franklin's eyes lit up the minute Gabriela stepped into his office. While giving his memorized speech about the company, he surreptitiously examined every inch of her body.

Gabriela missed nothing. Before she opened her mouth, she knew she had the job.

"You've had some good experience selling in that men's department store in Mexico City," said Franklin, his eyes on her legs. "We have a highly valuable and growing Hispanic customer base here. Someone like you on the floor who speaks Spanish would be a huge plus."

"*Bueno. Estoy muy encantado de estar aquí hoy y feliz de hablar con los clientes,*" said Gabriela, crossing and recrossing her tan legs while flashing her hundred-watt smile.

Robert Franklin smiled back, imagining what it would be like to kiss her full pouty lips. "Ms. Harmen, I don't know what you just said but whatever it was, it sounded charming. I'd like to give you a try here."

"I'd be very proud to work for such an amazing American institution such as Thayer and Company. So you know, my goal will be to become your best salesperson. Not just here in Manhattan but in the whole of the USA."

"I have no doubt, Ms. Harmen," said Franklin. "No doubt at all."

Minutes later, with a smile on her face, Gabriela slowly sauntered through the main floor of the store, winking at the young, handsome salesman who had greeted her when she arrived. Before she reached the door, she was pre-empted by that salesman who raced across the floor to catch up to her.

"I was wondering," he said, "would you like to meet me for a coffee or a drink later?"

"Isn't it against company policy for employees to date?" said Gabriela. "Since I start working here on Monday and because I'm also married, I'll have to say no."

Once outside, she walked down Madison Avenue and over to Fifth, stopping at Saks to buy herself a small celebration gift. To commemorate her new job, she selected a green-and-red ribbon-patterned Gucci key ring with a brown leather fob with her signature double G's. It was expensive for a key ring but she was sure her husband wouldn't begrudge her a little indulgence after landing a position with such a prestigious company. Standing at the Gucci counter running her fingers over the key ring while the female clerk showed her a few other styles, Gabriela remembered her first exposure to the Italian luxury brand.

She had been on an early shopping trip at one of Mexico City's poshest stores with her then benefactor, Senor Rodriguez. Having grown up poor she wasn't familiar with designer labels, though she soon developed an unquenchable thirst for them.

"*Mira, mi angel,*" said the elderly Sr. Rodriguez, holding up a gold necklace while they stood together at the Gucci counter. "Gucci's signature is the entwined double G's, just like your name, Gabriela García. I'm going to buy this for you. You should always wear Gucci, my dear. It suits you."

When Sr. Rodriguez placed the gold necklace around her slender, elegant neck, she had looked at herself in the oval standing mirror on the glass counter and knew he was absolutely right. From that day on, the Gucci brand became a regular staple of her wardrobe — with the financial help of gentleman friends.

"This is one of our most classic designs," said the Saks Fifth Avenue clerk holding up the colorful keychain, trying to make the sale. "It's sporty and screams understated class."

"Wrap it up," Gabriela said without hesitation. "I'll take it."

CHAPTER TWENTY-THREE

After Zoe and Sean left the police station, Daryl climbed the fire stairs to the second floor of the building.

"What did those two want?" said Heather, sitting at her desk, working on a report when Daryl entered the bullpen.

"They *want* to play Sherlock Holmes," said Daryl. "Civilians don't understand that police work is slow, tedious and methodical, not like on TV."

"Tell me about it," said Heather not looking up from her computer.

"It's about checking and rechecking information and then, checking it again," continued Daryl, talking to himself. "It's not like an episode of *Law and Order* where everything wraps up in an hour."

"What did the two nutcakes have to say?" said Heather shaking her head. "Let me guess, they wanted to know if we caught their mystery killer yet."

Daryl smiled and filled his partner in on the new information Sean and Zoe had shared regarding Gucci and Thayer and Company.

When he finished, Heather pursed her lips. "I don't think any of their *new* info about Gucci and Thayer moves the needle any further."

"Humor me. I'll do an interdepartmental form to get customer and employee lists from those two stores. Let's see if something pops," said Daryl. "I know it sounds crazy but something about their story . . . I don't think they're making it up."

"Personally, I think Zoe Brandt is a little delusional," said Heather, making a swirly movement with her finger next to her head.

"There's no doubt Ms. Brandt has a close and personal relationship with conspiracies and hyperbole but my gut says there's something there."

"Our priority is the seven women who've been strangled over the past six months. Real crimes with real victims," said Heather. "Not fantasy murders seen through binoculars."

Five minutes later, Daryl sent an official request for NYPD access to personnel lists from the two stores and then turned his attention back to the Strangler inquest.

The recent murder of Karina Kubiak in Central Park had thrown the police for a loop given that the murder profile was so different from the others. With multiple precincts on the task force now, opinions differed. Until they knew for sure, Karina Kubiak, victim number seven, would stay on the list.

* * *

"What do you want to do now?" asked Sean as the two friends headed uptown to Zoe's apartment after a second unsuccessful meeting with the police. "Detective Williams didn't sound very promising."

"He said he was still looking into a few things," said Zoe.

"I think he was blowing smoke. He's involved in the West Side Strangler investigation. He's not going to spend any time on our convoluted story."

"It's not convoluted," said Zoe, her eyes flashing. "I know what I saw, it was a murder plot."

"If the police aren't going to do anything, you've got to talk to Conner."

"You know how he is about this kind of stuff. Last night on the phone I just mentioned something funny was going on with the bookkeeper at the restaurant and he lost his mind."

"Occasionally, you do get slightly carried away," said Sean, "but that's part of your charm."

"I know, right? Conner doesn't *get* that part of me."

"Look, we know this isn't a joke. The fact is, it's a matter of life and death. Once Conner hears the whole story. He'll *want* to help us."

"I'm not so sure about that," said Zoe, casting her eyes downward and wringing her hands. "He thinks my crime investigations and any communication with police will come back to bite him with the bureau."

"There *was* that thing last year," said Sean, quietly looking away.

"You're siding with him?"

"No, but things did get kind of crazy."

"Only because the FBI is so rigid about confidentiality protocols," said Zoe with a scowl.

"But don't you think if Conner knew someone might die, he'd want to help?"

Zoe puffed up her cheeks and let out a breath. "You're right. I need to give my husband more credit. I'll have to risk pissing him off to save that man's life. Even if he gets mad at me, it's my duty as a citizen of the world to stop that murder from happening. I'll talk to him when he calls tonight. And if he bites my head off?"

"You can blame it on me."

"Don't worry, I will."

CHAPTER TWENTY-FOUR

As the hiring manager at Thayer and Co had suspected when he offered Gabriela a sales job, the voluptuous saleswoman had been a hit with the male clientele. Their male customer's relationship to clothing and fashion was tricky. Some men got it and enjoyed wardrobing themselves and the whole experience of shopping. But, the vast majority of men, particularly the older ones, were clueless or exceedingly insecure about their clothing and accessory choices. That's why so many men brought their wives or girlfriends with them.

Gabriela changed the shopping game for all those fashion-phobic men. Acting as their beautiful and stylish surrogate wife while they were in the store, she selected and recommended a shirt with a jacket, and then matched it with a belt, and a pair of pants or two. She turned her male customer's shopping experience into a happy though expensive occasion — one they wanted to repeat again and again. The better they felt, the more they'd spend and the more commission Gabriela would make. After the men were sufficiently mesmerized, she'd insist their new outfit would look great with a particular pair of expensive Italian shoes that happened to be on sale that same day. After a little cajoling and a healthy smattering of compliments, the men would usually buy the shoes in two colors.

When a male client came out of the dressing room to model a sweater or suit for her discerning eye, she'd beam at him approvingly, saying things like "You look like you stepped out of the pages of *GQ*. That color is wonderful against your complexion." Then, she'd look deeply into his eyes and hold his gaze for a very long time, saying nothing. After the unspoken exchange, she would own him. When the shopping spree was over, the man would pull out his plastic and pay whatever it cost to impress her. It worked almost every time and Gabriela made a bundle. Her commissions gave her that extra money to buy the expensive things she craved and put a little aside in a secret bank account.

After a few years of marriage, Greg proved to be a huge disappointment on every count, sexually, personally and financially. During the first six months of their marriage, Greg appeared elated at having such a pretty wife and congratulated himself on his good fortune. In a short amount of time, though, his attention reverted back to his computer and online gaming which soon took priority over his new bride. Greg also hadn't been completely honest with Gabriela about his financial situation, having led her to believe that he had many more assets than he really did. That didn't sit well with his wife.

When she married him, Gabriela had been under the impression that Greg earned far more. Soon after the wedding she learned the bank owned three quarters of his apartment. While she never thought Greg was loaded, the reality was, he was barely getting by. But, it was the fact that he showed more interest in gaming and bidding on eBay than in her that she couldn't get past. While her marriage to Greg had been a necessary stepping stone and nothing more, it irked her that he didn't place her at the center of his universe the way other men did. She concluded he must have a mental defect and looked forward to the day she would be rid of him. That was when she stepped up her game to find and secure husband number two.

With no intention of remaining a store clerk for the rest of her life, the next man she married would have to be significantly wealthier, handsomer, and much more devoted than the first. *I didn't come this far to end up in a tiny apartment looking at a crumbling brick wall.* She intended to marry someone with wealth and power and live in the high style she believed she deserved.

From then on, whenever a new male customer entered the store, she'd size them up. First, she'd check for a wedding ring. If he wore one, it wasn't a deal-breaker, just an annoying complication. After working with that customer, and observing how much money he spent and how easily he parted with it, she might move him to the next level, laying on the compliments like thick honey. Within minutes she could tell which ones only wanted a little in-store flirt and which ones might be up for more serious extra-curricular activities.

Over time, handfuls of older well-to-do men coming into the store regularly asked for her. After her initial encounter with any eligible male customer, she'd do extensive background research on him to get a general sense of his net worth.

"Why Mr. Granger, are you here again?" said a smiling Gabriela with her sultry, gravelly voice. "You practically bought everything in the store last week. The shelves were so empty after you left that we had to order new merchandise. Did I forget something?"

Slightly flustered, the overweight, fifty-eight-year-old married father of three sputtered, "I figured I could use a few more white and blue dress shirts and maybe a pair of cufflinks, Gabi. We didn't look at any of the cufflinks when I was last here."

"Of course," said Gabriela, putting on her most sorrowful face, "why didn't I think of that? I always say that a perfect pair of cufflinks makes a man. They give him that little something extra. Come with me, I know the perfect pair for you."

Granger smiled. Gabriela gently touched his arm, letting it linger for a moment, long enough to cause Granger's breathing to become labored. She physically guided him to the glass display case of men's jewelry. He bought two pairs, one in silver and one in gold, and promised to return the following week to get a new suit for a friend's wedding.

From Gabriela's research and solid background checks, Granger had the money she was looking for. When she googled him and found his wife and kids on Facebook and Instagram, she decided he wasn't the right one. Not because of his wife, who in her opinion looked old, dull and puffy, but because of his kids. Gabriela could suffer a lot of things but she did not enjoy children. *Separating a man from his wife is quite easy but kids are another story,* she often reminded herself. Granger's kids were on the younger side, too, which from Gabriela's perspective meant they'd be hanging around the second Mrs. Granger for far too long. She also considered all the money that would be funneled in their direction for college and weddings. Based on the Facebook pictures of his snaggle-toothed kids she figured they would all need an orthodontist. Three kids, three sets of braces, ka-ching! Granger was crossed off her potential husband list.

Over time she narrowed down her criteria and ultimately determined husband number two should not have any children at all. She must be the center of his world and not have to compete with demanding, annoying and expensive children. If husband number two had an untimely death, which he no doubt would, she didn't want to share the money with his offspring.

Shortly after her "no kids" revelation, a tall, good-looking, well-dressed man walked through the main door of Thayer and Co. When Gabriela spotted him, she raced towards the front of the store at the same time as two of her male colleagues.

"He's mine," she hissed as she pushed past the two salesmen, nearly knocking one of them over.

"Forget it," said one salesman to the other, stopping in his tracks as he grabbed his co-worker by the shoulder. "Vampira already has her fangs out."

Plastering an unctuous smile on her face and thrusting her chest up and out, she walked confidently towards her new customer like a jaguar homing in on an antelope. "Welcome to Thayer and Co," she said, "I'm Gabriela, what can I do for you today?"

From the minute he saw her, he was stunned by her beauty and she knew exactly what he was thinking by the way he looked at her. While the tall stranger attempted to explain he had just started a new job and needed to update his wardrobe, it was clear his mind was on one thing only, and it wasn't new clothes.

"I attend all sorts of high-level financial meetings," said the tall man with an air of accomplishment. "I'm in a position where I'll be judged not only by what I say and do but the image I portray. It's critical that I look like a million bucks."

Gabriela looked down at his hands and saw he was wearing a gold wedding band. "With your well-developed physique, you must work out a lot," she said breathlessly, "it won't be difficult to find the right clothing to make you stand out in a crowd. I hope you'll let me be your personal fashion consultant. I have an excellent eye. You can ask me anything and I'll tell you the truth."

"Anything?" said the man, playing along.

Gabriela smiled and laughed. Her mark had taken the bait. "Anything," she purred as she took him by the arm and walked him over to the suit racks.

With the skills of a crackerjack reporter, Gabriela casually interviewed the tall man without him realizing he was being evaluated. She learned he was married but had no kids. *Perfect.* He lived in Manhattan, worked in finance and like her, enjoyed nice things. As she rang his shopping up at the register, counting her hefty commission, she asked him if he'd be needing any more assistance.

"Actually," said the tall man with a wink, "I'll need a lot of assistance from you. I have to get a whole new wardrobe. New job, new look."

"Then, of course I must help you, just like I did today," she said. "I get off in twenty minutes, would you like to go for a coffee so we could discuss your needs in more detail. That way I could put a collection together for you and have it ready for the next time you come in."

"It's nearly five," said the tall man, his breath shallow as he drank in every inch of her. "How about a glass of wine instead?"

"I adore wine. That sounds perfect. Meet me at the bar in the lobby of the Hyatt on 42nd Street in half an hour," said Gabriela with a smile. As she turned and walked away, she felt his eyes on her and wondered if she might have just met her next husband. From that first meeting, she was fairly sure he'd do just about anything she asked. Which was good because one day, she'd ask him to kill for her.

CHAPTER TWENTY-FIVE

Settled on her couch that evening with her glass of bourbon and Jeopardy on the TV, Zoe waited for her husband's nightly call. Conner had been in the FBI for fifteen years and held a variety of positions, some more dangerous than others. Two years before they met, he had been held at gunpoint for ten hours by an unhinged cracked-out drug dealer. After that, Conner decided to move into a less physically dangerous division.

"I'm getting too old for this," he had said to Zoe right before they got married. "If we have kids, I'd like to live long enough to see them grow up."

It was then that he had applied for a job in the white-collar crime unit. The WCC department had been established in 1974 and accounted for over $300 billion annually in illegally gained funds but was a far less dangerous job for agents. They wore suits, dined at great restaurants, and their most dangerous activity was attending corporate meetings. The special agent's job in that division was to infiltrate corrupt organizations and gain enough solid intelligence to eventually bring them down. There were no flying bullets, drug dealers, terrorists or bombs. His team worked on crimes like embezzlement, insider trading, securities fraud, Ponzi schemes, and corporate espionage like the case of the woman who tried to sell Pepsi's cola formula to the competition.

WCC's cases also often took long periods of time to resolve. An undercover role in one of these humongous sting operations might last months, sometimes years. An agent slowly gained the trust of people on the inside, understood the inner workings of the operation and then when they least expected it, pulled the rug out from under before they knew what hit them. There were no guns, everything was done with a pen, subpoenas and warrants. If the agents did their jobs right, it often led to long prison terms for those caught with their hands in the golden cookie jar.

After putting his life on the line for so many years, Conner Brandt was more than ready for a less hazardous role within the bureau. Shortly after he and Zoe got back from their honeymoon, Conner had received the transfer.

"Guess what happened today?" he said with a big smile as he walked through the front door of their apartment and dropped his work bag on the kitchen counter with a thud.

With her back to him at the kitchen sink washing vegetables for dinner, Zoe shut off the faucet, and turned around. "From the smile on your face, I'm guessing it's good news."

"You, Mrs. Brandt, are looking at the newest member of the white-collar crime unit," said Conner grinning from ear to ear. "From now on, no more wandering through back alleys and sitting in cars by underpasses. Now, I'll be in corporate dining rooms and budget meetings, and probably getting fat eating expensive lunches at the top restaurants."

"Aren't you going to miss being out on the streets arresting the bad guys?" she asked. "Do you still get to carry a gun?"

"Agents are required to be armed at all times, you know that," said Conner. "Why do you look like you lost your dog? I thought you'd be happy about this. This is one of the best jobs at the bureau and very high profile."

"I'm thrilled for you," said an unconvincing Zoe. "I guess I thought of you more like a vigilante sheriff rounding up the bad guys."

"I was never a vigilante sheriff," Conner had said, shaking his head and laughing. "And, I'm still going to be rounding up bad guys, people like Bernie Madoff or the Enron crew. They're bad guys in a different way. They do it with a smile and a wink while they cheat millions of people, many of whom lose their life's savings. In my opinion, they're as bad as the drug dealers, they just wear better clothes, drive nicer cars and belong to country clubs."

Zoe leaned back on the couch and smiled, remembering how excited her husband had been when he had told her about his new position. Conner's special ringtone sounded from her phone and it startled her. As she picked it up she looked at the time — exactly 8 p.m. Conner as always, was right on time.

"Hey babe, I was just sitting here thinking about you and missing you," said Zoe into the phone while sneaking a sip of bourbon.

"It's good to hear your voice," said Conner. "They've given us so many new protocols and procedures this week, my head is spinning. This particular training has been brutal but we've got to learn it."

"Aww, I'm sorry. If you were here right now, I'd give you one of my super special foot massages, maybe even a full body rub."

"One of your massages would feel really good right now. My head is pounding. My eyes hurt I'm so tired."

"What did you learn about today?" asked Zoe.

"Babe, you know I can't tell you these things. Why do you always ask?"

"You can't tell me anything? Okay, what did you have for lunch?"

"I could tell you that, but then I'd have to kill you," said Conner with a laugh. "A soggy corned beef sandwich and some fries."

Wondering whether she should mention the masked woman and the murder plot, Zoe gently tested the waters.

"Corned beef, yum. So, did you hear about what happened last night? Another woman was found strangled this morning in Central Park," said Zoe.

"I saw it in my news feed when we broke for lunch."

"People are saying it might be the West Side Strangler? I'll bet it was him. What do you think?"

"I doubt it. From what I read, the park murder doesn't fit the MO of the previous homicides," said Conner. "All the other women were killed inside their apartments. This new homicide was outside. The question they need to ask is, why would a private school teacher go into that park alone late at night? She was asking for trouble."

"But she was strangled on the *west* side of the park," said Zoe plunging forward, unable to stop herself. "I was out for a run this morning and when I left the building, I saw all these flashing lights and squad cars. Then I ran up Central Park West and there were even more police. I saw this crowd so I went over and talked to the officer on duty who was securing the crime scene. I asked him if he thought it was the West Side Strangler because it seemed to me that it was a possibility and I—"

"You did what?" said Conner, anger creeping into his voice. "You stuck your nose into another police investigation? We've been down this road so many times. Zoe, you've got a real problem. If there's a crime in New York, you can't keep your hands off of it."

"But I was going for a run. Is it my fault the murder happened right near our apartment?"

"If it happened in Brooklyn, you'd have found your way there. Hell, if it happened in LA, you'd be on a plane."

"That's totally unfair," said Zoe, taking a big swig of her bourbon.

"Last year, you looked at a confidential FBI case file in my bag and nearly screwed up an entire six-month long FBI investigation. Do you know what would have happened if anyone had found out? I could have lost my job and who knows what else."

"I know. I know," said Zoe, swirling the ice in the glass and taking another sip. "But you didn't lose your job and I've apologized for that a million times."

"Are you drinking bourbon again?" said Conner suspiciously.

"Why do you ask that?" said Zoe, looking around for hidden cameras.

"Because you sound a little wonky and I heard ice banging against glass."

"I'm having an iced tea," said Zoe, her eyes round as she put her glass down on the coffee table.

"Do you remember what Dr. Eisdorfer said? How you needed to get control over yourself and stop making things up. No more obsessing over crimes or secret plots that may or may not have happened. I think maybe you should go back into therapy."

"I don't need therapy," said Zoe, her voice getting more animated. "I'm fine. Don't make me out to be crazy. A woman was murdered in the park only a few blocks from our apartment. Everyone in New York is talking about it. It's front-page news, Conner. I'm not allowed to talk about a murder that happened right near my home when everyone else in the city is?"

"That's the problem. You don't just talk about it, you live it. You investigate it. You get in the middle of things you shouldn't be involved in. It's not normal."

After the rebuke from her husband over the murder in the park, Zoe made a quick decision and decided not to ask him about *her* murder investigation of the masked woman and man.

"Anything else?" said Conner with an irritated sigh.

"Babe, I don't want to end this call on a sour note," said Zoe. "Honestly, I wasn't chasing after a crime. I literally went out for a run and it was all there in front of me."

"Maybe I overreacted. It's just that last year, you were so out of control, constantly obsessing. Theorizing, phoning tips into police, going to crime scenes."

There was a long silence.

"Zoe?"

"I promise, this week I wasn't obsessing. I swear," said Zoe.

"Okay. Let's call it a night. I've got an early start tomorrow."

"Are we good?"

"I'll call you tomorrow night, regular time," said Conner. "Did you remember to call the locksmith about fixing the lock on the front door?"

"Oops. I'll do it tomorrow. I promise."

"C'mon, Zoe. Please take care of it, the door is getting worse," said Conner. "Sometimes you think it's locked and it isn't, and sometimes you can't unlock it. That's not good security in New York. What if there was a fire and we couldn't get out because the door wouldn't open?"

"I promise. First thing tomorrow, I'll call the locksmith. Okay? Love you."

"Me too," said her husband just before he hung up.

When the call was over, Zoe replenished her empty bourbon glass and FaceTimed with Sean.

"Hey. What's up?" said Sean, noticing the strange expression on her face. "Why do you look all weirded out? Did you ask Conner about helping with the masked woman?"

Zoe shook her head. "I couldn't. I barely mentioned the story about the murder in the park last night and he totally kitchen-sinked me and pulled out all the old dirty laundry."

"Like what?"

"How I get obsessed with things and he could have gotten fired last year. That I should see a therapist. All the usual stuff."

"Oh."

"After that icy conversation, no way could I bring up the masked woman. If I told him about the binoculars and the murder plot, he would have reserved a room for me at a mental hospital."

"Sometimes you get a little carried away," said Sean, barely audible.

"You're agreeing with him?" said Zoe. "I thought you had my back. You know the murder plot is real. You saw it too."

"Not exactly."

"What do you mean? We both followed them."

"Don't take this the wrong way," said Sean, "but I never actually saw the texts about the murder. You *told* me about the texts when we were FaceTiming but I didn't see them myself."

"But you saw the woman and the man in the park," said Zoe. "We followed them onto the subway."

"Yes. But to me they looked like an ordinary couple wearing surgical masks," said Sean. "They went window shopping."

"But we tracked them to Gucci, remember? You don't believe I saw those texts?"

"I do believe you," said Sean. "I mean, I think you believe you saw them."

"You think I made it all up?" said Zoe. "That I'd go to the police and report a bogus crime?"

"No," said Sean, "of course not. I believe you or I wouldn't have helped. I was just pointing out that *you* were the only one who actually saw the text conversation of the murder. Sometimes your imagination takes over and you get a little wound up."

"I only got 'wound up' because that man on the bench is probably going to be killed by his Cruella de Vil wife on Thursday," said an incredulous Zoe. "Sean, you've got to believe me."

"Okay. I must be insane but okay."

"Yay," said Zoe, giggling.

"So, what are our next steps for tomorrow?"

"After our morning meeting at Villa d'Luna, we'll call Blue Crest Financial and track down the origin of that white bag with the red lettering that the masked woman was carrying," said Zoe, pouring herself another half glass of bourbon. "Then, we'll go downtown to the Lower East Side where we lost them yesterday and snoop around. Maybe we'll spot them."

"What are the odds of us randomly finding them?" said Sean, giving her a dubious look.

"Slim to none, but a man's life is at stake. We have to do whatever it takes to stop that murder."

CHAPTER TWENTY-SIX

Later that evening, when Zoe climbed between the soft cotton sheets on her empty king-sized bed, she felt tiny. Tossing and turning for half an hour, she groaned and reached in to her nightstand drawer, retrieving the nearly empty bottle of Ambien. She shook the container and removed the plastic cap. There were two pills left. *Good thing I picked up my new prescription this week.* Taking a single pill out, she popped it into her mouth and put the bottle back in the drawer. Lying down, she replayed the contentious phone call she had with her husband that night. It hadn't gone at all the way she had planned.

Conner jumped down my throat before I said anything. "You get in the middle of things you shouldn't be involved in. It's not normal. I think you should make an appointment with Dr. Eisdorfer like we talked about."

She sighed and rolled onto her side. What am I supposed to do? Let that man die without doing anything? That would be so wrong. Conner doesn't understand.

Folding her arms across her chest, she brought her knees up to meet them as she recalled her first sessions with Dr. Eisdorfer nearly a year before. Conner had accompanied her on that first meeting.

"What brings you here, Zoe?" asked the smiling Dr. Emily Eisdorfer, a petite woman in her fifties with curly, black, shoulder-length hair.

Before she answered the therapist, Zoe had picked up a Jolly Rancher candy from the bowl on the coffee table between them. She popped a green sour apple candy into her mouth and then looked over at her husband. His single raised brow signaled that she should speak. Zoe took a deep breath and exhaled. "Well, my husband thinks I get too excited and involved in certain activities."

"What kinds of activities?" asked the therapist.

"News and crime stories," said Zoe.

"Can you be more specific?" said the doctor.

"I have a natural curiosity and an interest in justice for all," said Zoe. "I probably should have gone into law enforcement but that ship has sailed. I find crime and criminals and what makes them tick fascinating."

"And this has become a problem?" said Dr. Eisdorfer.

"Not a problem for me, but my husband thinks I get too obsessed over criminal investigations."

"Do you mean reading about them?" asked the therapist, crinkling her brow. "Or do you actually get involved?"

"Well," said Zoe, swallowing, "that depends—"

"May I interrupt," said Conner, exasperation evident in his voice because of his wife's lack of candor. "I'm a special agent with the FBI. My wife and I have been married for two years. During that time, she has become increasingly enmeshed in crime, murder investigations, drug cartels, and dark money."

"I'm not enmeshed," Zoe protested. "That's a very strong word. It implies I can't separate myself from the crimes I investigate. I totally can. It's just my hobby."

"Tell Dr. Eisdorfer what you and your friend Sean do for entertainment on your mornings off," said Conner.

"We hang out, drink coffee. Go shopping."

"And . . . ?" said Conner staring her down.

"We walk around the neighborhood and people-watch," said Zoe. "Take a stroll in Central Park."

"It feels like we're dancing around an issue," said Dr. Eisdorfer gently. "Why don't you just tell me why you're here, Zoe."

"My wife isn't telling you the full story," said Conner, jumping in as Zoe's face fell. "She and her friend don't only drink coffee and take long walks. They think they're Sherlock Holmes and Dr. Watson. They read the local papers, go to crime scenes and try to solve cases in their spare time. They get in the way of law enforcement. Most of the time, it's benign, but occasionally, they go too far and get in the way of real criminal investigations. I've received several complaints."

"I see," said Dr. Eisdorfer, making a note. "Getting involved in criminal investigations is probably not a great idea, Zoe."

"She and her friend make pests of themselves with the local police stations, spin conspiracies where there are none and last year she almost caused an international incident with the Peruvian government. The US Department of Immigration had to get involved."

"Hmm," said the therapist, at a loss for words and wondering what she had gotten herself into.

"She and her friend follow people, spy on stores and pedestrians. Last month," said Conner, "she looked at one of my confidential FBI case files and attempted to insinuate herself into a federal investigation. She showed up at the undercover site and could have blown the whole sting operation wide open. Fortunately, I found out about it before she did any real damage. If it had gotten out that my wife was there, I would have lost my job."

"That's serious, isn't it, Zoe?" said the therapist.

"Nothing happened," said Zoe. "I didn't mean to get in anyone's way. Sean and I were just having some fun and I thought I had a lead on something that was going to help the FBI."

"It seems like your 'activities' could have some serious real-life consequences," said Dr. Eisdorfer. "If you were interested in the medical profession but didn't have a medical license, would it be okay for you to diagnose or operate on patients?"

"But that's totally different," said Zoe. "Sean and I are just playing around. I'm not posing as a police officer. We supplement investigations. We're extra eyes and ears on the ground. Sometimes the police miss things."

"It's clear you have an extremely active and creative imagination," said the therapist. "However, that seems to be causing problems for those around you, in particular your husband. It sounds like you need to rein in some of those impulses before there are some serious legal consequences."

"Thank you," said Conner. "That's what I've been trying to tell her."

The remainder of that first therapy session revealed more of Zoe's antics and unearthed her husband's continuing frustration. By the end, it was mutually decided that Zoe would start seeing Dr. Eisdorfer once a week so the therapist could help the young woman put things into perspective.

Lying in bed finally feeling the Ambien starting to kick in, Zoe rolled onto her other side and forced herself to think only happy thoughts. She reminisced about her first six wonderful months of marriage before Conner started chastising her about her amateur detective work.

Weeks before their wedding, Conner had moved from his studio apartment in Brooklyn into Zoe's palace on the park. He didn't bring much, mainly personal items and a few small pieces of furniture. The pull-out couch he had used as a bed in his one-room apartment had been left behind. Though he had been in Zoe's place hundreds of times, it wasn't until the day he moved in and dropped his bags in the large entrance foyer, that it finally felt like his home. She remembered him walking slowly through the entire apartment, room by room that day.

"What are you doing?" she had shouted from the kitchen as he walked past her.

"I can't believe I live here. This place is amazing."

"You act like you've never been here before."

"I was only a visitor before. Now, I'm a resident," said Conner smiling, "living here with the love of my life."

Zoe had smiled back and they got busy finding space for all of Conner's things. She loved having him there and not being alone anymore. The next few weeks were consumed with the last-minute details of the upcoming wedding and they had talked of nothing else. It was on their honeymoon in Key West that Conner first suggested fixing up the apartment.

"We've got this amazing home but it's in disrepair. Don't take this the wrong way, but it looks pretty tired," said Conner. "When was the last time anyone did any work on the place?"

Zoe shrugged. It had always been that way and she hadn't noticed it was "tired".

"The entire apartment needs painting," said Conner. "I noticed tiles are broken in a couple of the bathrooms and should be replaced. The wood floors are scratched and dull and need sanding and refinishing. I think we should put marble counters in the kitchen and replace the old white appliances with stainless."

"That's all going to cost a lot of money," said Zoe. "Our basic carrying costs are already steep."

"With my salary, and the money you still have left from your father's inheritance, we can start making changes, a little at a time," said Conner. "We can do all the painting ourselves, maybe even the floor sanding. This apartment is our biggest asset, babe. We have to take care of it and right now, it's a wreck. The place is falling apart."

After further discussion, Zoe came around to her husband's way of thinking. Conner is right, she had told herself. The apartment hasn't been updated in forty years.

As soon as they got back from their honeymoon, he got to work. Over the next few months, all of Zoe and Conner's free time and money had been dedicated to fixing up their home. They spackled and sanded, painted and polished. Furniture was moved around and rooms restaged.

The remainder of Zoe's inheritance had been used to update the kitchen.

"If we use the last of this money to redo the kitchen we won't have any cushion," said Zoe as she wrote a check to a contractor to begin the work. "This is the last of it."

"We'll be fine," Conner had said. "Between the two of us, we'll make it work."

Those early days were full of joy and their future was so bright that they even talked of having a baby in another two years.

"What did I do to deserve you?" said Conner one Sunday evening when they had finished painting for the day. "Love you, Zoe."

"Love you, more," she had replied as she picked a splatter of dried paint off of her husband's cheek.

With those happy memories, curled up alone in her bed in a fetal position, Zoe finally drifted off to sleep with a smile on her face.

CHAPTER TWENTY-SEVEN

That night in his hotel room in Virginia, Conner tossed and turned. The contentious call he had earlier that night with his wife was keeping him up. *Two more days of training and then home. Zoe is going off again. Bird-watching? Give me a break.*

Between his training at Quantico, the long-term white-collar crime case he had been working undercover in Manhattan, and his wife's possible slip off the sanity wagon, Conner Brandt was stressed out.

He'd been working on the Citizen's Investment Group (CIG) case since the previous fall. Jordan Spaulding, the CEO and grand wizard of the company was considered a Wall Street investment phenom. What put CIG on the FBI's radar was that Spaulding's clients consistently made higher returns on their investment than any other investment company in New York. It had been going on for more than a decade. No matter what the market was doing, Spaulding's clients always made a bundle. The secretive financial wizard was historically selective about who he let into his relatively small circle of investors. He only wanted the high rollers. Minimum investment to become a CIG client — a sweet five million. Anything less than that and CIG and Jordan Spaulding were simply not interested. The company kept their clients happy by giving them an unbelievable return on their investment and in exchange for that, their clients didn't ask any questions. Trouble was, nobody could figure out how CIG brought in those high returns so consistently.

There had always been rumors about Spaulding, but no hard evidence had ever surfaced. With a variety of business divisions employing over a hundred people, CIG was a mystery to outsiders. Within the company, only a small circle of executives were privy to their investment algorithms and portfolios. Those files were kept top secret and were not accessible to most employees.

Things at CIG would have continued that way had it not been for a pretty young assistant named Sabrina Foster who had filled in for Jordan Spaulding's admin during a long-term, high-risk pregnancy leave. Sabrina, a five-year CIG employee, was moved into the inner sanctum, and given a strong speech about confidentiality and SEC regulations. She was then assigned to work for CEO Jordan Spaulding for a nine-month period. An opportunist at heart, Sabrina was aware that she had a narrow window of access to the most confidential CIG files. She recognized this could be her golden opportunity. Her first week in the new job working for the CEO, Sabrina made copies of investment documents with the intention of studying them at home and mirroring the same CIG investments using her own funds. *Why should they be the only ones making huge profits in the market? It won't hurt anyone if I invest my own money and build my own little nest egg. Nobody gets hurt and I can put some money away for my future.*

For nearly a month, Sabrina tracked CIG investment portfolios each day and bought and traded her own money accordingly. Much to her surprise, her savings of $28,000 dwindled to $15,000.

At first, she thought she had misunderstood some of the investments and took another hard look at the data. She had bought and sold the same stocks on exactly the same days as a group of CIG clients only they had tremendous returns. All of them were up by thirty-six percent in the same period of time while Sabrina was down by nearly fifty percent.

Devastated and furious over her massive losses, she pored over all the confidential financial documents trying to figure out where she went wrong. *It makes no logical sense.* She double- and triple-checked the dates and stock prices and couldn't find the problem. Every investment purchase she had made had been executed perfectly and still, nothing added up. *My return should have been nearly $20,000 by mirroring CIG's other investors. They're all way up but I'm down. How can that be?*

Spitting mad at herself for losing so much of her hard-earned savings and unable to go to Jordan Spaulding to complain, she called her cousin in New Jersey whose next-door neighbor was an analyst with the FBI. After the FBI neighbor listened to Sabrina's story, he strongly advised her to speak to someone in the white-collar crime unit in the Manhattan FBI field office.

"Everything you've told me is right up their alley," he had said to Sabrina, encouraging her to make the call to the FBI.

For the longest time, the bureau had had their suspicions about CIG and Jordan Spaulding. When Sabrina Foster sat down with Conner Brandt and told him her story, Conner and his boss thought they might have a shot at getting the goods on Spaulding. If Sabrina Foster worked from the inside, they could finally put a nail in Spaulding's coffin.

"I don't know if I can do this," said Sabrina wringing her hands after Conner suggested she work undercover with the bureau. "What if they find out? I'll lose my job."

"If everything you say is true," said the director of the white-collar crime unit, "CIG is nothing but a house of cards. You won't have a job to go to when things come crashing down. From what you've told us, Ms. Foster, that's absolutely what's going to happen. Trust me, CIG is going down. Maybe not today, but soon. You can take that to the bank."

"That's the thing about Ponzi schemes, you can't keep them going forever," said Conner picking up the conversation thread. "At some point, the rent always comes due.

Spaulding has been on top of the world for years and now the party is over, if you help us."

After two more meetings, Conner convinced Sabrina that it was her patriotic duty to bring down the fraudulent financial operation. "Remember, it's not only fat-cat millionaires and billionaires who give their money to Spaulding. CIG invests for teachers' pension funds and children's hospitals too. What happens to them when this scam blows up? Those teachers are going to lose all their retirement money."

Sabrina nodded her head. "My mom's a teacher," she said softly. "What CIG is doing is messed up. Okay, I'll do it, for my mom."

Conner turned over on his uncomfortable hotel mattress and looked at the clock. It was after midnight. He went into the bathroom and poured himself a glass of water. His whole CIG sting operation was scheduled to go down in less than six weeks. Sabrina Foster had proved to be invaluable and had done an excellent job feeding him and his team everything they needed to shut CIG down. Now, the FBI had almost everything they needed to put Jordan Spaulding and half the executives at CIG behind bars. Climbing back into bed, Conner closed his eyes and tried to clear his mind so he could fall asleep. The phone conversation with his wife echoed in his head again. After another half an hour of restlessness, he acknowledged what he already knew — his wife was losing her grip.

CHAPTER TWENTY-EIGHT

Wednesday — June 3, 2020

Fighting off an Ambien/bourbon hangover the next morning, Zoe forced herself to get up at seven to go for her daily run. Breezing past the doorman in the lobby, she headed out into the warm spring air. The sun was up and the birds chirped as she hoofed her way up the sidewalk along Central Park West.

At 110th Street, she made a right turn and within a minute found herself running past the still cordoned-off crime scene. Twice as many looky-loo pedestrians in masks were there now and a significant police presence was evident in and around the park. Additional reporters and photographers gathered in a separated press area. As she jogged by taking everything in, Zoe spotted the reporter, Tommy Devlin again with his cameraman near a bunch of other reporters. She had read his most recent article about the park murder in *The New York Echo* right before she left her building.

* * *

THE NEW YORK ECHO — Wednesday, June 3, 2020
WAS KARINA KUBIAK VICTIM OF WEST SIDE STRANGLER?
by Tommy Devlin

Her name was Karina Kubiak. She was a 28-year-old middle school teacher for The Dover Academy, an elite private school on West 51st Street. Like the other victims of the West Side Strangler, Ms. Kubiak was single and killed on the West Side of Manhattan.

Ms. Kubiak grew up in Greenwich, Connecticut, graduating from Greenwich High School and received her BA in education from UConn in 2014. According to Dover Academy school officials, Ms. Kubiak had been employed there for the past three years. At the school, she was generally well liked by faculty and students, and no problems were ever reported. In the last yearbook, Ms. Kubiak was listed as "favorite teacher" by the seventh grade and she ran the after-school theater club. She lived in a studio apartment on West 85th Street, paid her bills on time and primarily associated with other professionals in her neighborhood.

Preliminary canvasing of Ms. Kubiak's friends and associates by this reporter found everyone in shock.

"I can't believe Karina would go into the park at night alone," said a female English teacher at The Dover Academy. "She and I were good friends. We'd eat lunch together once or twice a week. Someone must have forced her into the park. I can't imagine her going in alone, not her, she was pretty straight-laced."

Ms. Kubiak's profile, history and where she was found have baffled the police. Her behavior two nights ago doesn't fit her profile. Preliminary toxicology reports showed high levels of methamphetamine in her system which supports the theory that she went into the park to buy drugs.

"How does someone go out on a Monday night, get messed up on meth and then function the next morning in a classroom with twelve-year-olds?" said a Dover Academy

French teacher who knew the victim. "You know how rough middle-school kids are? The last thing in the world I'd want is to deal with twelve- and thirteen-year-olds with a hangover. That would be a living hell."

Because Ms. Kubiak's death may be connected to the West Side Strangler and because she was killed in the park, the Central Park Precinct is now being brought into the larger WSS investigation.

"According to the medical examiner, the way she was killed, the method of strangulation, appears to be similar to the other Strangler victims," said NYPD lead detective, Heather Kim. "There are two distinct differences between this new murder and the other six. Ms. Kubiak was killed outside while all the other murders were inside each victim's domicile. Secondly, the six previous West Side Strangler victims were all killed on the fifteenth of the month. Karina Kubiak was killed sometime between the night of June 1st and the early morning hours of June 2nd. That doesn't fit the previous pattern. However, given the seriousness of this crime, we can't rule anything out."

The question that remains in everyone's mind — will the West Side Strangler strike again in two weeks on June 15?

Zoe stopped running and bent over to catch her breath, inhaling deeply several times to regulate her pulse. "Hey," she said, smiling as she walked towards Devlin. "I read your new piece in *The Echo* this morning. Horrible story. That poor girl. It made me so sad. What would make a school teacher take a chance like that? None of it makes any sense."

"It does if you're looking for drugs," said the photographer. "Happens all the time."

"But Karina Kubiak had money, connections, a good life. She could have gotten drugs in a much safer way. She didn't have to go into Central Park alone in the middle of the night. You know what I think?"

"I can't wait," muttered Devlin, looking around to make sure he wasn't missing something important.

"I've heard there's a Polish gang that hangs out at the north end of the park at night," said Zoe with confidence.

"I've never heard that," said Devlin. "Polish, you mean from Poland?"

"That's usually where Polish people come from," said Zoe matter-of-factly, causing the photographer to snort. "I'm quite sure about this because this is my hood," said Zoe. "The north end of the park is filled with Polish people drinking vodka all night."

The photographer snorted again as Devlin's face contorted. "Drinking vodka all night?" said the incredulous reporter.

"And selling guns and drugs, too. Maybe Karina Kubiak was a Polish spy passing information through the thugs in the park," said Zoe. "That would explain why she was there."

"What are you talking about?" said Devlin. "The police think this was a simple case of being in the wrong place at the wrong time. They think she was trying to score some drugs for herself, not pass on international nuclear codes. And, they haven't ruled out that she was a victim of the West Side Strangler."

"I understand," said Zoe, "but think about it. Her name was Karina Kubiak. Kubiak is a Polish name."

"Having a Polish name doesn't make someone a Polish spy. My name is Devlin, that's Irish. That doesn't make me a member of the IRA. My partner here is Phil Boniglio, he's Italian-American. Phil, are you in the mafia?"

"Not anymore," said the photographer, laughing.

"Ms. Brandt, you have way too much time on your hands," said Devlin as he signaled to the photographer to move away.

"Just keep that Polish connection in the back of your mind. I have a hunch I'm right about that," said Zoe as she waved and ran off towards her apartment.

* * *

Two long tables covered by white tablecloths had been set up outside in front of Villa d'Luna. Plastic plates and cutlery were piled at one end and wicker baskets brimming with muffins, scones, jams and butter were at the other. Coffee urns, juice and selections of regular and herbal tea were placed on a round table. A dozen chairs had been moved from the inside of the restaurant and placed at socially distant intervals along the sidewalk. It looked quite festive for what they all knew was a sad occasion. Their friends — and maybe they themselves — were going to lose their jobs.

At ten o'clock on the dot, Miranda, her bright-red hair piled up on top of her head, wearing a green mask that had Villa d'Luna printed on it in white, stepped out from inside the restaurant. "Good morning, all you wonderful people," said Miranda, her arms up high in the air as she looked around at her beloved staff. "Thank you all so much for coming. We've had a rough few months and I've missed you. I've been giving the next phase of Villa d'Luna a great deal of thought during these many weeks of lockdown."

"Here it comes," Sean whispered to Zoe, "the guillotine is about to fall on a few necks."

"Shhh," said Zoe, her eyes glued to Miranda.

Villa d'Luna's owner shared the official details of New York City's latest plans and rules for outdoor dining and how it was going to work. "Based on the size of our restaurant and the amount of street space we've got, I figure we'll be able to put fifteen tables outside, maybe one or two more but that's it. We'll bring in large white tents and appropriately space the tables to provide a healthy distance between customers."

Applause and whistles emanated from the staff.

"Sounds pretty good, right?" Miranda continued. "I'm thinking we'll fill the outside café with tiny white Christmas lights and greenery. With a little elbow grease, we can make it look spectacular. Better than ever."

The entire staff applauded and cheered.

"I'm glad you all agree. As I said, we'll have max fifteen or sixteen tables as opposed to our normal forty-two that we had inside. That's a huge difference, one third of our previous volume."

A nervous murmur trickled through the crowd. "Obviously, our table service will be significantly smaller than what it had been," said Miranda. "When it starts to get cold, we'll bring out heat lamps. That's my plan. I'm happy to officially announce that starting next week through the end of October, Villa d'Luna will be open again for business."

After more applause and murmuring Miranda continued. "In November, if it's really cold, even heat lamps won't do the trick. When the temperature goes below fifty, we'll have to shut down for the winter."

"Get more heat lamps," shouted one of the waiters.

Miranda smiled. "I like your enthusiasm. New Yorkers love to eat out but they won't enjoy fine dining when they're freezing to death. Unfortunately, the best-case scenario is we'll be closed from Thanksgiving until mid-April."

After a series of questions from the staff and Miranda's firm commitment to keep Villa d'Luna open as long as possible, she moved on to the sad business of the day — who would stay and who would go.

"You are all like family to me. The reason I asked all of you to come today is that I didn't want those who I have to cut to simply fade away without a send-off, without a proper goodbye. I wanted this to be a little going away party of sorts. Of course, once things go back to normal, I'd hire every single one of you back, if you're still so inclined."

Miranda pulled out a piece of paper and regretfully read the new staff list to the crowd. If you weren't on the list, you were out. When she finished reading the names and gave a few of her employees an elbow bump instead of a hug, a few of the girls who had been cut began to cry.

Zoe looked at Sean. "Thank God," he said through his mask with a sigh of relief. "We're both safe. I don't know what I would have done if she cut me. I've only got about $700 left in my bank account."

"Conner and I would have been in deep trouble too. His income covers our home expenses but my paycheck is how we eat. We blew through all our savings fixing up the apartment. Anything that was left from my father went into our kitchen. Without this job, it would be a real struggle." As the two friends congratulated each other on their good fortune, Zoe spied Juliet Pasternak on the other side of the crowd glaring at her.

"Don't look," whispered Zoe loud enough for Sean to hear. "Juliet's over by the front door giving me a death stare." Sean turned his head.

"Are you going to say something to her?" he said upon seeing Juliet's scowl.

"I guess I should," Zoe replied as she turned and walked over to Juliet standing six feet in front of her.

"Congratulations, looks like Princess Zoe still has her job," hissed Juliet through her mask, her eyes narrowed.

"I'm really sorry," said Zoe. "One of us was going to get cut."

"Like you thought it was going to be you who got sacked," said Juliet. "You've always sucked up to Miranda. I'm not surprised she chose you. You're the only one here who doesn't need this job."

"What are you talking about?"

Juliet laughed with superiority. "Are you kidding? You own a freakin' multi-million-dollar apartment on Central Park West."

"How do you know what my place is like?"

"Duh," said Juliet, "people talk. I've heard your place is worth millions."

"That's none of your business," said Zoe. "This is about Conner, isn't it? You've had it in for me ever since I went out with him."

"Get over yourself," said Juliet as she turned and marched away.

Walking up beside Zoe, Sean caught the last few words of their exchange and shouted, "You don't have to be so mean, Juliet. Maybe if you weren't such a miserable wretch you'd still have a job."

Without turning around, Juliet held up her middle finger and continued walking. Tears welled up in Zoe's eyes.

"She's only taking it out on you because she's upset. Forget about Juliet."

Zoe let out a breath and shook her head. "You're right. She didn't mean it. She's just upset. I get it. People don't understand about my apartment. I grew up there, it's my home. Everything I make goes into it. It may be worth a lot but . . ."

"I understand. You don't have to explain to me," said Sean. "Let's try to be happy right now. We still have our jobs."

Zoe nodded, bit on her thumbnail and stared off into space.

"Hey, remember, we have more important things to worry about today," said Sean. "There's only two days left to stop that man's murder."

Sean's sober words snapped Zoe out of her funk. "You're right. Time is ticking. We've got to stop them from killing him."

CHAPTER TWENTY-NINE

Minutes after the Villa d'Luna meeting ended, Sean and Zoe went to Zoe's apartment to make phone calls to Blue Crest Financial. First order of business — trace the origins of the Blue Crest Financial white canvas tote bag carried by the masked woman on Monday. After that, they would head downtown to the Lower East Side and hunt for the woman and her unsuspecting husband in what they believed was the couple's home neighborhood turf.

Breezing by Zoe's doorman, the two amateur detectives rode the elevator to the third floor. Once inside the apartment, Sean ripped his mask off. "I can't breathe in this thing," he said, gasping.

"Join the club," said Zoe, taking off hers but keeping her distance from her friend. "I've seen people running and biking in the park wearing masks. I don't know how they do it. You can't get enough air in your lungs when you're wearing one."

She poured them each a glass of iced tea and they settled on opposite couches in the large living room to make phone calls. Zoe started with Blue Crest's HR department while Sean tried to get hold of someone who worked in Blue Crest's merchandising and promotions group. After an hour's worth of dead-end calls, Sean got lucky.

"Good morning, I'm writing a story on promotional materials, you know like mugs and pens with company logos," said Sean, laying it on thick so the woman on the phone would buy his story. "I saw someone carrying a lovely white canvas tote bag with the Blue Crest Financial name and logo printed on it in red. Can you tell me if those bags are sold or given away to the public or are they only for employees? Maybe they're used as premiums for new customers opening accounts?"

"This is an odd question," said the woman on the phone. "Who did you say you were with?"

Sean bullshitted his way through the conversation telling the woman he was with PremiumGold.com, unsure if the website even existed. By the time he finished the call, he had learned that the white bags with the blue logo were produced in the hundreds of thousands for Blue Crest customers but the white bags with red lettering were given *only* to employees.

"If the masked woman works at Thayer and Co," said Zoe, "that means her husband could work at Blue Crest. Maybe her husband makes a boatload of money and the wife wants to bump him off so she can have the whole enchilada and be with her paramour."

"You're making a big leap to the husband working at Blue Crest," said Sean. "All we know for sure is that the masked woman has *some* connection to a Blue Crest Financial employee."

"We should share what we learned with the detectives when we stop at the police station later," said Zoe.

"We're going to the police station again?"

"There's only one more day to stop this heinous crime," said Zoe, her voice going up half an octave. "If we walk through the park on our way to the subway, you never know, we might see the woman in the park again."

"Highly unlikely, but okay," said Sean playing along.

The two sleuths cut through Central Park eyeing every passer-by carefully. With the beautiful weather, the park was once again filled with people in masks but no one resembled the couple they were looking for. Exiting at the south-eastern entrance, they grabbed the Lexington subway at 59th Street, heading back to the Lower East Side.

"You really think this is a good use of our time?" said Sean as they climbed to the surface from the subway station and looked around. "Wandering aimlessly around 14th Street?"

"We have a very specific agenda. Any better suggestions? We know the couple lives somewhere around here," said Zoe. "Why don't we split up? That way we can cover more ground."

"What if we run into the masked couple? You want to tackle them alone?"

"If I run into them, I'll call you and if you see them, you call me. We'll walk on parallel streets. We won't be more than a block apart. How does that sound?"

"Not nearly as much fun as doing it together," said Sean making a face.

"It's not about fun right now, Sean, it's about saving a life," said Zoe emphatically. "That woman is around here somewhere. I can feel her."

CHAPTER THIRTY

That first time, when the tall man invited Gabriela to join him for a glass of wine at the Hyatt, he knew nothing about her, not even her marital status. Conversely, before they were seated in the hotel bar, she knew almost everything there was to know about him. Before their rendezvous, she spent half an hour looking him up on people-finder sites and paid the ten dollars to have a quick personal, financial and credit check done. What she found, she liked. He had the kind of assets she had been searching for and no kids. After carefully reviewing his net worth, and adding bonus points for his good looks and height, Gabriela decided he could be "the one" — at least for a few years.

When the tall man watched the Latin bombshell select ties for him behind the Thayer and Co counter that first day, she took his breath away. She was the most beautiful woman he had ever seen. Her body was all curves and she had a mane of thick brown almost black hair that cascaded down her back. All he could think about was running his fingers through it. Her dark, sultry eyes flanked by thick, curly, black lashes and her full red lips sucked him in. He had to keep himself from grabbing her right there in the sport jacket aisle.

Even on that first day, he was vaguely aware that there was nothing he wouldn't do for her.

"Do you always go out for drinks with your customers?" said the tall man hoping she said no, as he held up a glass of Cabernet and took a sip.

"Never," said Gabriela feigning shock at such a question. "You're the first."

"I'm flattered."

"You were so nice and sweet and all the sales today made me eligible for the T and Co monthly sales bonus."

"I'm just a dollar sign to you," he said, making a pretend hurt face.

"Of course not," said Gabriela, pouting while making a clicking sound with her tongue before she slid it across her top teeth. "Since you walked into my store I haven't been able to stop thinking about you. You are a very attractive man, but you know that, don't you?" Gabriela kicked off one of her heels and rubbed her bare foot up and down the man's calf sending a shiver to his groin and causing his breathing to slow. "You know what else? I think you like me too," the confident woman said breathlessly as she continued to move her foot up past his knee towards his thigh. "Am I right? You like me too?"

"Oh, yeah."

"Maybe we should go someplace more private so we can talk?"

Twenty minutes later, the couple was upstairs in a room at the Hyatt. With the drapes closed, Gabriela pulled out every trick in her sexual toolbox, giving the tall man a ride to remember.

An hour and a half later, when they walked out of the hotel onto 42nd Street, it was getting dark.

"I should be going," said Gabriela looking up into his eyes.

"Wait," he said as she started to turn away, "I have to see you again. You take my breath away. I've never met a woman like you before. I'll do anything for you."

That's the moment she knew she owned him. She had gone fishing, caught her guppy and slowly reeled him in. Next step — her big handsome fish needed to get rid of another fish that was in the way of her future. She smiled up at him. "To be totally transparent," said Gabriela, "you should know, I'm married."

"Since we're being honest," said the tall man, "So am I."

"Nobody's perfect," she replied with a smile. "So, what do we do now?"

"I've never done anything like this before. When I saw you, I couldn't stop myself."

"I feel the same," said Gabriela breathlessly. "I've never done this either. Maybe we're soulmates?"

They made plans to meet the following week. Before they parted, he bent his head down and kissed her one last time.

Later, boarding the Lexington Express train to go home, Gabriela's brain fired on all pistons. *There's so much still to do and I've got to play him exactly right. Bonus for me, the sex wasn't terrible.*

Arriving at home, Greg was where he always was, sitting in front of his computer bidding on eBay while simultaneously gaming on the TV. "How was your night out with your friends from work?" he said, not taking his eyes off his screen.

"Fine," said Gabriela as she shuffled through the pile of mail on the kitchen counter. "It's good to let off a little work steam. I think we're going to make it a weekly thing."

"That's nice," said Greg half listening and still glued to his game. "I'm bidding on an antique Masonic orb pendant. There's only a few minutes left on the clock. Some asshole has been bidding it up for the last two hours."

Standing behind him, Gabriela rolled her big eyes. "Don't you get tired of doing this all day?"

"That's how I make the money to keep you in style."

Gabriela looked around at their tiny, cluttered apartment and made a face. "If you got a real job, you'd make more money and we wouldn't have all this junk lying around. This place is like a pen for pigs."

"Damn! That other jerk just outbid me. Damn it!" said Greg, pounding his hand on the desk.

"You need to calm down. It's always the same. Every day you sit at that computer and scream, then packages come in the mail and crowd me out of my own house. I'm going to bed. Don't wake me, I have a headache from all your screaming."

"I'm going to be up late anyway. I'm bidding on cases of shirts from China," said Greg. "I'll make a killing on those. You'll see."

Gabriela went into her bedroom. It had been an excellent day. She had sold a ton of merchandise to her new tall customer, hooked him in her snare, and had a relatively pleasant sexual encounter. Soon, her new boyfriend would become her new husband and upgrade her lifestyle significantly. Everything was going to plan.

She brushed her teeth and gazed at her glorious reflection in the mirror as she plotted out her next move. She wondered if her new paramour was up to the task. Then she remembered his words, "You take my breath away . . . I'll do anything for you," and she knew the answer. From the way he looked at her and responded to her lovemaking, she was fairly certain he'd kill for her — if she asked.

CHAPTER THIRTY-ONE

The Central Park Police patrol 843 acres, seven bodies of water, fifty-eight miles of pedestrian paths, six miles of road and a five-mile bridle path. Despite the expanse of the area, murder in the park was rare and the Central Park Precinct had one of the lowest crime rates in the city. The CP Commanding Officer liked it that way. Their park was safe and that's how he wanted it to stay. But with the murder of Karina Kubiak, his precinct had been added to the taskforce hunting for the Strangler.

A press conference had been scheduled for that afternoon. Detectives Daryl Williams and Heather Kim briefed seventy reporters in front of City Hall.

"We're not 100 percent certain the recent murder in Central Park was committed by the same person responsible for the other attacks on the Upper West Side," said Detective Williams, fielding reporters' relentless, rapid-fire questions. "Given a few similarities; age of victim and method of murder, we'll assume they're connected until proven wrong."

"Where are you on making an arrest?" shouted Tommy Devlin from the center of the mob of eager reporters, "Is this another Boston Strangler situation? The Boston police chased their own tails for two years on that one while women continued to be murdered."

"There are some parallels with the Boston murders but overall, the two cases are very different," said Detective Williams. "The Boston Strangler raped before he killed. In some of his later attacks, he also used a knife. Our killer only uses his hands and so far, there's been no evidence of any sexual assault."

"You got any intel on the psyche of this degenerate that I can share with my readers?" said Tommy Devlin.

"According to our NYPD psychologist, serial killers are usually particular and precise," said Daryl Williams. "They're into patterns and schedules and get a weird thrill leaving clues for the police to solve like a puzzle. In many cases, doing that somehow increases their sense of power and I guess, pleasure. In the 1970s, the Son of Sam sent letters to a *Daily News* reporter. Basically, some serial killers get off on playing cat and mouse. They believe themselves superior to the rest of us mortals."

Tommy Devlin and the other reporters nodded and took notes while Daryl continued.

"We assume the people who commit these crimes have some deviant psychological disorder that precludes them from rational thought. We hope that at some point they'll get sloppy and leave a crucial piece of evidence at the scene," said Darryl. "According to our police psychologist, very few serial killers are deranged in any medical or legal sense. Many are highly competent and sometimes extremely intelligent. What they lack is a conscience. Plain and simple, they're sociopaths. But, the world is full of sociopaths who operate and function in society. There are probably a few right here."

His last comment caused some laughter in the crowd of newsmen with several pointing and jostling the others as to who qualified.

"We must remember that this stalker isn't some raving lunatic," said the detective. "He's calm and calculated. One more possible personality trait — serial murderers are often motivated by the pure fun of it."

A murmur trickled through the crowd.

"When I want to have fun, I watch a ball game and have a couple of beers," shouted Devlin.

"That's not what I heard, Devlin," shouted a reporter from the *NY Post* in the back of the crowd. "I thought your idea of a good time was going moose walking. I never saw a grown man run so fast. How cold was that lake anyway?"

Laughter and jeers erupted from the reporters as Tommy Devlin's face turned red.

"My kids played that video a hundred times. You're a rock star at the Fair Oaks, New Jersey Middle School," said the *NY Post* reporter. More laughter and catcalls ensued.

"As far as this Strangler's patterns go," said Detective Williams, ignoring the comments, "our killer has established some. He always kills on the fifteenth of the month. There's obviously some significance to that date but so far, we don't know what that is. If we're correct about that pattern, another young woman may likely be attacked in twelve days."

"Our killer has also stayed roughly within a ten-block playing field to commit his crimes," said Heather Kim jumping in, "but we haven't figured out the significance of that — yet. Maybe he lives in the neighborhood? Maybe he works there? Or, maybe he used to live there? Right now, everything is on the table."

"Any possible connection between the victims?" asked a red-haired reporter from the *NY Daily News*.

"We did a background check on all of the women and there doesn't appear to be any relationship," said Williams. "In each case, except for the Central Park murder, there was no forced entry. We have to assume that all the women willingly let him in."

"What we don't know is *why* they let him in," said Heather. "The bottom line is this killer has some kind of inside track on all these women which we still don't understand. He knows them really well."

"Trial and error?" said the red-haired female reporter from the *Daily News*. "Maybe he spots the women on the street, strikes up a conversation and somehow gets into their apartment."

"We thought of that but it doesn't fit with his pattern," said Detective Williams. "He kills late in the day or at night on the fifteenth. Based on the time of all the murders, it's not likely he follows multiple people home. He wouldn't have the time to make mistakes if it's going to happen on that specific date. We believe he targets a specific individual and leaves nothing to chance. Our theory is that he identifies his victim well in advance of the crime."

The detectives shared the last remaining details of the West Side Strangler case with the press.

"What about all the Argus cameras? Any usable footage?" asked Tommy Devlin.

"On the most recent murder the cameras aren't of much help. They're located throughout the park but with all the trees in full bloom this time of year, visibility is poor," said Williams. "Go off the paths and roads, you get no visuals. Combine that with the darkness and we got next to nothing on Karina Kubiak — only maple trees and squirrels."

"What about footage from the neighborhoods of the first six murders?" shouted Tommy Devlin over the crowd.

"We've looked at all the street images from each homicide," said Daryl. "That's another puzzling piece. It appears the killer knows the neighborhood like the back of his hand. We've got film that's timestamped around each murder and we're pretty sure we've captured him but we never get an identifiable shot. It's like he knows exactly where the cameras are and when to cross a street or turn a corner so he won't be seen."

"Even with the pictures," said Heather, "an ID is challenging because everyone is wearing a mask. Add a baseball hat and sunglasses and you literally can't tell what someone looks like. That's the reality we're dealing with these days."

The crowd of reporters nodded and murmured in agreement. "That's about all we've got," said Daryl wrapping things up. "The police commissioner has asked that we do regular briefings with the press whenever there is new information. We're waiting on DNA test results on Karina Kubiak. Hopefully, that will give us the lead we've been waiting for."

When the press conference was over, the detectives returned to their precinct uptown. When Daryl got to his desk in the bullpen, a large envelope was there waiting for him. It contained the personnel records for all of Thayer and Co's New York metro stores. An electronic version had also been sent by email.

Waiting for the DNA results from the Central Park murder, Daryl opened the Thayer and Co files despite his partner's objections. "Are we really going to jerk around with Zoe Brandt's mystery woman when we've got an active serial killer?" said Heather.

The older detective pursed his lips. "Humor me. We won't spend a lot of time on it. Something about her story . . . I can't get Zoe Brandt out of my head."

Daryl opened a file containing detailed lists of employees at thirty-nine Thayer and Co stores in the New York area. Looking for female employees with Italian last names because of the Italian flag connection, he and Heather cross-matched those names with addresses of employees living around 14th Street. When they finished, they had a list of nearly seventy women. Separately, they created a second list of all female employees with first and last names beginning with G. When they compared the two lists, they were left with twenty-two names.

From Zoe Brandt's description, the masked woman was likely in her twenties or thirties. Checking birthdates, they ruled out those who were too old or too young. That left fourteen. Overlaying marital status, ten of the fourteen were single, now they were left with four. After a few phone calls they learned that one of the four women broke her leg in May and two of the others had left New York City in April when the pandemic got really bad.

That left one name — Gina Garicelli. For a few minutes Daryl thought they had hit the jackpot. After a phone call to her employer, he learned Garicelli had been in the hospital for the past four weeks with the virus. She couldn't be the masked woman. Frustrated, he pushed the files to the far corner of his desk and sighed.

"Are we done with this goose chase?" said Heather staring at her partner, "Because while you were on the phone about Garicelli, I got a message that the commissioner's office wants us to come in to do a briefing."

"I'm done with it," said Daryl, adjusting his mask and heading towards the fire door to go down the back stairs. Walking behind her partner, when the gray metal door swung open into the lobby, Heather spotted Zoe and Sean standing by the front desk. She tried to pull Daryl back into the stairwell, but it was too late. Zoe had already seen them.

"Detectives," Zoe shouted with wild eyes, a broad smile and an exaggerated wave as she ran over to them. "We came here to see you."

Trapped, the two detectives moved over to the row of wooden chairs for a brief powwow. Detective Williams quickly explained that there were no matches on the employee list from Thayer and Co.

"But that's impossible. I know that woman works there, I just know it. What do we do now?" said Zoe, a frantic look creeping into her eyes.

"We," said Heather making air quotes, "don't do anything. You need to leave the investigating to us."

"But—" said Zoe.

"There's not much more we can do given the limited information," said Daryl. "Unless you have something else for us to go on—"

"We do, actually," said Sean stepping forward. "That Blue Crest Financial tote bag the masked woman was carrying. We found out that specific design was only given to employees."

"Do you have any idea how many employees Blue Crest has in the New York area?" said Heather, obviously annoyed. "Thousands, maybe tens of thousands."

"Oh," said Zoe, tears welling up in her eyes. "We thought it was a really good clue."

Daryl Williams cleared his throat, signaling his partner to dial it down. "Ms. Brandt, I'll give the Thayer and Co list another pass tonight, but no promises."

CHAPTER THIRTY-TWO

Sr. Bello considered himself a confident man, comfortable in his own skin, someone who almost always did the right thing. He didn't cut corners, cheat on his taxes or use bad language — at least not too often. His life was neat and orderly. He had a nice wife, a beautiful home, a solid job where he was well respected by his colleagues. He paid the majority of his bills on time and even remembered to send a birthday card to his mother once a year. In short, he had everything a man could want — or so he had thought until the day he met Gabriela.

When their all-consuming affair started he lied to his unsuspecting wife in an effort to keep his relationship secret, unsure where it was headed. In the beginning, he'd occasionally have pangs of guilt and take a moment to reflect on his actions. As the affair continued and became more intense, his soul-searching grew less frequent until he stopped examining and questioning how far off-course he had strayed. Gabriela was his drug and he couldn't and wouldn't give her up. Her demands only made him want to please her more, and in time, he knew he would do anything to keep her. Eight months into their relationship, she gave him an ultimatum neatly packaged as a request.

"My darling, you promised we would be together soon," she purred as she lay next to him in bed. "We snatch a few hours here and there. That's not enough for me. Is it enough for you?"

"Of course not, but it's complicated," said Sr. Bello as he rolled over and caressed her thigh. "You've got a husband, I've got a wife. It's not just us and there are financial considerations too."

"I've been giving this problem a lot of thought," said Gabriela as she started to unpack her plan. For the next half hour, she talked and explained while he listened without interrupting, partly because he was in shock. When she finished, a chill went down his spine.

"Makes perfect sense, no?" she said. "It's the only solution. We will get what we want and then we can be together."

"There's got to be another way."

"There isn't," said Gabriela, climbing on top of him and leaning in for a kiss that he couldn't resist. "Not unless we lose everything and I'm not willing to do that. I can't stay with Greg a minute longer. If you don't want to do what it takes to be with me, maybe I should find someone else. Maybe I should find a man who is less complicated and more willing to do whatever it takes."

The smell of her skin addled his brain and eventually he heard himself agreeing to do what she had asked. That was the moment he fully surrendered to her. For a man who otherwise revered order, when it came to Gabi, he was merely a passenger on a runaway train with no engineer — scared but thrilled at the same time.

"How long will it take you to make this happen for us, my love?" she asked as if she were ordering a cup of coffee at Starbucks. "I can't live in that tiny apartment filled with garbage for much longer. All night long he plays those stupid video games. I've got to get out of there."

"If we do this, we've got to do it right or I'll end up in jail and so will you," he said as he caressed her skin. "It will be soon, I promise. You'll have to trust me and be patient."

* * *

If someone wants to anonymously buy guns, ammo, drugs, credit card numbers, counterfeit money or codes to hack into other people's computers they can find it all on the dark web. It's like no other shopping experience in the world. One can order services from vendors who will do or get whatever the customer wants. Providing it's all anonymous and paid for with crypto currency.

Kiddie porn — no problem. A slave — sure, get two for one. A paid killer — easy-peasy. The dark web is a veritable mall for evil featuring the latest hits from the black arts. Every bottom feeder and lowlife on the planet with something illegal to buy or sell eventually finds their way there. It's *the* place to hock merchandise be it human or other. Once in business, customers from around the globe drop in to do a little shopping. They even have sales and promotions. "Hurry, hurry, going fast. Weekly special — kidnappings are half price for only one thousand euros! Buy two!"

After his promise to Gabriela, Sr. Bello educated himself, reading as many articles on the dark web as he could find before he made a move and put his plan into motion.

Downloading the Tor browser, the way to get into the dark web, he was initially surprised that it looked so normal — a collection of marketplaces that sold a variety of products to the highest bidder. Except, once you scratched the surface and looked deeper into what they were actually selling, you knew you weren't shopping at IKEA.

The dark web was a digital crime candy store. One vendor offered login credentials to a bank account that had more than $100,000 in it. Pay the fee for the credentials and you were in. Another was offering two for ones on counterfeit dollars, pounds, shekels, any currency you wanted — such a bargain. Vendors offered usernames and passwords, and pornography of all kinds, much of which most people didn't know existed.

As Sr. Bello scrolled through each section with names like White House Market, Monopoly, Dark Market, Versus, Vice, and Enigma, it became evident that each group had their own specialty — their unique selling proposition. He dug further, searching for one that provided the services he specifically needed.

After clicking around for hours, he stumbled upon the Death Star Market. They had a range of vendors — credit cards, cocaine, and bomb materials but they also had a marketplace for soldiers of fortune, more commonly known as people who would do *anything* for a buck.

For obvious reasons, no one used real names on the dark web. All transactions were done using euphemisms — the drug seller might be called "Dr. Happy" and the counterfeiter might be called "The Printer." Sr. Bello scrolled through all the listings until he found one that seemed like it might fit his needs. The person called him or herself "Pest Control."

In order to communicate with Pest Control, Bello used Jabber, a chat program that worked on the dark web. He wrote and rewrote his message a hundred times before he finally sent it to Pest Control.

> *Hello. I've seen your ad on the Death Star Market and you look like you provide the kind of services I'm looking for. I have a terrible pest problem in New York City. — Sir Lancelot*

Several hours later, Sr. Bello received a response.

> *SL — what did you have in mind? I get rid of things, make them disappear, can clean out your attic. After my exterminating service, you won't have a problem again.*

Sr. Bello and Pest Control went back and forth for weeks until both were satisfied the other one wasn't a member of law enforcement. Sr. Bello sent him a picture of the intended victim. Then, he created a digital wallet using Bitcoin and deposited half the payment for the job. They agreed the other half would be sent when the job was completed. A date was selected for the extermination service: Thursday, June 4th, 2020.

CHAPTER THIRTY-THREE

A few weeks earlier while sitting at his desk in the CIG corporate offices in Lower Manhattan, Sr. Bello pulled together his final notes in preparation for that morning's executive meeting. The gathering would be long and he'd likely be called on to speak about his department's numbers. His quarterly goals had been achieved which he considered a minor miracle given that he had been completely preoccupied with *her*.

Forcing himself to focus on his work, he had to make a conscious effort to stay on task or his mind immediately drifted back to Gabriela. He had long ago accepted his obsession with her, believing that they were inexplicably tied together and he didn't want it any other way.

Looking out of his office window, he thought back to the first time they had met in the men's footwear department of Thayer and Company. He remembered the sweat seeping out of his pores when he got up the nerve to ask her to meet him for a drink. When she had suggested a hotel bar, his knees had nearly buckled. Later, over their wine, when her naked foot crept up his thigh, he wanted to take her right there at the table. The air between them was so thick he was more intoxicated by her scent than the alcohol he had consumed. That first time they made love he knew there was nothing he wouldn't do for her. From that day forward, his only desire was to be in her orbit and he'd do whatever it took to stay there.

Since his affair began, his wife had noticed on more than one occasion that he seemed preoccupied. "Lately, you've been in another world," she had said, her comments jolting him out of the mind movie he was playing of his last sexual encounter with Gabriela. "You've been so quiet these past few months. Is everything okay?"

"Work is really intense, that's all," he had said to alleviate his wife's concerns. She had accepted his explanations given his high-pressure job. Whenever he had little pangs of guilt, he distanced himself even more from the woman he had married.

Because of the pandemic, most people had curtailed socializing altogether but it didn't stop Sr. Bello and Gabriela from their trysts. "I can't bear being away from you," Gabriela had purred in bed one evening while drawing a line down the center of his chest with her finger. "When I'm not with you, I feel like half a person. Do you feel the same?"

"How can you ask me that? You know I do."

"When are we going to be together? I can't wait anymore."

"Trust me," he had replied, her naked body in his arms rendering him helpless, "I've put a plan in place."

When Gabriela had first suggested their only way forward was murder, he had been shocked. But she was a persuasive woman, and he eventually agreed that murder was their only viable path. With the wheels now set in motion, he was in deep and there was no turning back.

A colleague rapped on Sr. Bello's open office door as he passed, signaling it was time for their meeting. Gathering his files, he stepped out into the long glass hallway, nodding and smiling to several CIG employees walking by. Ahead, at an intersection of corridors, another department head waved to him.

"Morning," said the co-worker as Bello caught up and the two continued to the conference room together.

"Morning," said Sr. Bello. "You ready for the meeting?"

"Ready as I'll ever be. I heard Spaulding's going to sit in today," said the co-worker.

"Is that unusual?" said Sr. Bello, having only joined the firm a couple of months earlier and not yet met Jordan Spaulding.

"He runs hot and cold," said the co-worker, shrugging. "Sometimes he doesn't come to the meeting for months and then he shows up every week. I prefer it when he's not there. He makes everyone nervous."

Sr. Bello pushed open the glass door to the conference room. Eleven other managers were already seated around a large, glossy wooden table. He found an empty seat and got settled as the glass door opened again. A tall man entered the room sheepishly and quietly took a seat.

"Who's that?" whispered Sr. Bello to the person on his left. "Haven't seen him before."

"I forget his name," said his colleague. "I think he's a senior analyst from Chicago. I guess that means you're not the new kid on the block anymore." Sr. Bello nodded to the new analyst across the table who responded with a smile and a quick but subtle wave.

Outside the conference room door there was a commotion as the CEO of CIG, Jordan Spaulding, blasted into the room. "Good morning everyone," said the CEO in a booming voice as he took his seat at the head of the table. "The sun is shining. It's a beautiful day. No doubt you all have wonderful numbers for me. Let's try not to ruin my good mood."

"Good morning," murmured several people in the room.

"I see some new faces since I was last here," said Jordan looking down at a piece of paper. "Which one of you is Kevin Bishop?"

Conner Brandt raised his hand. "I'm Kevin Bishop. Nice to finally meet you, Jordan."

Undercover on the CIG case for months, Conner expected the FBI would soon have enough solid evidence to put Spaulding and all of his minions behind bars. From what they had discovered so far, Jordan Spaulding was a bigger fraudster than anyone had dreamed.

CHAPTER THIRTY-FOUR

At his desk at 2 p.m. that Wednesday, Daryl Williams' eyes were glued to a spreadsheet of Thayer and Co employees.

"Here's that report you wanted," said Manny Perez, one of the young police officers on the Strangler task force as he placed a large brown envelope on Daryl's desk. When Daryl minimized the Thayer document it revealed another image underneath — a flag. The picture caught the young officer's eye.

"You planning a little trip to Mexico, detective?" said Manny with a smile.

"Mexico?" said Daryl looking up at him. "What are you talking about?"

"You have a Mexican flag on your screen."

"It's an Italian flag," said Daryl, opening the large envelope the young man had just placed on his desk.

"Hate to tell ya, but both of my parents are Mexican. I've been there every Christmas since I was born and spent half my summers there when I was a kid. I know what the Mexican flag looks like. That's a Mexican flag, not Italian."

Puzzled, Daryl turned back to his computer and did a google image search for the Italian and Mexican flags.

"Would you look at that," said Daryl, when he had pictures of the flags side by side. "They're almost identical, except the Mexican flag has a brown bird in the middle. Otherwise, the colors are the same and in the same pattern. From a distance, if you didn't notice the brown circle in the center, you might think the Mexican flag was the Italian flag."

"Italians and Mexicans wouldn't make that mistake," said Manny Perez, still grinning.

"All this time, I've been looking for an Italian name when she might be Spanish."

"Whatever you say," said the young officer walking away when Daryl offered no further explanation.

"What are you working on?" said Heather Kim as she placed a fresh cup of coffee on her desk. "I'll regret this when I go to bed but it was either another shot of caffeine or I was going to pass out."

"I could use your help with something," said Daryl as he split the Thayer and Co list in two and handed half to Heather. "Circle all the women who have Spanish names."

"I thought we were done with this?" said Heather. "Weren't we were looking for Italian names? What's going on?"

"It's a long story. Just trust me on this," said Daryl scratching his head. "Something about Zoe Brandt's story feels like we're on the cusp of something."

"The Strangler is our priority."

"I know, but I think the Brandt woman is telling the truth. If we can prevent another murder, don't we have to try?"

Heather's face softened. Her partner's dogged pursuit of the truth was one of the reasons she liked working with him. She looked at her watch and she rolled her eyes. "Okay, what do you need me to do?" she said as she sat down next to him. For the next thirty minutes, they combed through all the Thayer employee lists. Out of the 3,000 people the company employed in the New York metro region, they narrowed the list down to sixteen women with a Hispanic name with a first and last name that started with G.

Daryl whistled. "Now we're getting somewhere," he said and explained his revelation to his partner.

"I thought Zoe Brandt told us the woman was wearing a hat with an Italian flag," said Heather.

"She said it was green, white and red," said Daryl, "I led the witness. I assumed it was an Italian flag and she went along with it. It was my mistake. We've been looking for a pizza when we should have been hunting for tacos."

"In that case, we made another wrong assumption. Sr. Bello isn't Italian as in, Signore Bello, it's Spanish for Senor Bello," said Heather. "I'm pretty sure the word *bello* means the same thing in Italian and Spanish — beautiful. Eww, the masked woman calls her murderous boyfriend Mr. Beautiful. I think I'm going to be sick. If Brandt and McAllister were right, our masked Lady Macbeth has to be one of these sixteen women."

After a string of phone calls the detectives deduced that none of the women on the new list with double G names fitted the new profile. Gabriela García's name didn't show up because when she applied for the job, she had used her married name — Gabi Harmen. Frustrated, but still convinced there was something to Zoe's story, Daryl Williams had another idea. "If Zoe Brandt is right about this murder happening tomorrow on June 4, in about twenty-four to forty-eight hours a man's corpse is going to turn up," he said to his partner. "We know the masked woman has a G name, right? What if we expand the search to women with first or a last name beginning with G?"

"Worth a shot," said Heather as she reached for the stacks of employee rosters and pulled out a red pen. "What about the Mexican-Italian connection?"

"Look for both."

When they finished, they had identified five new names at different Thayer and Co stores around the city — Gloria Sala, Maria Gonzalez, Gabi Harmen, Ellen Grassi and Vicki Garistino.

"Gloria Sala was born in 1956. That would make her sixty-four. She's definitely not the masked woman," said Daryl crossing off her name. "Same with Vicki Garistino, too old."

"Gonzalez and Grassi fit into the Spanish-Italian bucket," said Heather, "and both women are under forty. That moves them to the top of the list."

"What about Harmen? Harmen doesn't sound Latin."

"Give me a second," said Heather as she turned back to her computer and entered an access code into the Thayer digital file. Seconds later she let out a yelp.

"Here we go," she said, smiling. "According to the personnel records, Gabi Harmen is her married name. Her middle name is García. There's your double G and García could definitely be of Mexican descent."

"Let's pick up Zoe Brandt and Sean McAllister and do a drive-by on these women and see if they can ID her," said Daryl as he grabbed the phone to call Zoe.

CHAPTER THIRTY-FIVE

By 3:45 p.m., Zoe and Sean were in the back seat of Daryl and Heather's unmarked police vehicle on their way to a Thayer and Co store in Lower Manhattan.

While cruising south, Daryl showed Zoe and Sean employee ID headshots of the three women they were going to see that morning. After stopping in front of the store in a no-parking zone, they walked towards the entrance while Daryl gave the amateur sleuths last-minute instructions. "We don't want to tip anyone off that they're being watched. All the stores will be empty because of the virus. There's probably only a handful of employees inside and possibly no customers. Keep a low profile. Clear?"

Zoe gulped as she and Sean nodded their heads.

The first store was where Ellen Grassi worked. Everyone inside was masked. Zoe and Sean, acting like serious shoppers, gave Ms. Grassi a hard look while they circled the store while pretending to examine and comment on different merchandise. Staying out of their way, the detectives quietly perused the shoe department. When they all met up outside, Zoe and Sean were unsure.

"It could be her," said Zoe, "but like I said, the woman I saw in the park wore a mask, sunglasses and a hat. I never saw her face. I can't be sure the woman we just looked at was the same person."

Next, they drove to the Thayer store in Midtown on the east side to get a look at Gabriela Harmen. "Dial it down a little this time," said Daryl with a weary look in his eyes. "At the last store, you looked like you were going to steal something. Their security man was watching you like a hawk."

Zoe and Sean nodded and walked into the store ahead of the detectives. As soon as they entered, a masked salesman raced over and offered to help.

"We're just browsing," said Sean grandly through his mask waving the salesman away. Wandering through the aisles, the two friends passed the detectives several times and eventually headed towards a petite, dark-haired saleswoman standing behind a counter. Masked, with long, wavy brown hair and thick, black eyelashes, the saleswoman looked up at them as they approached. "Can I help you find something?" she said with a sexy, gravelly voice and a thick, syrupy Spanish accent.

"We're just browsing," said Sean again, his eyes darting around the store.

"I'll leave you to shop on your own. Let me know if I can be of help," said Gabriela as she walked away. She hated waiting on couples: making far better commissions when a man was alone and she could really work it.

"What do you think?" said Sean as he and Zoe moved down the aisle.

"I don't know," whispered Zoe, "could be her, but it could also be the woman we saw at the last store. The day we saw the masked woman, she was so far away and she had her sunglasses on the whole time. This woman here has killer eyelashes. I'd remember those lashes but I never saw the masked woman's eyes."

The detectives lingered for a while near the front entrance looking at socks until Zoe and Sean walked out the door shrugging their shoulders. The two detectives looked at each other and shook their heads. "This is such a waste of time," said Heather under her breath.

"One more store," said Daryl, "then we're done. I promise."

The four drove to an Upper West Side store where they examined and had a brief conversation with another saleswoman, Maria Gonzalez. Once again, she looked very much like the other two. Small to average height, long, dark-brown hair, thin and most of her face covered by a mask.

"Anything familiar?" said Daryl once they were outside and half a block from the store.

"I'm sorry. All the women looked the same," said Zoe. "I couldn't identify any of them."

"Me neither," said Sean shaking his head.

"Where do we go from here?" asked Zoe.

"We've gone as far as we can go, given the information we have," said Daryl.

"So, that's it?" said Zoe. "We're just going to let him die?"

"Ms. Brandt," said Heather losing her patience, "Do you realize what's going on in this city right now? Take a look around. The streets are practically empty. Everyone is in masks. We shouldn't have given you as much time as we did. You provided information that was absolutely impossible to follow up on and yet, my partner has been up late at night trying to figure it all out. Detective Williams is correct, we've run down all the info and until there's something new, there's nothing more we can do with your story."

"But—" said Zoe.

"Come on, Zoe," said Sean pulling her arm. "It's time for us to go. Thank you for trying, detectives. It was a long shot and we appreciate what you've done."

"If anything else comes up, you know where to find us," Daryl said as Zoe and Sean walked away.

"You need to cut back on all that coffee," said Daryl to Heather as he watched Zoe and Sean turn the corner.

"I shouldn't have lost my temper but that woman got under my skin. She's like a rabid dog with a bone."

"She's persistent, I'll give her that. I'm satisfied we did all we could with what we had. Let's get back to our other case. June 15th is only twelve days away."

CHAPTER THIRTY-SIX

After leaving the detectives, Zoe and Sean went to Central Park. It was nearly 6 p.m. when they stopped and sat on the same bench where Zoe had witnessed the masked woman plotting her husband's demise.

"We're at the end of the road," said Sean. "I don't know what else we can do."

"We can't give up. A man's life is in our hands," said Zoe. "What about trying to track down the husband through eBay from when he bid on that antique lamp? If we can find the item, maybe we could get his name from eBay and warn him?"

"eBay is not going to release that kind of personal information," said Sean. "Even if the police ask for it, they'd need to get a court order first and there's no time left for that. If what you saw through your binoculars was correct, the hit on the husband is going down in less than forty-eight hours."

"We've got to do something," said Zoe, biting her lip. "What if we try the Gucci store again tomorrow morning?"

"That salesperson wouldn't give us the information the last time we were there, why do you think she'll give it to us tomorrow?"

"Because, I have a brilliant idea."

"I've got to hear this," said Sean with one raised eyebrow.

"We'll tell her the truth. The whole thing, the masked woman, the murder plot, the binoculars, the works."

"On Monday we told her you were looking to purchase a Gucci bag because you admired one a friend had," said Sean. "Now, it's because of a murder plot you learned about using binoculars from your apartment window."

"Exactly," said Zoe, her eyes afire, a huge smile on her face.

"You're delusional," said Sean. "No way that store clerk is going to risk her job over that story."

Zoe groaned. "You're right. I was desperate. Maybe Detective Williams will still come up with something."

"There's still one more option you haven't tried," said Sean. "You could ask your husband, aka the FBI agent, to help us."

"I could never," said Zoe. "If Conner had any idea I've been all over New York asking questions, trying to get confidential data from companies, talking to detectives and reporters, it would be the end of my marriage."

* * *

At 7:15 p.m. that night, eating broiled salmon and a spinach salad, Zoe took a sip of her white wine while she watched the local evening news. The weatherman had predicted a heatwave starting that coming Saturday. The weather report was followed by an update on the West Side Strangler case. Detective Williams and Kim's faces were suddenly in the center of her TV screen.

"It's still unclear whether there is any connection between the young teacher found in Central Park this past Tuesday and the murders of six women on the west side of Manhattan," said Detective Williams into a microphone as a map of all the murder locations flashed across the left half of the screen.

Heather Kim stepped up to the podium. "We're doing everything we can to stop this predator. We've got officers working in twenty-four-hour shifts and that will continue until we catch him."

* * *

After Zoe finished her dinner, she went into the kitchen, poured herself her nightly glass of bourbon and climbed back onto the couch to wait for her husband's call. At 8 p.m., her phone rang. It was Conner. "Hello there, stranger," she said as she swirled the ice cubes in her glass. "Right on time, as always. I like a punctual man."

"I've only got a few minutes to talk. The team is going to meet tonight at some outdoor beer garden," said Conner.

"That sounds fun. Don't get too close to people."

"I'm always careful. Did you call someone to fix the front door lock?"

"No, but I'm writing myself a note right now," said Zoe reaching for a pen and writing LOCK on the palm of her hand in black ink.

"What's the problem, Zoe? You're not working right now. The only thing you had to do this week was to get that lock fixed. Or are you too involved with Sean on all of your 'investigations' to have time for anything else?"

"I don't know what you're talking about. There's been a lot of stuff going on at the restaurant. We're reopening outside next week and this morning Miranda let half the staff go. I still have my job but—"

"I got a call from Juliet Pasternak today."

"Juliet? How does she have your number?"

"From the bank robbery investigation, I guess. She told me she was concerned about you, that you were talking about conspiracies at the restaurant today," said an exasperated Conner.

"I never even spoke to her," said Zoe. *That bitch.* "She's mad because she lost her job and I didn't. Conner, you've got to believe me. You know Juliet and I never got along."

"We'll talk about it when I get home. I've got to go. I'm getting a ride from someone and they just pulled up outside.

Get the lock fixed. I'll be home in three days and we can talk then."

"I swear, Juliet is making stuff up."

"Okay."

"Love you."

"Gotta go."

She put her phone down and stared at the word LOCK written on her hand. *I can't believe Juliet called Conner. What is she up to?* After one last text check, she turned off the living-room lights and walked back to her master bathroom to brush her teeth. Opening her cabinet, she took out the brand-new prescription of Ambien that she had picked up earlier that week.

Conner was so cranky tonight. He's still mad about all that stuff from last year. Now, he's blowing everything way out of proportion. He wasn't going to be fired. Does he believe Juliet over me?

She opened the new bottle of Ambien, popped a single pill in her mouth, and washed it down with her last sip of bourbon. Changing into her nightshirt, she put her new prescription bottle back into the bathroom medicine cabinet and climbed into bed. *At least I'll get some sleep tonight. I'll worry about Conner and the masked woman tomorrow.*

CHAPTER THIRTY-SEVEN

Before the effects of the Ambien totally kicked in that Wednesday night, Zoe's mind remained busy. She reviewed the activities of her day and made a list of plans for the next morning as she waited for the sleeping pill to send her off to dreamland. Thoughts of Conner and the irritated tone he took with her on their calls that week crept into her mind. *He says he's over what happened with the embassy, but I don't think he is. If he wants me to go back to Dr. Eisdorfer, it means he's still upset. I don't need therapy. I only went to make him happy.*

"Why do you think you insert yourself into other people's lives, Zoe?" Dr. Eisdorfer had asked in one of their early sessions.

"I don't," said Zoe. "I have extremely heightened senses. I notice things other people don't."

"Like what?" said Dr. Eisdorfer smiling warmly.

"Most people walk around caught up in their own thoughts, moving from one place to the next, one meeting to another. I move through the world with all my senses open and available. I look, listen, smell, touch, and really feel my environment," said Zoe passionately. "That's why I detect things — a blink of an eye, a whisper between strangers, a secret document passed from a Central European man to a South African woman on a bus."

The therapist's face remained still as she took a long deep breath in and exhaled. "It must be wonderful to have such an acute sense of the world, but it also has to be very distracting and exhausting," said the therapist in earnest. "Don't you get tired of always being so attuned to your environment?"

Zoe smiled and leaned forward. "It's invigorating most of the time. Although, I sometimes find it difficult to focus with so many things happening around me."

"I can imagine."

"But you know what they say, if you see something, say something, right? If you see a potential crime, you have to let the authorities know, don't you? You *have* to report it."

"Alerting law enforcement to a crime *is* one's civic duty. But, let me ask you, how has all of your investigating ended up? Have any of the perpetrators you reported actually been arrested?" asked Dr. Eisdorfer.

"Not exactly."

"Do you think it's possible your imagination exaggerates little things and makes them seem bigger or more nefarious than they actually are?"

"Look at me. I'm a restaurant shift manager," said Zoe blinking back tears. "My imagination is what makes my otherwise pretty dull life seem exciting and full of color. I wake up every morning ready for my next great adventure. That's why I write. Does that make sense to you, Dr. Eisdorfer?"

"An active imagination is a wonderful thing," said the therapist, "but it seems to get you into a bit of trouble. Your husband is frustrated and worried about you, especially after that incident with the Peruvians. What if we channel your imaginative thoughts into your writing?"

"What do you mean?"

"What if instead of calling an embassy, the CIA, the Department of Health, or the Drug Enforcement Agency, you started by writing things down."

"You mean like a short story?"

"Exactly," said the therapist. "Instead of involving the law, some government agency or the United Nations, what if you wrote a short story and then brought it with you to our session? Together, we could bang on it before you alerted the Pentagon, the Department of Homeland Security or some other official organization."

"I suppose I could do that."

Dr. Eisdorfer smiled. "Let's try it for the next few weeks and see how it goes."

That's exactly what Zoe did. For several months she threw herself into her writing and every time she had a notion about a potential crime or something that just didn't look quite right, she'd turn it into a short story and bring it with her to the therapy session. For four months Zoe dutifully brought her stories to Dr. Eisdorfer who marveled at her creativity. Together they examined how some of the incidents or people Zoe "noticed" might have been a coincidence or nothing at all.

When her conspiracy theories were funneled into her writing, things between Zoe and Conner moved into a much better place. He stopped micromanaging her and she was generally more relaxed.

All that changed when Zoe witnessed the masked woman plotting to murder her husband from her living-room window. No matter how hard she tried, she couldn't ignore what she had seen. Convinced the incident in the park was real and believing a man's life was at stake, Zoe was committed to seeing it through even if it did cause problems in her marriage.

CHAPTER THIRTY-EIGHT

Thursday — June 4, 2020

"There's an order to this," said Heather Kim sitting at her desk in the bullpen, shaking her head and staring up at a giant map of the Upper West Side pinned on the wall. "I keep coming back to this map. My gut says the answer is right there in front of us."

"We've looked at the map a thousand times from every angle," said Daryl Williams, taking a sip of his fourth coffee. "If it's saying something, it's not talking to me."

Heather moved closer to the map with a red ruler in her hand and pointed. "Humor me, let's do this one more time. The first murder was Lisa Eng on 95th Street, right? Next, Carly Faircloth on 104th Street, which means our perp went uptown by nine blocks. Third, Nicole Barrett on 96th Street, which means he goes back downtown by eight blocks."

"Then in March it was Rosie Florio on 97th and Columbus," said Daryl.

"Which is only one block north of the previous murder," said Heather. "The killer stayed in the same neighborhood. That's significant, right?"

Daryl shrugged his shoulders. "I've looked at this thing so many times, I don't know what's significant anymore."

"The fifth victim was Michelle Rothberg on 103rd and Amsterdam; and victim number six, Katie Tierney, on Central Park West and 100th Street," said Heather, walking in front of the map like a college professor giving a lecture. "The killer goes uptown then downtown then uptown then downtown. A big zigzag. Maybe that's something? Maybe that's part of his pattern?"

"If it is, I don't know what it means. Any theories?"

"Not a clue," said a frustrated Heather plopping down in her desk chair. "We've checked every retailer in the areas surrounding each crime scene and there's no connection."

"What's your gut on the teacher in the park as a seventh victim?" said Daryl. "I'm not a hundred percent on that."

"Part of me says yes and part of me says no. Medical examiner said the strangulation technique appears the same but everything else is wrong."

"Let's re-interview a few people," said Daryl as he picked up a file on his desk. "We've missed something. Tomorrow, we'll go back over to Katie Tierney's neighborhood and rattle some trees until something falls out."

As the two detectives dug into their own individual paperwork, a bald, middle-aged mailman who was clearly lost entered the police bullpen.

"I'm looking for a Detective Daryl Williams," said the postman loudly, lugging his overstuffed mailbag, visibly sweating through his face mask. "It's so hot outside and this mask keeps all the heat in. No global warming? Ha! I'm dying out there."

"Wait until August," said a young officer passing by. "We're all going to bake in those masks. Be glad you're not a traffic cop standing in the sun."

"I'm Williams," said Daryl raising his hand.

"The man of the hour. I've got two letters for you that need signatures," said the postal worker, pulling two envelopes out of his bag and handing them to Daryl.

As the detective reached for a pen, the mailman looked around the busy room. "Looks like you've got a lot going on here," he said.

"You could say that," said Heather without looking up.

The mailman nodded appreciatively as his eyes settled on the big map hanging above Heather's desk. "That's weird," said the postman.

"What's weird," said Daryl as he signed his letters.

"That big map up there with the red marks looks just like my old postal route," he said.

Daryl looked over at Heather who was already looking up at the mailman.

"What did you just say?" said Daryl.

"That's my old mail route you have circled there on the map," said the mailman, pointing and moving closer. "I used to deliver from 96th to 104th between Central Park West and Amsterdam. That's what you've got outlined on your map, isn't it?"

"Wait a second," said Heather standing up, "you're saying that's your exact mail route?"

"My old one. Got a way sweeter route now. I cover 42nd to 55th between Eighth and Ninth," said the mailman. "A lot less mail to deliver. That old route took forever and everyone was so particular about everything."

On their feet, the two detectives faced the mailman. "When did you leave that route?" asked Daryl.

"A few years ago," said the mailman, backing up as the detectives invaded his personal space. "I put in for a different territory over on the east side when someone over there retired. I worked the east side for a couple of years and then someone died, so I put in for the route I have now. Most people don't know this but when you have a good mail route, you never give it up . . . unless you die. The only time the good routes come available is when somebody bites the big one. The longer you stay at USPS, the better your routes get, if you don't keel over first."

"Do you know if the same person who took over your old West Side route is still there?" asked Heather.

"No clue," said the mailman shaking his head. "People at the postal service move around a lot and besides, I check in at a different sorting facility now. It could be someone new, or not."

"Thank you," said Daryl to the mailman who was enjoying being the center of attention. "Thank you very much."

"If he's right," said Heather, "this takes *going postal* to a whole new level."

Minutes later, the two detectives assembled the entire West Side Strangler team in the war room. With the other precincts on the task force on speakerphone, they briefed everyone on what they had just learned.

"This may be a total boondoggle but it's the first goddamn time that map has any meaningful context," said Daryl. "Detective Kim and I think it's extremely possible our perp is a mail carrier. It makes total sense. A mailman knows who lives in a building, who lives alone, when they come, when they go, what they buy, when they're on vacation."

"They know who's getting divorced," said Heather, "or who's getting foreclosed on, having surgery, overdue on their bills."

"Michelle Rothberg had foot surgery," shouted one of the younger officers as everyone else in the room nodded.

"Exactly," said Daryl as he handed each member of the team their assignments. "We need to find out who has that same Upper West Side postal route now. And, we need it fast."

"With the whole country working remotely," said Heather, "I don't know where to start. All my usual channels are out of whack because of this virus. Who would we call to get postal routes?"

"I'll get the postmaster general of the United States on the phone, if I have to," said Daryl. "We're going to find out who has that route — today."

The entire team jumped on their phones, texting and calling around to find out which department controlled the mail-carrier schedules in Manhattan. After leaving dozens of messages, they still had no answers.

"This is the break we were waiting for," said Daryl rubbing his hands together. "I'll brief the captain on this. Let's see if he can get a postal inspector on the phone. This can't wait until tomorrow. If he can't help, I'll take it right up the line to the police commissioner."

CHAPTER THIRTY-NINE

When the alarm on Gabriela's phone rang at 6:30 that Thursday morning, she opened her eyes and smiled. She had been waiting for this day for a long time. Sr. Bello had promised that everything would be taken care of and the problem neutralized before the day was over. He also pledged that they would finally be together in October. *In five months, I'll be on my way to my perfect life. I should plan a little surprise October celebration getaway for the two of us. Hmm . . . where should we go?*

Her husband's side of the bed was empty. He had an early dentist appointment that day. She heard sounds of banging cabinets coming from the kitchen. *He's so annoying. Why must he slam the doors all the time?* She put a pillow over her head to block out the noise and remained quiet. *If he thinks I'm sleeping, he won't bother me.*

Pulling up the cool cotton sheets around her flawless neck, she thought about her life's journey. After all the years and all her struggles, everything was finally coming together. Images of her childhood outside of Mexico City, and their broken-down family home flashed across her mind. When thoughts of her stepfather and the way he touched her intruded, her forehead furrowed. Her only wish had been to get away from that place, convinced she was destined for far greater things.

In her early teens she had gone to a movie with her best friend, Martá. The American film *Enchanted,* about a princess transported from a magical kingdom to the streets of New York City had been playing. Sitting in the darkened movie theater drinking in scenes of the Big Apple, Gabriela was struck by a thunderbolt. *I'll go to New York. One day I'll live in a penthouse in Manhattan.* As she and Martá left the theater, elaborate plans of her New York dream formed in her mind.

"Don't you think Nueva York is the most amazing city in the world?" she said to Martá as they walked from the theater out to the street.

"There are lots of crazy people there," said Martá. "I would be scared. My papa said they have so many guns in Nueva York. People walk around with machine guns and will shoot you dead if you look at them the wrong way."

"You're such a baby. I'm not afraid of guns. I'm going to live in Manhattan just like the princess in the movie. Maybe I'll even get my own gun."

Martá's mouth dropped open.

"Close your mouth, Martá or the mosquitos will fly right in and go down your throat," said Gabriela as she sped up her pace, walking ahead of her friend.

From that day forward, everything Gabriela did furthered her plan for a life in New York. Studying English at school became her priority and soon her teachers considered her to be the best English-language student in the school.

"I've never seen another student take to languages the way you have, Gabriela," said her older male English teacher as his eyes took in every inch of her blossoming body. "You are so motivated. You're not just a beautiful girl but you're smart too."

"It's only because you are such a wonderful teacher, senor," she replied with a smile.

She didn't want to just *visit* New York, she wanted to *live* in New York and live large. Her perfect life included amazing homes — plural, expensive designer clothes, fine jewelry, European cars and trips all over the world. She wanted to go to the most exclusive restaurants, attend fashion shows and wear only $800 shoes — the ones with the red soles.

At 7:05 a.m. she heard Greg open the front door and pull it shut making a loud bang. *Always slamming things. At least now I won't have to look at his stupid doughy face again.* Despite her growing disgust, Greg had been earning more money lately. His online tutoring business had blown up in a lucrative way since the pandemic started. Children being homeschooled turned out to be great for his business. Wealthy New York parents made sure their progeny kept up with their studies and hired tutors for their kids. Greg even had to turn down a few jobs because of the high demand: there were not enough hours in the day. Despite that, his moderately increased income would never be enough for Gabi.

Peeling off the bed sheets, she stood up and walked to the single open bedroom window that faced the red-brick wall. Just the sight of the bricks irritated her. It was not the glamorous view she longed for and had expected when she married him. She thought back to her teenage years, a time when she had worked so hard and saved everything she made for her eventual getaway to New York.

No one had known about the *special* relationships she had back in Mexico. A few times her mother had looked at her sideways after discovering an expensive bracelet or a pair of gold earrings in her daughter's room. "Where did you get this jewelry from? These things cost a lot of money. You didn't steal it, did you?" her mother had said suspiciously.

"No Mama, I don't steal. I earn whatever I have."

"Then, where did this come from?" her mother said, holding up a sparkly bracelet.

"Some boy gave it to me," said Gabriela turning away.

Her mother squinted and stared at her daughter. "If a boy gives you a gold bracelet, he expects payment."

"You're so old-fashioned," said Gabriela, making a tsking sound with her tongue. "He was an ugly rich boy. I met him while I was working at the department store. He had so much money. The cost of the bracelet meant nothing to him.

He only wanted to show off to impress me, so I let him buy it. What do I care?"

What Gabriela didn't tell her mother was that the "rich boy" was actually a seventy-nine-year-old man who she had grown rather fond of. Senor Rodriguez was refined. He had always been kind and charming, and he never pushed her to do anything she was uncomfortable with. He did, however, reward her when she pleased him. She was simply doing a job, it was a way to save up for her move to America. She rationalized that anything she did for the senor was perfectly all right if it got her closer to New York and far away from her sad little town.

Now, so many years later, she smiled at her reflection in the mirror of her tiny New York City bedroom. *Everything is about to change for me and soon I will have the life I've always dreamed of.* By the end of the day, the first obstacle between her and her glamorous life would be eliminated. Taking a deep breath and exhaling, she marveled at how everything had finally come together and congratulated herself for being patient and careful. All the hard work was about to pay off. Her face darkened as she wondered how long Sr. Bello would be enough for her. In time, she knew she'd want more. It was her curse, she always wanted more. Pushing the dark thoughts out of her mind, she told herself that for now, Sr. Bello was perfectly fine. And when he wasn't — she'd trade up again.

It was only 7:30 a.m. and she wondered if *it* had been done yet. Sr. Bello hadn't told her what time, where or even how. He only said it would be sometime on Thursday. *I suppose it might not happen until this afternoon or even later tonight.*

The last time she and Sr. Bello had communicated he had implored her to follow his instructions. "There's no way you'll be implicated, Gabi, but to be on the safe side, make sure you're out in public and seen by people that entire Thursday."

"But I don't know anything," she had said. "You haven't told me about the plan. How could I be implicated?"

"Do what I tell you, Gabi," he had replied. "Create an alibi for yourself. Trust me, it will protect you."

"Everyone is in masks, no one will remember seeing me."

"You're wrong. They'll all remember your body and those eyes," Sr. Bello had said as he kissed her. "Meet a friend for a walk in the park. Go shopping, talk to as many people as you can in the stores that day. You know how to attract attention, you're very good at that."

Gabriela admired herself in the mirror one last time before putting on her most form-fitting top. The thin-knit shirt hugged her breasts and its low-cut neckline revealed an ample amount of cleavage. She chose one of her shortest skirts, providing anyone who looked the chance to see all her not-so-hidden wonders. Combing her lustrous dark-brown hair into a ponytail, she completed her makeup adding extra mascara, put on a bright-pink face mask and by 8:05 a.m. she was out the front door headed towards the uptown subway station.

Wandering along 14th Street, she waved to the owner of the dry cleaners she and Greg used. The man recognized her and waved back enthusiastically.

She smiled through her mask and shouted through the open shop door, "Good morning, it's a beautiful day," and kept on walking. She took a few steps and turned her head.

The dry cleaner was standing in the doorway watching her walk away.

She smiled. *Couldn't resist another look, could you?*

CHAPTER FORTY

When Zoe woke that same Thursday morning, she reached for her phone on the nightstand. Fishing around, she knocked over two half-filled iced-tea glasses. Jumping out of bed, she looked down at the tea seeping onto some clothes piled on the wooden floor.

"Shit," she said as she looked around for something to mop it up.

Picking up one of her dirty sweatshirts off a doorknob, she threw it on top of the tea to soak it up. At 7:15am, after cleaning up the mess, she walked to the living-room window to look out at the park and city street below. It was another beautiful sunny day. Though it had been three months since the city had gone into lockdown, it still shocked her to see so few cars and hardly any pedestrians outside.

Back in her bedroom, she picked her white cotton robe off the floor and noticed it was covered with stains. *Still good for one more wear.* Putting the soiled robe on, she shuffled into the kitchen, fixed herself a cup of coffee and settled in by the living-room window to FaceTime with Sean.

Moments later, his groggy and unshaven face appeared on her phone.

"What?" he said, obviously still in bed half asleep. "It's not even 9 a.m. yet. I didn't sleep well last night. Right before I went to bed I was examining my face in the bathroom mirror and noticed that there's a little ding on the inside of my lower right eyelid. Look." Sean moved the camera of his phone up to his eye so it filled Zoe's entire screen. "What if it's that flesh-eating disease? What if it eats my eye?"

"Your eye looks bloodshot, but other than that, I don't see any evidence of flesh-eating bacteria," said Zoe. "Can we get back to business? Today is Thursday. We're nearly out of time. We've got less than twenty-four hours left."

Sean ran his fingers through his hair. "It's a lost cause."

"We have to try. You promised."

Sean let out a breath of surrender knowing Zoe wasn't about to let this go. "Okay, what's our first move?"

"I was thinking," said Zoe, taking a sip of her coffee and glancing out the window, "we should go back downtown and walk the blocks between the 14th Street subway stop and Bleecker Street. If we're lucky, maybe we'll run into him and can warn him."

"The odds of us bumping into him on the street are slim to none," said Sean. "Besides, the restaurant is opening on Monday and I've got a ton of things to do before we go back to work. This investigation has consumed my whole week."

"We can't just do nothing."

"We've talked to the police numerous times. What else can we do?"

Zoe let out a defeated breath as she lifted her binoculars to her eyes and looked out the window. "I feel so helpless. I keep thinking about that poor man and how he . . . Oh my God . . . Sean, she's here, the woman, she's sitting across the street on that same bench."

"What woman?"

"The masked woman!"

"No way. Are you sure it's her? Is her husband with her?"

Zoe looked around the park. "I don't see him anywhere. Do you think they already killed him?" she gasped. "Do you think he's dead?"

"They said they were going to kill him today."

"What should we do?" shouted Zoe, standing and bouncing on the balls of her feet, the binoculars still glued to her eyes.

"We should call the detectives like they told us," said Sean.

"But the police won't get here in time. She could walk away at any second. I'm going to follow her. Give me thirty seconds to put on some clothes," said Zoe, dropping the binoculars on a living-room chair and running to her bedroom. Forty seconds later she was back in a T-shirt and a pair of shorts. "I'm dressed," she yelled to Sean, still waiting for her on FaceTime. Running over to the window with her sneakers in one hand, she picked up the binoculars and looked out. "Thank God, she's still there. Sean, get over here, now!"

Jamming on her shoes, she grabbed her phone and was about to run out the front door when she remembered she didn't have her keys or wallet. Running back to the bedroom she hunted for her bag. Her clothes were piled up all over the room and finding anything was nearly impossible. When her husband was at home, Zoe was more mindful of picking things up and putting stuff away. When he was off on assignment, she let things go. She sprinted back into the living room to check that the masked woman was still outside — she was.

Zoe tossed the binoculars back on the chair and ran to the dining room — no bag. Back to the bedroom she pulled out all of her drawers — no bag. *The kitchen!* Racing down the long hallway, she found her bag slung over the back of a kitchen chair. Grabbing it, she dropped her phone in but noticed her wallet wasn't inside. *Shit, where did I leave my freakin' wallet? If that woman gets on a subway or takes a cab, I'll need money. Where's my wallet? Wait . . . the black shoes with the studs on the heel.* The night before she had been shoe-shopping on her phone in bed and used her credit card to buy a pair of shoes. Galloping back to the bedroom she dropped onto the floor, shimmied under her bed and retrieved her wallet.

Seconds later and out of breath, she flew past the lobby doorman and out to the street. Now at ground level, she couldn't see the bench where the woman had been sitting. Dodging the few cars driving on Central Park West, she ran across the street and into the park. The bench was empty and the masked woman was gone. *No!*

Looking up and down Central Park West, she jogged south on one of the walking paths inside the park. With no sign of the woman, she turned in the opposite direction and ran frenetically north. Minutes later, sweating, gasping for air and not knowing which way to turn, she pivoted again and ran head first into Sean.

"What the hell are you doing?" he said after she nearly knocked him over. "I saw you from across the street running in circles."

Tears of defeat welled up in Zoe's eyes. "I lost her. I couldn't find my bag and when I finally did my wallet was missing. I finally found my wallet under my bed and by the time I got out here, she was gone."

"Following her was a terrible idea anyway," said Sean. "Remember what the detectives said? The masked woman could be dangerous."

"It's over then," said Zoe, sitting down on the same bench the woman had been perched on only fifteen minutes before. She buried her head in her hands. "We're out of time. We didn't stop it. How can we live with ourselves?"

"I'm not owning that," said Sean sitting down next to her. "We did everything possible. Even the cops said there was nowhere else to go. Besides, we don't even know if he's still alive or not. From the texts you saw, it didn't sound like the woman was going to do it herself, so following her wouldn't have led us to the murder."

Zoe rubbed her eyes. "I really thought we were going to save him. What if he was a scientist just about to find the cure for cancer or the coronavirus? He'll never have the chance to complete his experiments because we failed and now, millions will die."

"Seriously?" said Sean incredulous as he looked at her. "If he were a scientist working on a vaccine for Covid-19 or a cancer cure, I don't think he would have been hanging out in Central Park on Monday bidding for hideous lamps on eBay."

They sat without speaking for a minute until Zoe broke the silence. "Let me ask you something. If the masked woman lives all the way down on 14th Street why would she come all the way up to the north end of Central Park to hang out. There are plenty of parks downtown like Washington Square. Why does she come up here?"

"None of the other parks are as big or as nice as this one," said Sean. "When you're here, you almost forget you're in the city."

"That's true, but it's still peculiar."

CHAPTER FORTY-ONE

A stocky mail carrier with an olive complexion parked his mail truck in a commercial loading spot on West 97th Street. Waiting for his favorite country song to finish on the radio, he adjusted his face mask, put on his sunglasses and pulled his official USPS hat over his curly black hair. Before getting out of the truck, he looked at his reflection in the large rear-view mirror. His image with a mask, hat and glasses made him laugh. *I'm a postal ninja, silent and lethal.*

Climbing out of his truck, he walked around to the back and opened the doors. He slid his mail cart out, and made sure the sorted mail packets were locked and loaded. The district supervisor had warned all postal employees about a marked increase in local mail theft. A number of his colleagues had their mail trucks vandalized and packages stolen. A couple of USPS handcarts filled to the brim with mail had been taken while carriers were distracted delivering a package or getting a signature for a certified letter.

The mailman took a long look down the street to make sure no sketchy people lurked nearby. *I've got a switchblade under my left pant leg and a Glock 42 in the waist of my pants. Screw with me or my mail cart and you'll be sorry, sucka.*

After carefully examining the neighborhood and the people in it, he locked his truck and pushed his full cart down the street to the first building on his route. Stopping in front of a medium-sized elevator building, he opened the unlocked outer glass door and went into the foyer leaving his cart outside. Using his master key, he opened the brass frame that surrounded the mailboxes. Once unlatched, the open wall revealed a cubbyhole for each tenant's mail. He placed letter packets into slots, starting with the top row. As he worked, he scrutinized various envelopes.

That's nice, Diane Mattioli in 3B got her social security check on time this month. That was terrible when it was so late last time. How was that poor woman supposed to eat? She looks very good for ninety. He placed a few envelopes into Ms. Mattioli's mailbox along with some coupons for cat food that he had collected for her and reached for the next packet. *More parking tickets for Bill Gibbons. One day they're going to arrest him. He must have over 500 outstanding tickets. You can run, but you can't hide, Mr. Gibbons.* He placed Gibbons' mail in the appropriate cubby along with a flyer for an attorney and reached for the next packet of envelopes.

Oh look, Nadine Vail has jury duty again. Poor woman's been working two jobs since she kicked her husband out and got that restraining order. She always gives money to all kinds of food banks. She's well rid of him with all his porn magazines. He put most of Nadine Vail's mail into her box but held back one envelope that looked interesting and placed it into his special "after hours" mail bag. At home that night, he'd have a look at the contents like he did every night. Once he got the letter open, and consumed its contents, he'd deliver it to Ms. Vail the following day like he did with all of his customers. He liked to know how they were all doing and no one had ever suspected. He kept tabs on everyone on his route who was interesting and he only found out which were the interesting ones after he reviewed some of their correspondence. Moving to the other end of the slots, he pulled out another packet and examined it.

What a surprise, another lawyer writing to John Keane. Must be that real estate scam he was running. No wonder his wife moved out. I have twice as much room in my cart since she left with all her clothes and makeup catalogs. How much of his money did she spend on all her garbage? Note to self: check his bank statement the next time it comes.

Reaching for several colored envelopes addressed to Anna Pabst, he held them up to the light. *Looks like some cards. If I'm not mistaken, I believe today is Ms. Pabst's birthday. Happy birthday, Anna. If you were younger I might let you be my girlfriend for a night, but since you're over forty, congratulations, you'll get to enjoy another year.* Whistling 'Happy Birthday', he completed his mail delivery for that building and locked up all the boxes.

Pushing his cart to the next building, he daydreamed about his upcoming *date*. He had selected the lucky girl only recently but was satisfied she was the perfect one for June. From the first time he read her mail he had been enchanted but when he finally saw her, it was love at first sight. He smiled ruefully. *I always think the next one is going to be "the one" and I'm always so disappointed. But this time, I really think she could be my soulmate.*

He shook his head to bump any negative thoughts out as he entered another building and unlocked the metal mailbox case. *I have a very good feeling about my June date. I might even ask her to marry me if she behaves. Of course, it will have to be a very short engagement.*

* * *

After losing the masked woman in the park, Sean walked a still shaken Zoe back to her building.

"Listen," he said when they arrived, "the restaurant opens on Monday and it's going to be batshit crazy having the whole operation outside. I suggest you get all your loose ends tied up because come Monday, it will be all hands on deck."

Zoe nodded, waved goodbye and pushed open the front door to her building.

Later, while staring out her window at the empty bench in the park and still determined to save a life, Zoe left a series of messages for Detective Williams. Each subsequent voicemail sounded more anxious and convoluted.

On the first one, Zoe reported the sighting that morning of the masked woman in the park. Her second message warned the detectives that they were running out of time. Her third voicemail was nonsensical, worried and teary. When several hours passed with no response, she called Detective Kim and left two messages. Frustrated, at five o'clock, Zoe called Detective Williams a fourth time.

"It's me again, Zoe Brandt. I wanted to find out if there was *any* possibility of you locating that man before something happens to him," she said as she cleared her throat and took a sip of her bourbon. "We've got to stop this." With her voice cracking, she started to cry. "I can't stop thinking about him and I don't know how I can live with myself if I just let him die. Maybe it's still not too late."

* * *

In hot pursuit of the West Side Strangler, the detectives were on their way to meet a postal inspector and go over mail routes and carriers. Zoe Brandt's nonsensical murder mystery was no longer on their radar.

"She's relentless, I'll give her that," said Daryl shaking his head as he put his phone back in his breast pocket and turned the car onto 34th Street. "I just got my fourth message from Zoe Brandt."

"She's called me twice," said Heather. "She should have been a detective. Tenacious is an understatement. You do know she's got a screw loose."

"That thought crossed my mind several hundred times but I still think she's telling the truth."

"Maybe she just *thinks* it's the truth," said Heather. "We can't get distracted by the Zoe Brandts of the world."

"I'm on the same page," said Daryl as they pulled abruptly into a parking spot. Leaping out of the car the two detectives walked briskly into a USPS building.

CHAPTER FORTY-TWO

On the couch in her living room that evening, Zoe FaceTimed with Sean.

"It's 7:15," she said, "the man is probably already dead. We completely failed. We're the world's worst detectives."

"Look at it this way, if someone turns up dead today or tomorrow, the cops will know his wife was behind it," said Sean.

Zoe squinted her eyes at him and shook her head in disbelief. "How does that help the dead man? He's already dead. You can't unring that bell."

"Back up, Miss Thing," said Sean. "We did the best we could. We tried everything."

"Tell that to the dead guy."

"I'm officially changing the subject," said Sean. "So, this gorgeous person moved into my building today. I think I'm in love. He lives one floor above me. I met him when I walked into my building by the mailboxes."

Still obsessing about the murder plot as Sean waxed poetic about his new neighbor, Zoe looked over at the clock on the end table. "Can we put a pin in this for now," she said. "It's almost eight. Conner will be calling in a few minutes and I want to give your new neighbor conversation my full attention."

They ended their chat, promising to FaceTime later to watch reruns of *Friends* on TV together — a regular late-night activity they engaged in whenever Conner was away.

Zoe poured a little more bourbon into her glass, settled onto the couch and waited for her husband's call. At 7:57 p.m. her phone rang.

"Hey babe," said Zoe, looking around at the mess in the apartment and glad they weren't doing a video call. *Oy, I have to clean this whole place before Conner gets home.* "I can't wait to see you."

"Same here," said Conner, "been a long week. They scheduled all of our sessions with practically no breaks and we even had some evening classes. It's been non-stop, my head feels like it's going to explode. Will be nice to get home."

The buzzer from the lobby sounded. "That's weird," said Zoe as she got up holding the phone and walked towards the intercom by the front door. "Hang on a sec, babe, the doorman just buzzed from the lobby." She pushed the intercom button.

"Ms. Brandt, I've got a flower delivery for you. Okay if I send him up?"

"Flowers? Sure, won't say no to that," said Zoe, smiling.

She put the phone back to her ear. "Conner, did you send me something else? I thought you were mad at me after our call last night and I was feeling a little anxious about that. That was so sweet of you."

Before Conner could respond there was a sharp knock on the front door. "Hold on a second, babe," she said to her husband as she walked down the hall. Looking through the peephole, Zoe saw nothing but flowers on the other side and let out a little squeal. Turning the top and bottom locks, the door swung open. A burly man with dark wavy hair, wearing a delivery uniform, gloves, a face mask, glasses and hat stood in the hall holding a large pink-and-white flower arrangement.

"Zoe Brandt?" he said.

"That's me. Come on in. You can put them on the hall table on the other side of the foyer." She whispered into the phone, "Conner, thank you, they're beautiful. I'm going to put the phone down for a minute while I get him a tip. Be right back." She placed the phone on a side table in the large entrance hall.

The burly man placed the flowers on the hall table near the living room and turned around to face her. "You're my last delivery for the night," he said.

"Wait here, I want to get something for you," said Zoe as she ran into the kitchen to get her wallet. Her bag wasn't there. "Just a minute," she said as she dashed past him down the hallway to her bedroom.

Her large leather bag was on the floor near the walk-in closet. She grabbed it. As she headed back down the hall towards the front door she hoisted the strap of the bag over her head cross-body style, leaving her hands free to dig for money inside the deep satchel. When she got back to the foyer, the front door was closed and the man was gone. *He left before I gave him his tip.* She opened the front door again and looked out. "Hello, are you out there?" No one was in the hallway. She closed the door and picked up the phone she had left on the hall table.

"The deliveryman left before I could give him a tip," she said to her husband still on the phone. "People are so impatient these days."

From behind her a male voice called out. "I'm still here," called the deliveryman from the living room. Confused, Zoe spun around. "Oh wait, good, he's still here. Conner, hold on. I'm going to put the phone down again to finish up with the delivery guy," she said to her husband before she placed the phone back on the hall table.

Standing in the living room, the flower man's back was to her as he looked out of the big picture window. "Nice place," he said, looking around. "Must cost a bundle."

"I have a tip for you but let me walk you to the front door," she said as her hands groped for money inside of the large bag. Using both hands to hunt for her wallet or some loose bills, she kept one eye on the deliveryman as he walked past her towards the front door.

Halfway down the foyer, the man abruptly turned, took her by the shoulders and knocked her to the floor. Stunned, Zoe tried to get up but he leapt on top of her and grabbed her by the throat. She tried to scream but only managed a loud frightened moan.

Still on the phone, Conner heard strange muffled sounds. When he heard a woman groan, he knew it was his wife and he shouted, "Zoe, what's going on? Are you okay? Zoe? Zoe!"

The deliveryman's hands were tight around her neck and were crushing her windpipe while she struggled to get free. For a second, he moved to one side and she kneed him hard in the groin, causing him to double over, allowing her to get away. She pushed herself up and ran towards the front door and tried to open it. Frantically turning the knob over and over, it wouldn't open. *Shit. I never called the locksmith.*

From the other side of the foyer, the intruder had recovered and was on his feet, moving towards her. He grabbed Zoe from behind and dragged her into the living room. She shouted into the air hoping Conner would hear her, "Help! Conner. Help me. He's trying to kill me."

"Zoe, what's happening?" yelled Conner. "Zoe!"

Before she could get out another word, the man slapped a big meaty hand over her mouth and pushed her onto the couch. This time when he jumped on top of her he made sure he had a better grip. He was heavier and stronger and she could barely move underneath him. As he squeezed her neck tighter and tighter her hand groped for something, anything, that she could use to fight him off.

With her open bag still strapped across her chest, her right hand reached deep inside the leather opening. As the man squeezed her throat, she looked up into his dark, cold eyes, unable to take in any air when her fingers found something T-shaped. On the verge of passing out, she gripped the implement in her hand knowing she'd have only one shot. With all the strength she had left in her body, she swung her right arm up, out, and down, plunging the corkscrew Sean had given her into the neck of her assailant.

Then the corkscrew by some miracle landed in his jugular vein. At first, the man appeared stunned and let go of her throat as he reached for his own. Within seconds, blood gushed out, running through his fingers. When he gripped the handle of the corkscrew and pulled it out, blood spurted in every direction. It hit the picture window that overlooked the park, the couch, and the marble-topped coffee table. Still choking and gasping for air, Zoe tried to get up. With one last clumsy attempt to grab her as blood poured out of his wound, he seized up and fell on top of her, knocking her backwards and causing her to smack her head on the side of the marble coffee table. Moments later, he was dead and Zoe lay unconscious in a pool of his blood.

Still on the phone, Conner now heard only silence. Shouting his wife's name over and over he finally hung up to call for help.

"911, what's your emergency?" said the dispatcher.

"You've got to help me. I think my wife was attacked in our apartment in New York City," said a frantic Conner.

"Why do you think that, sir?"

"I'm in DC and I was on the phone with my wife when the doorbell rang. She put her phone down to answer it and then I heard a scuffle. My wife screamed 'help' and then it sounded like there was a fight. I kept shouting to her and then suddenly, all the noise stopped. I didn't know what else to do so I hung up and called you. Please, you need to send someone over there right away. Something's happened. Please."

As soon as Conner finished the call to 911, the dispatcher put out a call to local police in Manhattan and officers were sent to the Brandts' building. Conner grabbed his overnight bag, jumped in his car and began his four-and-a-half hour drive to New York. Going way over the speed limit, he tried Zoe's phone over and over but it only went to voicemail.

Fifteen minutes later, while Detectives Kim and Williams were in their car heading back to the station to sign out for the night, Daryl William's phone rang.

"You're kidding me?" said Daryl as he listened to a police dispatcher. "What's the address? Did you say Brandt? There are officers on site already? Is she all right? We're on our way." Daryl ended the call and looked at his partner. "Change of plans. Drive to Zoe Brandt's apartment," he said.

"Another murder mystery? I thought we were signing out?" said Heather as she turned the car around.

"911 got a call from Zoe Brandt's husband. He's in DC and was on the phone with her. He says the doorbell rang and after his wife answered it, there was some kind of a struggle. That's all I know."

"I knew that woman was going to get herself into trouble," said Heather as she put on her siren and hit the gas pedal. "Is she all right?"

"She's okay. A patrol car is already there. They reported that her apartment looked like a bloodbath," said Daryl. "They thought it might be the Strangler, that's why they called us."

"Civilians should not be out chasing bad guys," said Heather shaking her head as she blew through a red light.

When the detectives arrived at the Brandt's building two squad cars were already parked out front, lights flashing. The detectives adjusted their masks and walked up to the front door of the building at the same time as a police photographer.

"That you, Detective Williams?" said the photographer, recognizing Daryl from other cases. "It's hard to tell who anybody is these days. What are you doing here?"

"Long story," said Daryl as all three entered the lobby. "Could be related to the Strangler investigation."

"Right," said the photographer. "I saw your recent press conference on TV."

As they approached the obviously rattled doorman, Daryl flashed his badge. "We need to get into the Brandts' apartment," he said.

"Four officers are already up there," said the doorman. "Third floor, 303."

"Was there anyone here with her tonight?" said Daryl as he walked towards the elevator.

"Like I told the other officers. Ms. Brandt had a flower delivery about an hour ago," said the doorman. "Come to think of it, I never saw him leave. Of course, I might have been helping one of the other tenants and missed him."

Standing outside of Zoe's slightly ajar front door, the detectives pushed it open, the photographer following behind them. From the large octagonal foyer, they could see furniture had been overturned indicating a struggle had taken place.

"Ms. Brandt," Daryl called out. "It's Detective Williams."

"Ms. Brandt," shouted Heather, as the three slowly walked down the hall towards the living room. "Zoe."

A male voice called out. "We're back here."

When Daryl and Heather walked under the tall, rounded archway leading into the living room, blood splatters covered one full wall. A heavyset man with dark hair lay face down in a puddle of blood next to the couch, a corkscrew with the word *Justice* printed on the handle was still in his hand.

"Holy shit," said Heather looking around at the blood-covered room. "It's like the prom scene from *Carrie*."

"How did you get wind of this already?" said one of the three police officers in the room.

"Good news travels fast," Daryl said as he and Heather walked towards the dead man's body.

The photographer waved, showed his credentials and started taking pictures.

"Looks like he bled out from the wound in his neck," said one of the police officers. "She got him right in the jugular. Lucky shot."

"Where's Ms. Brandt now?" said Heather, kneeling down next to the dead man, trying to avoid contaminating the pools of blood on the floor.

"In the shower," said one of the officers. "Woman was covered in the victim's blood. My partner, Helen, is waiting for her in the bedroom to make sure she doesn't touch or move anything."

"Why did you report this to the Strangler task force?" asked Heather.

"When the lady came to, she said the man tried to choke her," said the first officer.

CHAPTER FORTY-THREE

Anxiously parading around her neighborhood and wandering further throughout Manhattan that Thursday, Gabriela had done exactly what Sr. Bello had told her to do. For fifteen hours she made sure she had contact with store merchants or street vendors. Stopping to chat with men in every shop, she shamelessly flirted with each one to make sure they'd remember seeing her that day. Using a credit card in numerous stores, she bought many small, inexpensive items to create a timestamped paper trail.

"You've got to have an alibi, Gabi, just in case," Sr. Bello had said firmly. "It's unlikely anything would ever be traced to you, but I still want you to have contact with as many people as possible. Make sure you're seen all day long and into the evening. It's just a precaution."

That Thursday morning, she was surprised how her nerves had gotten the better of her. Strolling and sashaying through the Lower East Side streets she took the subway uptown to the park in the morning. From there she worked her way downtown, stopping and shopping on almost every block. Once in her neighborhood after her uptown jaunt, she took a deep breath, walked into her local vegetable market and greeted the proprietor.

"*Buenos tardes*, Sr. Santiago," said Gabriela when the owner looked up and smiled. "*Un buen día, no? Que es un especial hoy?*" Chatting amiably with the older Dominican man, she complimented him on the quality of his produce. During their conversation he revealed his age.

"I'm nearly sixty," he said proudly.

"*No es possiblé!* I don't believe it. You look like a young man in his thirties. You must have very good genes, senor," said Gabriela holding a small bag of avocados. She touched his arm. "I will think of you tonight when I mix up my guacamole." His eyes crinkled above his blue surgical mask. He'd remember her visit that day.

By 9 p.m., exhausted and weary of wandering, she stopped at a wine store and bought a bottle of champagne — tonight she would celebrate. On her way home, she sat on a bench and took out her special phone used only for communication with Sr. Bello.

"Can you talk?" said Gabriela in a loud whisper.

"For a moment," said Sr. Bello.

"Is it done? Can I go home now?"

"Yes, but after this, we won't be able to talk or text for a while. There could be a lot of blowback and we don't want to make a mistake," he said firmly. "It's better if we don't have any contact for a few months."

"Months?" said Gabriela. "But I thought . . ."

"Gabi, trust me. I know what I'm doing. I'll be in touch when it's safe. We've come too far to screw this up by being sloppy. Be patient."

"It will be terrible being apart from you for so long."

"You know I adore you and being away from you will be torture. I said I'd do anything for you. Guess I proved that, didn't I? We'll be together soon, I promise."

"When? You promised October," said Gabriela. "I've got something special planned."

"Yes, October."

* * *

Zoe was taken to the 24th Precinct by the detectives to make a statement, while Conner drove at dangerously high speeds on I-95 towards New York. Having tried his wife's phone thirty times, he still had no idea if she was all right or what happened. He called 911 again, but couldn't get connected to anyone who could provide any further information. Desperate for answers, he called a colleague from the FBI.

"It's Conner," he said breathlessly as his car crossed through Delaware.

"You still at Quantico?" said one of his FBI colleagues.

"Listen, I've got an emergency," said Conner frantically. "I was on the phone with my wife when someone came to our front door in New York with flowers. There was a scuffle and she screamed and then I heard nothing. I'm driving back but I won't be in New York for a few hours. Can you help me?"

"Oh my God," said the other agent. "Sure. What do you need me to do?"

"I tried 911 again, but I still don't know what happened to my wife. Can you go over to my apartment and—"

Conner's phone beeped. "Hold on a second, there's another call coming in. Get over to my apartment and see what's going on and call me?"

"I'm walking out the door now," said his friend.

Conner picked up the other call. "This is Conner Brandt."

"Mr. Brandt, this is Detective Daryl Williams with the NYPD. I'm calling about your wife."

Conner held his breath. "Is she okay?"

"We've got her here with us at the police station," said Daryl. "She had a nasty blow to the head but she's all right now and giving her statement."

"Thank God. I was on the phone with her and I heard a fight going on."

"Someone attacked your wife but she fought back. She wound up killing her attacker."

Stunned, Conner let out the breath he had been holding. "Oh my God. Did he hurt her? But she's okay, right? Can I speak to her?"

"She'll be fine. According to your wife, the man tried to strangle her. Like I said, she's giving her statement right now, but she was adamant that I call you and let you know she was not in any danger," said Daryl. "She had to leave her phone with forensics so she doesn't have a phone at the moment."

"I'm in Jersey now driving north on the turnpike going as fast as I can. I should be in Manhattan in a little over an hour. She's really okay?"

"She's shaken up but she's fine. I can't say the same for the man who attacked her."

"You said he tried to strangle Zoe?" said Conner. "Was this the West Side Strangler?"

"I can't discuss an ongoing investigation, Mr. Brandt."

"Detective, I'm a special agent with the FBI," said Conner, switching lanes on the road to pick up more speed.

"I'm aware of that, but we're still putting all the pieces together and I can't comment," said Daryl. "We have descriptions of a man seen in the area of the other attacks. The man your wife killed has a similar physique and hair color. Street camera footage from a few of the other murder locations show a masked man with the same body type as the person who attacked your wife."

An hour later, Conner Brandt raced into the 24th Street Precinct, flashed his FBI badge and was admitted immediately. A police officer escorted him to a small interrogation room. Zoe was sitting inside talking to the two detectives. When the door to the room opened and she saw her husband she broke down in tears and sobbed. He rushed over to her and held her in his arms. A white bandage with gauze was fixed on the back of her head and her neck and arms had already started turning purple.

"I was so scared," she cried, clinging to him. "I thought I was going to die. I thought he was going to kill me."

"Shhh. I'm here now. Everything is going to be all right," said Conner with his arms wrapped around her. "You're going to be okay."

"Looks like we've got what we need for the moment," said Daryl, making one final note on the paper in front of him.

"Are we free to go?" said Conner.

"I can't go back into our apartment right now," said Zoe, clinging to her husband.

"I'm afraid you can't go home, anyway, Ms. Brandt," said Daryl. "Your apartment is a crime scene. Until we're finished with our forensic collection and the investigation is complete, you and your husband will need to find another place to stay."

"One of my co-workers just left for a six-month assignment in California. He asked me to pick up his mail. I've got the keys to his apartment," said Conner to his wife. "We can go there for a few days, okay?"

Still in shock, Zoe nodded and allowed her special agent husband to take control as he escorted her slowly out of the police station.

CHAPTER FORTY-FOUR

Sunday — June 7, 2020

For the next couple of days, Zoe and Conner stayed in his colleague's apartment. When they got an early call on Sunday morning from the police saying they could return to their home, Zoe began to tremble.

"I want to go home," she had said nervously, her voice at a higher pitch than usual, "but I'm so scared. I don't know if I'm ready to go back in there. It was horrible."

"I'll be with you. I'll go over to the apartment today and make sure everything looks okay," Conner had said. "I promise, when you walk in tomorrow, everything will look normal."

"But . . ." said Zoe as Conner got up to leave.

"Trust me. We'll order in a nice dinner when I get back here tonight and watch a happy movie. I won't be gone long."

"Promise?" she said, gnawing on the cuticle of her thumb. He smiled, nodded and kissed her on the top of her head and then headed out the door.

Twenty minutes later, standing outside the front door of their Central Park West apartment, he pulled off bits of ripped, yellow crime-scene tape still stuck to the door frame and rolled them into a large sticky ball. Entering the apartment for the first time since the incident, he found the condition more horrific than he had imagined.

From the second he set foot inside, he had to sidestep around overturned tables and chairs. A blue ceramic hall lamp lay shattered on the floor. Walking through the elegant foyer and down the hall, he crossed through the archway into the living room. The scene in there took his breath away. Blood was splashed across the big picture window, the surrounding walls, floor, couches and rugs, making the room look like a crimson Jackson Pollack painting.

After a few deep breaths, Conner got to work. Grabbing some rags and a variety of cleaning supplies, he filled a plastic bucket with hot water and soap. He scrubbed the walls, windows, floors, and baseboards until no blood could be detected. Placing all the furniture back in their original positions, he attempted to get the bloodstains out of the gray couch cushions and decorative throw pillows. Unable to get all the blood out of the sofa, he flipped the cushions over so his wife wouldn't see the spots. Wiping down all the tables, he picked up pieces of broken lamps, glass and knick-knacks and swept all that remained into a dustpan. After three hours of cleaning, the place looked much like it had before the attack, minus a few lamps and odds and ends. The one thing he couldn't fix was the oriental rug. The stain was too large and the fibers too saturated. Rolling it up, he dragged it onto the elevator and took it down to the dumpster in the basement.

* * *

Monday — June 8, 2020

At 11:30 a.m., carrying two overnight bags, Conner escorted his wife into their building for the first time since she had been attacked.

"How are you feeling, Ms. Brandt?" said Don the doorman when they entered the lobby. "I feel terrible about letting that maniac up into your apartment."

"It's not your fault," said Zoe as she walked past him clutching her husband's arm. "I told you to send him up. Please don't blame yourself."

"Thanks for understanding, Ms. Brandt," said Don. "I'm just glad you're okay."

When they got to their front door, Zoe froze. "Are you ready?" said Conner gently. "I promise, everything looks fine."

Zoe inhaled and exhaled and then nodded as the two walked into their apartment. "Everything looks normal. You'd hardly know anything happened here," she said softly while standing inside the front door in the large foyer. "I can't go into the living room yet. I don't know when I'll be able to go in there." She turned to the right, bypassing the living room entirely and walked down the long hall to the master bedroom.

"Go at your own pace," Conner called out as he watched his wife disappear into their room. When he stepped into the bedroom a few minutes later, Zoe was already in bed with the comforter pulled up to her chin. Dropping their bags on the end of the bed, he sat down next to her.

"Listen to me," he said, gently rubbing her arm. "You've been through a terrible thing. You're probably still in shock. Don't push yourself. Do what feels good to you, okay? Let me take care of everything, I promise."

Zoe nodded, happy to have someone else in control.

"Why don't you take a shower? You'll feel better."

Her lips quivered and she started to shake. Conner moved closer and put his arms around her. "I'm here. I promise, I won't let anything happen to you," he said. "Look at me, Zoe. The man who tried to hurt you is dead. He can't hurt you anymore."

"But who was he and why did he come here? Why did he pick me?" said Zoe still shaking. "I don't understand any of it."

"The police think he could be the West Side Strangler. There's no rhyme or reason to any of his crimes," said Conner, stepping back and looking into her eyes. "Zoe, do you realize you may have stopped a serial killer?"

"How do we know it was the Strangler? What if it wasn't? What if the man I killed has friends and they come back for me to seek revenge?" she said, starting to hyperventilate. "They could be watching us right now. Maybe he was a member of an organized crime family or a gang? What if they saw me come back into the building?"

"You've got to calm down. Turn that vivid imagination off, it always gets you into trouble. No one is getting in here. Trust me, you're safe. This place is FBI certified," said Conner, giving her a little smile. "And don't forget, I always pack a gun."

After a little more coaxing, Zoe took a shower while Conner unpacked his wife's overnight bag and straightened up their bedroom. When he heard the shower turn off, he called out to her, "I'm going to the kitchen to get some water, I'll be right back."

She was in her pajamas and sitting on the bed when he returned. She looked up and smiled at him. "Despite everything that happened, it does feel good to be home," she said.

"The police called while you were in the shower. They want me to come down tomorrow morning to make a statement."

Zoe nodded.

"Also, there's nothing to eat in this place," said Conner as he opened his overnight bag on the bed and started to unpack. "What were you living on? The fridge is empty."

Zoe shrugged her shoulders as Conner sorted his dirty clothes into piles on the bed from his week out-of-town. "Need to take my dirty dress shirts to the cleaners tomorrow. I've got nothing to wear," he said as he took his shaving kit into the bathroom. Reaching over, she picked up one of his dress shirts and sniffed. *Smells like Conner.* She smiled. The label on the shirt said Brooks Brothers. She picked up another, it was from Thayer and Co. Three shirts were from Thayer and Co and three were from Brooks Brothers.

"Do you buy all your shirts from Brooks Brothers and Thayer?" Zoe called out to her husband, now inside of his walk-in closet.

Conner popped his head out. "Been shopping there since I was in college. Both those stores are expensive but I wait for the sales. Why?"

"I never noticed where you got your clothes from before," said Zoe.

"That's because you never do laundry."

Zoe smiled. "True."

"Since I'm taking time off this week because of what happened, my supervisor asked me to stop in today and sign-off on something for a case I'm working on."

"You're leaving me?" she said, worry in her eyes.

"Babe, you'll be fine. I'll be back in less than three hours," he said, sitting on the bed next to her and taking her hand.

"Three hours?"

"Also, since we've got nothing in the house to eat, I'll stop at the market and pick up something for dinner."

"I'm not hungry. I just want to take a nap," said Zoe, her face ashen.

"How about I make you a bourbon to help you fall asleep?"

"Okay," said Zoe, surprised by his offer of an afternoon cocktail. "That would be great."

Minutes later he returned with an extra-large glass of bourbon on the rocks. "Here you go," he said, handing her the tumbler. "This should send you off into dreamland. Take a nice long nap and I'll be back before you wake up. I'm going to leave now, okay? I'll lock the top lock. No one can get in and there's no way Don will let anyone up here after what happened. He'll probably make me show my ID when I come back."

After she heard the front door open and close, she texted Sean.

Just got home. Exhausted and stressed. Conner left to do something for work. Am going to take a nap. FaceTime tonight?

She opened the nightstand drawer and took out her old Ambien prescription bottle containing one last pill. Popping it into her mouth, she washed it down with bourbon and closed her eyes.

CHAPTER FORTY-FIVE

When he closed the front door to the apartment, Conner stopped in the hallway and did a mental checklist before summoning the elevator. Taking out his iPhone he ordered an Uber to take him downtown. A car driven by Enrique was only nine minutes away. *Perfect.* Reaching into his breast pocket, he pulled out a brand-new disposable phone and opened Gmail. Punching in Zoe's credentials, Zoefbrandt456@gmail, he keyed in the same password his wife used for everything — *AgathaChristie1890.* It was her favorite author and the year the famous mystery writer was born. When Zoe's email account opened instantly, Conner shook his head and smiled. He had told his wife to change her passwords a million times, but she never did it. Now, he was glad she hadn't listened. Opening a blank email, he left the subject line empty. In the body of the email he entered only two words and pushed send.

When Conner stepped out of the elevator into the lobby, the doorman looked up. "How's Ms. Brandt feeling? It was an awful thing that happened. If I had realized—"

"Don't beat yourself up about it," said Conner. "You couldn't have known."

"I know but—"

"We don't blame you," said Conner checking his iPhone to find out where his car was. "Do me a favor, Don. I have to go into the office to take care of something and then I'm running to the supermarket. My wife is upstairs taking a nap. She's a little depressed and completely exhausted. Under no circumstances is she to be disturbed. No one is allowed in for any reason. Is that clear?"

"Absolutely, Mr. Brandt. You can count on me. No one goes up."

Conner gave him a thumbs up as a car arrived in front of the building. "Looks like my Uber's here," he said, adjusting his face mask while Don opened the front door for him. Walking to the waiting car, Conner opened the door and stuck his head in. "Enrique?"

"That's me," said the masked driver. "Conner?"

"You got him. Conner Brandt, nice to meet you."

As the Uber headed downtown, Conner checked his iPhone again. "How's business been for you these past few months with this crazy virus?" he asked.

"Up and down," said Enrique shrugging his shoulders. "When it started, my wife didn't want me to drive anymore because she was afraid I'd get sick or get my kids sick, but we needed the money. For a few weeks nobody in New York was going anywhere. There were no fares. None. Now people are relaxing a little and moving around more."

"I hear you have a slight accent. Where are you from, Enrique?"

The middle-aged driver laughed. "I'm from Columbia. You ever been?"

"Never."

"You should go. I'm from Medellín, it's a beautiful city. Perfect weather all year round just like California."

"No kidding?" said Conner.

The two men chatted amiably for the entire trip downtown. When Enrique pulled up to the front of the FBI field office he handed Conner his business card.

"You in the FBI? If you ever need a ride to the airport or anything, call me direct and I'll give you a great deal," said Enrique.

Conner took the card and put it in his breast pocket. "Good to know. Nice meeting you, Enrique. You have a great day."

Inside the FBI building, Conner went through security and got on the elevator. Once on his floor, he passed another agent from his unit in the hall.

"Hey Brandt, I heard about what happened with your wife. Is she all right?" said the other agent.

"It was a crazy thing but she's holding up," said Conner. "She's depressed though. The whole thing has been a shock."

"I heard you were taking some time off?" said the agent.

"I am but I've been working the CIG case and the boss needed me to sign off on something today. I'm not technically here," he replied. "Just in and out. My wife was taking a nap so it was a good time for me to duck out for a few hours."

* * *

Still in bed nursing her glass of bourbon, Zoe got up, walked over to the dresser and picked up her hairbrush. Gliding it through her thick dark hair, she took another sip of her drink. As she stared at her reflection in the mirror her eyes went to the pile of Conner's soiled dress shirts behind her on the bed. Turning around, she picked one up, looked at the collar and ran her finger over the Thayer and Co label. *I never noticed he bought his shirts from that store before.*

They had separate walk-in closets and she rarely went into his unless she was hanging up his dry cleaning. A little tipsy from the drink, she ventured into his closet and took a hard look at her husband's wardrobe, examining the labels on all his suits. *Brooks Brothers, Bloomingdale's, Saks, Thayer and Co, Macy's. Clearly, my husband has zero brand loyalty.*

She straightened out a few of his jackets on their hangers. Many of them were new with their tags still attached, purchased compliments of the FBI for his undercover sting operation. As she touched a few of the sleeves on his new suits, she noticed a collection of face masks looped over a hanger. Four months earlier, there wouldn't have been a single mask in his closet. Now everyone in the country had their own collection.

She picked up a New York Mets mask. *I haven't seen him wear this one. I didn't even know he liked the Mets.* After taking another sip of her drink she noticed a navy-blue mask underneath the others. It looked vaguely familiar. She polished off the remainder of her large cocktail. The cozy effects of the bourbon and Ambien had already made her mind fuzzy. She took the blue mask off the hanger and stared at it. One side of the mask was embroidered with an emblem of a little white shirt and red tie. *Wait, I know this. It's the same mask the woman in the park had.* She flipped the mask over. On the inside it was stamped — "Property of FBI White-Collar Crime Unit."

CHAPTER FORTY-SIX

Zoe dropped the mask and stumbled out of her husband's closet, now feeling the intense effects of the drink and drug. When she saw all the dirty clothes scattered around the room she forgot about the mask and suddenly decided to do a load of laundry. Grabbing an armful of dirty laundry from the floor, she picked up Conner's overnight bag to empty it. She pulled out another wrinkled Thayer and Co shirt along with a half-dozen pairs of dirty socks and undershorts. Gathering it all under one arm, she took a last look inside his bag to see if she had missed anything.

That's when she noticed a black phone in an inside pocket of the bag and took it out. Conner forgot his phone? What if someone from the bureau needs to reach him? He's supposed to have it with him at all times. I should call him. Oh wait, I can't, he doesn't have his phone. Increasingly bleary-eyed and unsteady on her feet, she sat and examined the phone more closely. Wait, this isn't Conner's phone. He has an iPhone. This is an Android. Maybe it's a special FBI phone? Zoe smiled. A secret spy phone.

Even in her inebriated, addled state she was still unable to resist a mystery or the prospect of secret information. She wondered what fabulous nuggets of FBI data might be on the phone in her hand. Incapable of resisting the temptation, she leaned back on her pillow and turned the phone on. It was locked. She knew some of her husband's most frequently used passwords and tried his mother's birthday. It didn't work. She went through a half-dozen others he occasionally used. Nothing. She tried her birthday and then their wedding anniversary and the phone unlocked. Yay! Yawning again from the bourbon, she looked at the screen and noticed there was only one app on the phone called Jabber. What the hell is Jabber? She opened up the app and found a string of texts from a pest-control company.

—What kind of problem do you need help with?
—I've got a rodent infestation in my house.
—A large rodent like a raccoon or something small like a mouse?
—Small like a mouse. How soon are you available to take care of my problem?

Normally, finding a secret FBI phone would have been like discovering buried treasure or a unicorn, but at that moment, Zoe could barely stay awake. Her eyelids flickered and her head bobbed several times. She sat up straight and slapped her face to remain alert. Standing up and walking around her bedroom, she continued scrolling and reading the texts on the phone. *Rodent problem? What the hell is this? Does the FBI have a rat infestation in the New York office? Ewww. Conner never mentioned anything about rats at work. But why would he be taking care of that? Wouldn't that be the job of maintenance people? Maybe this is part of an FBI sting operation? Cool . . . I know what it is, rats must be code for criminals, like a dirty rat.* Zoe sat back and smiled, proud of how she had worked that out.

After she finished reading all the texts on Jabber she closed it and clicked over into the general messages. There was only one contact there—Wardrobe Consultant. *This is so weird. It must be part of the case he's working on.* The most recent message was from the previous Monday. She clicked on it.

—When will it be done?
—Soon.
—This week?
—We're confirmed for Thursday. Be patient.
—Soon it will be just the two of us in our amazing apartment overlooking the park.

* * *

Cruising through the halls of the FBI building, Conner had dropped by several different departments chatting with co-workers in his unit before he ducked into his unit leader's office.

"I really appreciate you giving me the time off," said Conner.

"You and your wife have been through something terrible," said his unit director. "You didn't need to come down here today. You could have reviewed the documents online."

"It was no problem," said Conner. "My wife was taking a nap this afternoon so it wasn't a big deal." He looked at his watch. "It's three o'clock. Guess I'd better head home."

In another Uber going uptown, Conner engaged in a lengthy conversation with the driver. Exiting the vehicle on West 96th Street, he waved as the car pulled away and continued on to his neighborhood market.

Chatting with the man behind the deli counter, he traded jokes as he ordered some sliced turkey. He asked a stock boy about the location of Dijon mustard and queried the woman behind the Plexiglas making sushi on how she made them look so pretty. He finished off his shopping trip by conversing with an older female cashier.

"I bought more than I planned," said Conner as the grocery bags were filled. "Hope I can get home with all this stuff. My wife's not feeling well and I'm in charge of dinner."

"Aren't you a peach," said the older cashier. "The last time my husband made dinner, Reagan was in the White House. Your wife is a lucky woman."

* * *

Zoe moved around her bedroom trying to fight off sleep but her legs were heavy as if she was walking through thick syrup. Stumbling into her bathroom, she turned on the cold water and splashed some on her face in an attempt to stay awake. Her brain wasn't working properly, partly from the cryptic nature of the information she had found on her husband's phone but also from the pill and booze.

She grabbed the sides of the sink and stood up straight looking at her reflection in the mirror. *What did all those texts mean? Who was Conner talking to? Is he having an affair? I've got to stay awake.* She blinked several times and opened the medicine cabinet to get some eyedrops. Reaching for the drops, she knocked her brand-new bottle of Ambien into the sink. The cap was slightly askew which caught her attention. Picking up the plastic container she shook it. It was empty. She squinted as she checked the date on the label to be sure it was the same prescription bottle she had picked up earlier that week. It was. *Where are all my pills?*

Deep in her drug-addled brain the neurons somehow still fired and ushered in a brief moment of clarity. She wobbled back into the bedroom, picked up her bourbon glass from the nightstand and examined it. That's when she saw little white particles settled at the bottom of the glass. *What is that? Is that my Ambien? Did Conner put Ambien in my bourbon? Shit.* On the verge of passing out, she grabbed Conner's secret Android phone and slipped it into the pocket of the yoga pants she was wearing, zipping it shut.

Fading fast, and now feeling nauseous and dizzy, she went back into the bathroom and knelt down in front of the toilet. Lifting the lid, she stared down at the water in the bowl. *Come on, you remember what to do.* Painful memories of her teenaged eating disorder flooded back as she took two fingers, stuck them down her throat and gagged a few times. Nothing came up but she tried again. Finally, there was that old familiar feeling as her body responded and brown liquid spewed into the white porcelain.

She tried a few more times but nothing more came up. Pushing herself up from the tiled bathroom floor, she used the walls for balance to get to her iPhone on the bed. Panicking, and not thinking straight but convinced she might overdose, she grabbed her phone and lay back on her pillows as she punched Sean's name into her phone. Unable to focus her eyes, she managed to type six words.

I know who the killer is.

She hit send and then called him but it went straight to voicemail. Losing consciousness before she could leave a voice message, her phone dropped from her hand onto the floor.

* * *

Sean turned off his shower and dried off in his steamy bathroom. Tucking a towel around his waist, he got a bottle of water from the fridge and checked his phone for messages. That's when he saw Zoe's strange text and missed call. Alarmed after reading the text, he called her back but there was no answer. He left a message and waited a minute and then called and texted a second and a third time. He tried FaceTime, no answer.

Fearing something was terribly wrong, he put on his clothes, grabbed a mask and bolted out of his building, sprinting the seven blocks to Zoe's apartment in minutes. While he ran he called Detective Williams and told him about the text message he had received.

"Zoe left me a message about half an hour ago," said Sean breathing hard as he ran. "She sounded loopy but said she knew who tried to kill her. I called and texted but she didn't respond. I'm really worried. I'm on my way to her place now."

"Where's her husband?" said Daryl getting up from his desk.

"Zoe told me earlier that he had to go to work. I don't have his number anyway," said Sean. "He never wanted Zoe to give it out. FBI stuff I guess."

"We'll meet you at her apartment," said Daryl as he signaled to Heather that they were leaving. Without asking any questions, she grabbed her things and followed her partner out the door.

"What's going on?" said Heather as she got into the passenger side of their car.

"It's Zoe Brandt," said Daryl, putting the car in drive.

"Now what?" said Heather.

Daryl filled her in as they sped up Central Park West. When they got to Zoe's building two minutes later, Sean was already there talking to the doorman.

"But you've got to let me get upstairs," said Sean.

"I'm sorry. Mr. Brandt left very specific instructions that no one was allowed up," said the doorman. "I just can't do it. Not after what happened."

"It could be a matter of life or death," Sean pleaded.

Daryl and Heather raced into the building flashing their badges. "Police. We need to get into the Brandt apartment immediately."

"Mr. Brandt told me no one is supposed to go up there," said the doorman.

"What about the word 'police' did you not understand?" said Heather. "Let's go. Now."

CHAPTER FORTY-SEVEN

For the second time in a week, the doorman let the police into the Brandt's apartment.

"Zoe," shouted Sean as he moved quickly through the foyer.

"Ms. Brandt," shouted Daryl. "Everyone spread out."

"I'll check the bedroom," said Sean running down the long hallway.

Heather had just entered the kitchen when she heard Sean shout, "She's here in the bedroom."

Within moments all three stood over Zoe, passed out on the bed. Sean gently slapped her face while Daryl took her pulse. Heather quickly scanned the room and then went into the bathroom.

"I don't like this," said Daryl. "Her pulse is too weak. Let's put her in the recovery position and get some help. Wake up, Zoe."

He and Sean lifted the unconscious woman into a semi-prone position as Heather raced out of the bathroom holding an empty bottle of Ambien. "I found this in the sink. It was filled for sixty pills a week ago. It's empty. Also, there's puke in the toilet. I think she threw up before she passed out which could be a good thing."

"Call 911," shouted Daryl. Heather pulled out her phone and walked into the hall.

"Do you know if Ms. Brandt uses Ambien?" Daryl asked Sean while they rolled her over.

"Occasionally, but only a half a pill and not every day. At least that's what she told me," said Sean.

"EMS is on the way," said Heather walking back into the bedroom with a phone to her ear. "The ambulance will be here in four minutes." Picking up an empty glass from the nightstand she noticed a sliver of an ice cube at the bottom. She sniffed it. "Smells like bourbon."

"Does Zoe take Ambien with alcohol?" said Daryl, one of his eyebrows raised.

"Sometimes," said Sean nodding his head. "I keep telling her it's dangerous but she never listens."

Daryl leaned over close to Zoe to feel her breath on his cheek. "Her breathing is very shallow. Zoe, wake up," he said, shaking her. There was no response. "If she took that entire bottle, this is extremely serious."

"EMS should be here any minute," said Heather, "I'll go down to the lobby to meet them."

"She was a little depressed about the attack, but I can't believe she'd take a whole bottle of pills," said Sean. "I didn't realize how upset she was. I should have seen it."

There was a commotion out in the hall as the EMS technicians and Heather ran in. Checking Zoe's vitals, they placed her on a wheeled gurney and hooked her up to monitors. The technicians got some basic info from Daryl and Sean and were given the empty bottle of Ambien to take with them to the hospital. Seconds later, they hustled an unconscious Zoe out the door and onto the elevator with Daryl, Heather and Sean following behind. "I'll ride in the ambulance with Zoe," said Sean.

* * *

Carrying his groceries up Central Park West, Conner saw an ambulance with its strobe lights flashing in front of his building. When he spotted the detectives and then Sean climbing into the back of the ambulance, he dropped his bags on the sidewalk and ran towards them.

"What's going on?" Conner shouted as he approached.

"Your wife may have taken an overdose of Ambien," said Daryl. "They're taking her to Regency Memorial Hospital now."

"I don't understand," said a stunned Conner watching the ambulance roar off with sirens blaring. "I left her just a few hours ago and she was fine. Is she okay?"

"She's still breathing. We're heading over to the hospital now. You can ride with us," said Daryl.

"I have to go upstairs to get my insurance cards and medical information," said Conner as he turned to go into his building. "I'll meet you in the emergency room in ten minutes."

Once inside the apartment, Conner went straight into his bedroom to get his insurance papers. That's when he noticed his overnight bag had been moved from where he left it. He reached inside the bag into the side pocket — the burner phone was gone.

It's got to be here. Dumping the contents of the bag out onto the bed, he sifted through all the items but there was no phone. *Zoe must have taken it. She can't keep her hands off anything. Shit.* Hunting around the apartment, he opened drawers and closets, and then rifled through his wife's clothes and personal items. Moving to the living room he rummaged through several end-table drawers and cabinets. He glanced down at his watch. Eight minutes had passed since the ambulance had left. *I have to leave for the hospital right now or it will look suspicious.*

When Conner arrived at the emergency room six minutes later, an ER nurse briefed him on what was happening with his wife. Daryl stood by Zoe's bed conferring with an ER doctor. Numerous tubes and wires had been attached to her body and a team of technicians and doctors were attempting to revive her. Because of the virus, Conner and Sean had been asked to wait outside by the ER entrance.

"What's going on? Is she going to be okay?" an anxious Conner asked when one of the ER doctors came outside to give him an update. "Are you going to pump her stomach?"

"We don't do that anymore," said the doctor. "We've administered charcoal. If we get to a patient soon enough, it encapsulates the drugs in their stomach before they filter through the organs and cause permanent liver damage."

"How do you know if you got to her in time?" asked Sean.

"We don't. According to the intake notes, no one's exactly sure when she took the pills or how many. We're hoping we got to her within the window. We'll have to wait and see how she responds," said the doctor as he turned and went back into the ER.

There was nothing more to be done until Zoe woke up. After three hours of waiting, the nurses informed Conner that they were moving his wife into a private room.

"But shouldn't she be in the ICU?" Conner said.

"We need to clear the ER and reserve the ICU for incoming Covid patients," said one of the older nurses. "Your wife is breathing normally, her blood pressure is good, pulse is strong. The ICU is full of very contagious and sick patients. Your wife is better off in a private room. That way you can sit with her. Give her a little more time to wake up: it hasn't been that long."

Thirty minutes later, Zoe's eyes still closed, Conner sat quietly next to his wife's bed. Seeing no change and wanting to speak to a doctor, he let Sean in to take a turn sitting with his wife. When Sean entered the room and saw all the equipment attached to his best friend, tears pooled in his eyes. Sitting in the chair next to her bed, he talked to her, hoping somehow she could hear him. After a few minutes, Zoe muttered something unintelligible. Sean smiled and ran out into the hallway to get a doctor.

Outside the ER main entrance, a small crowd comprised of friends and relatives of patients, police, EMTs and a few members of the press gathered. Daryl Williams stood off to the side on the phone next to his partner as he briefed their captain on the new developments in the Strangler case. When he hung up, he stared at his partner.

"What?" said Heather Kim looking at the strange expression on his face.

"The captain told me the man Zoe Brandt killed in her apartment may not be the Strangler. They're checking right now to see if—"

"Detective Williams," said Tommy Devlin walking towards the two police officers with his cameraman in tow, "what a pleasant surprise. What brings you down to the hospital?"

"Hello Devlin," said Daryl Williams, not hiding his disappointment at seeing the aggressive and often obnoxious reporter. "What brings you to Regency Memorial?"

"I've been keeping tabs on the Brandt apartment ever since Zoe Brandt flatlined her attacker last Thursday," said Devlin. "If she offed the West Side Strangler, that's big news. When are you going to call it? In an odd coincidence, I interviewed Ms. Brandt right after the Central Park murder of that teacher last week. What's going on? Why was Zoe Brandt taken out of her building by ambulance today?"

"It's a private matter," said Daryl shaking his head as he moved away.

"C'mon detective, there are no secrets from the press," said Devlin staying close to him. "It's my job to leave no stone unturned, to hunt for the truth until I get the story."

"Was that what you were doing in Alaska when that moose chased you into the frozen lake," said Heather, "hunting for the truth? When you got to the edge of the water and that moose snorted and went at you with his antlers, you were screaming like a freakin' baby. The look on your face was incredible. Last time I checked, that video had over a million views. Guess Alaska wasn't for you."

Devlin's photographer stifled a snicker.

"That video was very misleading," said Devlin gritting his teeth and shooting his photographer a look. "Most people don't know but moose are very dangerous animals. I told CNN that I was going back to my roots in New York. I'm only doing this gig at *The Echo* until I finalize my contracts with a different cable network. Pretty soon you're going to see my pretty face on the evening news every night."

"Thankfully, I get my news online," said Daryl.

"What do you say, detectives? The guy Zoe Brandt offed in her apartment last week, was he the West Side Strangler? Love to get the scoop and be the first reporter in New York to break the story."

"No comment," said Daryl just as he saw Sean waving to him from inside the ER doorway and signaled for Heather to follow him inside.

"I think Zoe's coming around. She said something," said Sean when the detectives approached.

"What did she say?" said Daryl, moving the three of them from the doorway and Devlin's prying eyes and ears.

"It sounded like she said 'mask.'"

CHAPTER FORTY-EIGHT

Wednesday — June 10, 2020

Zoe remained unresponsive in the hospital for two days.

"Doctor, can't you do anything? When is my wife going to wake up?" Conner asked at the end of the first day.

"We don't know," said the physician. "From the ER reports I received, it seems the encapsulation of the drugs in her system was only partly successful because her liver enzymes were somewhat elevated. We've been monitoring that closely."

"When will she regain consciousness?" said Conner.

"It's unpredictable," said the doctor. "All of her vitals are good. She could wake up in thirty seconds or it could be longer."

"She *will* wake up, right?" said Conner, alarm in his voice.

"I'll check back in later today," said the doctor. "She's in otherwise good health. Hang in there. This is a time game."

An hour later, Sean managed to sneak by security and into Zoe's room and asked Conner the same questions. "She'll wake up, won't she?"

"They're not saying," Conner replied. "I believe she will. Zoe's one of the strongest people I know."

Sean smiled weakly and looked over at his friend motionless in the bed. "She's a force of nature." Taking her hand, Sean talked softly, encouraging Zoe to wake up.

After a brief visit, Sean left for work and by 9 p.m., with no discernible change in Zoe's condition, one of the nurses suggested Conner go home and get some sleep. "You're no good to her if you get sick," said the kindly nurse. "When she wakes up she's going to need a lot of support. Go home and get some rest. We'll call if there's any change."

Conner nodded. He had much to do. The two detectives had already grilled him on his whereabouts on the afternoon Zoe took the overdose of pills. They asked him several times why he had left her alone on Monday when she had been violently attacked only a few days before.

"Look, detective," Conner had replied, indignant, "I'm in the middle of a huge FBI undercover operation that's coming to a head. When my wife was attacked, I asked for some time off. Getting that time required a lot of extra work on the part of my team so my cover wasn't blown. I *had* to go into the office for fifteen minutes and sign-off on something."

"But then you went out shopping," said Heather studying him.

"We had no food in the house," said Conner. "I didn't realize how depressed my wife was. If I had, I wouldn't have left her. I only saw the email she sent to me that day a few minutes ago."

"What email?" asked Daryl.

Conner pulled out his iPhone and opened his Gmail account. "She sent this after I left for my office on Monday. I didn't see it until today. I usually check my personal Gmail more frequently but with everything that was going on I didn't look until this morning." He handed his phone to Daryl.

An email had been sent from Zoe to her husband at 2:10 p.m. on the same day Zoe had overdosed. There were only two words in the email — *I'm Sorry*.

"Don't delete that email, Mr. Brandt," said Daryl. "It may become material."

When Conner got home that night exhaustion overcame him. He would have loved nothing better than to take a shower and go to bed but he needed to find that missing phone first.

For the next four hours, he ripped the place apart searching every inch of the apartment. At 2am, completely spent, he sat on a stool in the kitchen digging through one last drawer. *Where the hell did she put that goddamn phone? I was only gone for a few hours and no one else came in or out. It was definitely in my bag when I left. Zoe left the apartment unconscious on a stretcher. The phone has got to be here somewhere. Where the hell is it?*

* * *

Thursday — June 11, 2020

Because of the pandemic, each hospital had created their own set of safety protocols. Regency Memorial allowed only immediate family and no more than two at a time. Police were allowed in with proper PPE. Masquerading as her brother, Sean once again got past the hospital gatekeepers. When he arrived late that afternoon, Conner was already there sitting next to her bed.

"I'll stay with her for a while before I head into work," said Sean. "Why don't you go home? You look exhausted." Conner protested but finally agreed saying he'd be back in a few hours. After Conner left, Sean chattered on as cheerfully as possible about all the things happening at the newly opened Villa d'Luna.

"The reopening has been one disaster after the next," said Sean. "Trust me, running a restaurant outside is a whole different ball game. Miranda's hair is falling out in big red clumps and there have been several accidents with people bringing food in and out of the same front door. We totally need you back, so you really have to wake up, okay?"

Zoe's eyelids flickered.

"Zoe?" said Sean leaning closer. "It's Sean, can you hear me?"

Her eyelids moved again but there was still no response. Disappointed, he sat back in his chair, tears filling his eyes. "Please wake up, Zoe, I really miss you."

Almost as if his will had a telekinetic effect, Zoe's eyelids fluttered again and slowly opened. She blinked several times and Sean let out a squeal. "Zoe, can you hear me?"

"What?"

"Oh my God, you can hear me," said Sean, smiling. "You're in the hospital."

"What?"

"You took all that Ambien. Do you remember?"

"Where am I?" said Zoe, her eyes circling the room.

"Regency Memorial Hospital," said Sean again.

"Why?"

"You took some pills. Don't move, I'm going to get the doctor," said Sean as he bolted from the room. A minute later he returned with a man wearing a white coat who was trailed by a nurse.

"See, she's awake," said a smiling Sean as they walked over to Zoe's bed.

"She is indeed. I'm Dr. Hufnagel, Zoe. I'm in charge of your care," said the smiling doctor. "You gave us quite a scare. You've been out for a while. The longer a person remains unconscious the worse the outcome may be. Glad to see you're awake."

"Where's Conner?" said Zoe in a raspy voice.

"He went home a little while ago," said Sean. "He was here all day."

"I think it's best if you relax for the time being," said the doctor.

"What happened?" said Zoe groggily.

"Looks like you took a fair amount of pills," said the doctor, "and chased them down with a fair amount of alcohol."

"I would never do that," said Zoe obviously confused. "I don't remember doing that." She took a breath and tried to string her thoughts together but her mind was all a jumble. "I remember a man came into my apartment with flowers and he knocked me down and tried to choke me."

Sean stared at his best friend. "That's the last thing you remember?"

"Yes," said Zoe closing her eyes.

"That happened several days before we found her unconscious," said Sean looking at the doctor. "Is it normal to lose memory?"

"There's no normal when it comes to brain injuries," said Dr. Hufnagel. "Memory loss after what she's been through is not unusual. I've seen patients with months of memory missing and then I've had patients with none."

"Will she get it back?" asked Sean.

"Maybe or maybe not," said the doctor. "A nurse will be in soon to check your blood pressure and a few other things. I want you to rest now, Zoe. Okay? I'll be back in a little while."

Zoe nodded as the doctor left the room. "I want to see Conner," she said to Sean.

"I'll call him, but let me ask you something first. The night we found you, you texted me saying you knew who tried to kill you. That you knew who it was. Do you remember?" said Sean, pulling out his phone and showing her the text message.

"I don't remember writing that," said Zoe trying to focus her eyes. "But, I know I didn't take all those pills. The most I ever take is one."

"You sent Conner an email an hour before we found you that said, *I'm Sorry*."

"Sorry for what?"

"We assumed for taking all those pills," said Sean gently.

"Why would I do that?"

"I saw the email, Zoe. Conner thought maybe the depression you had as a teenager had returned."

"My mother had just died then. You know that. I'm not depressed and I didn't take an overdose of pills. I want to see Conner," said Zoe getting agitated as a female nurse entered the room.

"I'll need you to step out for a few minutes," said the nurse to Sean.

"I'll call Conner. I'll be right outside," he said, walking into the hallway and taking out his phone.

"She's awake," said Sean when Conner answered.

"Really?" said Conner. "When?"

"About ten minutes ago."

"How is she?"

"Groggy but she seems all right," said Sean. "I asked her about taking the pills and she has no memory of it. She doesn't remember anything after June 4th, the day she was attacked."

"That was a week ago," said Conner. "Tell her I'll be there in half an hour."

When the nurse left, Sean returned to Zoe's bedside. "Conner's on his way. I also called Detective Williams. He's going to stop by to see you in the morning."

"Detective Williams?"

"Don't tell me you don't remember him?" said Sean, his eyes wide.

"Of course I remember him," said Zoe. "But why would he be coming to see me in the hospital?"

Sean recounted the events and details that led to Zoe ending up in the ER.

"Both detectives were there when you found me?" she said.

"Yes."

"Where was Conner?"

"He had gone to his office and was walking up to your building with groceries when the ambulance was leaving to bring you here."

"I don't remember any of it. My brain is mush. I want to get out of here," she said, trying to sit up.

"You're not going anywhere right now," said a male voice from the doorway.

A look of relief crossed Zoe's face and she half-smiled. "Conner. You're here."

Walking over to the bed, Conner kissed his wife on the forehead. "We almost lost you," he said, gently brushing a lock of hair off of her face. "How do you feel?"

"I have a bitch of a headache," said Zoe.

"Why did you take all those pills?" said Conner.

"I didn't," she said. "Why would I do that?"

"You were so anxious and depressed the days after you were attacked," said Conner. "I should have paid more attention to it given your history."

"But I would never do that . . ."

"I see you've had a chance to visit your wife. I'm afraid I need time with my patient right now," said Dr. Hufnagel as he entered the room. "We have to run a few more tests. Then, most importantly, she needs rest. Why don't you come back in the morning — but not together, the hospital is only allowing one visitor at a time now because of Covid."

"Can I have a private word with you, doctor?" said Conner. Dr. Hufnagel nodded and the two men went out into the hallway. "A hospital social worker contacted me and said because this was a suicide attempt the Regency Memorial won't release Zoe to go home? Is that true?"

"That's correct, it's our standard protocol. When someone is a potential risk to themselves, our policy is to release them into a psychiatric care facility for a week or so for observation. They will evaluate and make the recommendation of when and if it's safe for the patient to return home. It's for her own protection."

"Is that really necessary?" said Conner.

"Second suicide attempts are extremely common," said the doctor. "People who try it once often do it again. We don't want that to happen, do we?"

* * *

In front of his computer in his bedroom, Greg Harmen let out a yelp. "Yessss! Nailed it. Sweet."

"Why do you always have to scream?" said a more annoyed than usual Gabriela sitting on the living-room sofa thumbing through a copy of *Vogue*. Gritting her teeth, she took a deep exasperated breath.

"Are you kidding? I just outbid MuddyMan45 for 5,000 soccer jerseys coming in from Beijing," said a grinning Greg now standing in the living-room doorway. "I'm going to make a killing on those. Wait and see, Gabi. Wait and see."

"Then we can have more boxes stacked up in the apartment?" said Gabriela looking around at all the bags and packages. "Do you know what a hoarder is, Greg? This is exactly what a hoarder does. There's useless junk everywhere. I can't breathe in here. The boxes stink. When are you getting rid of all this crap? I demand to know."

"I've got to play the game, Gabi. I need to hold onto the merchandise for a while and then strike when the market is just right," he said.

Bored with the conversation, she flipped the pages of her magazine, stopping at an ad for a new perfume. Pulling back the scent strip flap she leaned over and sniffed, making a mental note to buy it for herself the next time she was in Bloomingdale's. Checking the time on her phone, she stood and began to pace. *Why hasn't he texted me? It's been too many days. Something is wrong.* She reached for the burner phone in her bag and checked for messages. There were none.

"Gabi," shouted her husband from the bedroom. "Why don't you make some of your extra special beef empanadas for dinner tonight?"

Why don't you go kill yourself? "Great idea," she said, feigning enthusiasm. "I'll go to the store and buy what we need now."

Out of patience with both Greg and Sr. Bello, Gabriela left the apartment and whipped out her burner phone once she was on the street. She had promised her lover she wouldn't contact him, but it had been way too long and she had to know what happened. She texted:

What's going on?

CHAPTER FORTY-NINE

Friday June 12, 2020

Stopped at a red light on Broadway and 86th Street that morning, Heather tapped the steering wheel with her fingers while her partner finished his call.

"Got the ID," said Daryl as he took the phone from his ear and put it into his jacket pocket.

"On the flower deliveryman?" said Heather as she and Daryl sped across town towards Regency Memorial Hospital.

"Perp's name was Oscar Jaworski, aged forty-two. Long rap sheet. Started with petty crime, then assault and moved up to armed robbery. He'd been in and out of prison since he was a kid. In juvie when he was fourteen and spent more time inside than out. Jaworski was a busy boy, had his hand in a lot of pots — arson, drug trafficking, prostitution and pornography."

"He sounds charming."

"More recently, it looks like he's been a gun for hire selling his services on the dark web. A real jack-of-all-trades, Jaworski would do anything if the price was right."

"But is he any good for the Strangler?"

"That would have been too easy. Jaworski was in Rikers from January 8th until March 20th when his arrest was thrown out. No way he could be the Strangler, dates don't match up."

"Shit," said Heather as she parked in front of Regency Memorial. "I thought his MO was off with the flower delivery but I was hoping he was just getting more creative and he was our man."

"Unfortunately, our killer is still out there and in three days he'll be on the move again."

When the detectives entered Zoe's hospital room, her eyes were closed. "Ms. Brandt?" said Daryl gently.

Opening her eyes, she smiled when she saw the two detectives.

"We were on our way to interview someone and figured we'd stop in to see how you were doing."

"Detectives, I guess I owe you both a big thank you," said Zoe. "I heard you helped get me to the hospital."

"Glad we got you here in time," said Daryl. "How are you feeling?"

"I've been better, but I'm okay," said Zoe. "I don't remember much. Did you find the masked woman? Did an unknown man who lives around 14th Street turn up dead in the last few days?"

"We didn't find your masked woman and people turn up dead in New York City every single day," said Heather. "We'd have no way of knowing if one of them was your supposed victim."

"What about my attacker?" said Zoe, "Conner thought the man with the flowers might be the West Side Strangler."

"You must be feeling better if you're already trying to solve crimes," said Daryl with a slight smile. "Unfortunately, the flower man is not the Strangler. Would have been great if he was. The man who attacked you in your apartment was in jail during three of the Strangler murders."

"Oh," said Zoe.

"You want to tell me why you took all those pills?" said Daryl.

"But I didn't . . ." said Zoe.

"Your doctor told us you have no memory of the three or four days before you were brought to the hospital," said Heather. "How do you know you didn't take them?"

"At first, the last thing I was able to recall was the flower man in my apartment and him choking me. Then this morning, I remembered something new. Conner and I stayed at his friend's apartment for a few days after the attack," said Zoe, wrinkling her forehead. "I can visualize the place and I remember we took an Uber from there back to our apartment on Central Park West. Other than that, everything else is a blank."

"There was an empty pill bottle in your bathroom sink the night we found you," said Heather gently.

"I've never had any thought to kill myself, ever," said Zoe getting agitated. "Why won't anyone believe me?"

The detectives pulled two chairs over and sat by the bed. "Why don't you tell us everything you *can* remember," said Daryl.

"After I fought with the flower deliveryman, I must have hit my head. When I woke up there were police officers there. I thought I was going to die that night," she said slowly, running her fingers through her hair. "There was blood everywhere," said Zoe starting to cry. "Then I went to the police station and Conner came and took me to an apartment on East 95th Street. We stayed there for a few days. That part is kind of fuzzy, but I do remember it."

"Take your time," said Daryl.

"I was afraid to go back to our apartment, so Conner went alone to clean everything. The next day we took an Uber to our place on Central Park West together," said Zoe.

"Do you remember going into your apartment that day?" asked Daryl.

Zoe let out a frustrated sigh. "No . . . wait . . . Yes. Conner was carrying our bags. I didn't want to go into the living room so I went directly down the hall to the bedroom. I didn't want to see where the man died."

"Okay, that's good. You're starting to remember bits and pieces," said Daryl. "Anything else?"

Zoe shook her head. "No, the rest is a big gray blob."

"Hey Zoe," said a masked Sean standing in the doorway holding a large potted plant with a "get well" blue ribbon around its base. "How are you feeling?"

"Mr. McAllister," said Daryl, "I thought the hospital wasn't letting people in?"

"I have my ways," said Sean, his eyes crinkling as he walked into the room.

"As long as you're here, we've got a few questions for you too." The detectives turned back to Zoe while Sean placed the heavy plant on the nightstand.

"The evening you overdosed you sent Sean a text saying you knew who tried to kill you?" said Heather. "What exactly did you mean by that?"

"I don't remember. I've been trying," said Zoe, "but it won't come."

"Retrace your steps after you got back to your apartment," said Daryl. "You went into your bedroom . . ."

"I think I got into my bed when we got home. I was tired," said Zoe looking out the window. "Conner offered to make me a bourbon so I could take a nap. He had to go somewhere . . ."

". . . To his office," said Daryl.

"Yes, that's right. He had to sign something," she said with a smile. "I heard him leave and I wanted to go to sleep so I took . . . Ambien."

"Then, you did take the pills," said Heather glancing over at her partner.

Zoe's face scrunched up as she searched for an answer. "I did . . . but only one. There was only one pill left in my nightstand. That's all I took." She closed her eyes and spoke slowly. "Conner's dirty shirts were piled at the foot of our bed. I noticed some of them were from Thayer and Co, and it made me think of the masked woman. I drank my bourbon and went into his closet because I wanted to do a load of laundry."

"You took Ambien, had a bourbon and then decided to do laundry?" said Heather, squinting. "Damn."

"Guess I was a little drunk," said Zoe. "Laundry seemed like a good idea at the time."

"Then what happened?" said Daryl.

Zoe rubbed her eyes. "I don't know. It's a blank."

"Do you remember calling Sean?"

"No . . . wait, wait . . . I was in Conner's closet straightening his clothes and I found a face mask. It was navy with a white shirt and red tie emblem."

"Like the one you saw on the masked woman with your binoculars?" said Sean, his eyes wide.

Zoe nodded. "Yes. I remember looking at the mask and I started feeling really woozy. Then the room started to spin, which was weird because I've had bourbon with an Ambien plenty of times and that never happened before."

"Looks like there's a party going on here," said a half-smiling Conner standing in the doorway. "Good morning, detectives."

"We're just wrapping up. Anything else you can recall, Ms. Brandt?" said Daryl.

"Do you remember vomiting into the toilet?" asked Heather.

"No," said Zoe rubbing her temples. "Did I?"

"Detectives, I appreciate your concern, but my wife is supposed to rest. Can we pick this up at a later date," said Conner walking over to Zoe's bed.

"We've got another appointment now anyway. We'll check in with you tomorrow," said Daryl, waving as he and Heather left the room.

"The plant is so pretty," said Zoe looking at Sean.

"Everyone at the restaurant chipped in. We all miss you."

"What were you talking about with the police?" said Conner to his wife.

"They were trying to help me remember what happened."

"Did they?" asked Conner.

"Only little bits," she replied, "it's mainly all a big jumbled mess in my head."

"Nothing concrete?" said Conner looking down and checking his phone. Seeing him holding his phone jolted her memory. An image of the Android phone she found in her husband's overnight bag flashed in her mind. "Zoe, did you remember anything else when you were talking with the police?"

"No, nothing," she said quickly, confused by what she had just recalled.

"But you told me . . ." said Sean. Zoe shot her friend a look that stopped him in mid-sentence.

"That was all," said Zoe.

"I was hoping you might remember going through my work bag," said Conner. "I'm missing a few important items."

"Why would I go through your work bag?"

Conner pulled a face. "You've done it before."

"I don't remember anything," said Zoe looking over at Sean, signaling with her eyes for him to stay quiet.

Conner looked down at his phone. "Just got an email from work. I've got to go into the office for a few hours. Things are heating up on my case. I'll be back this afternoon."

"I've got to go, too, am working the lunch shift today," said Sean, adjusting his mask while giving Zoe a worried look as he got up to leave. "I'll stop by later. Try to get some rest."

CHAPTER FIFTY

After Conner and Sean left, Zoe closed her eyes, hoping to summon the missing puzzle pieces from her uncooperative brain. After a few minutes of nothingness, she heard the distinct ping sound of a phone alert and opened her eyes. She reached for her phone on the nightstand. There were no new messages. She heard the ping again.

Where's that noise coming from? Am I hearing things? Still very weak, she got up slowly, leaning on the walls as she circled the small room opening drawers and cabinets. She opened the closet door. It was mainly empty with only a few bare hangers. Lower down, a large white plastic bag with a yellow drawstring lay on the middle shelf. She opened it. The bag was full of her clothes — a pink top, gray yoga pants and gray socks. *That's what I was wearing before I passed out in my bedroom.* She pulled the drawstring closed, placed the bag back on the shelf, and was about to close the closet door when she heard that ping sound again.

The noise is coming from inside the plastic bag. Taking the bag over to the bed, she dumped the contents out. That's when she noticed something was inside the zippered pocket of her pants. Sliding the zipper to the left she found an Android phone inside. *Where did this come from?*

Staring at it, an image flashed in front of her. *I found this phone in Conner's overnight bag. Why did I put it in my pants pocket?* She wrinkled her forehead and groaned, trying to remember. *It had something to do with text messages.*

She tried to open the messages but the phone required a password. *Shit. What are the passwords Conner uses?* She punched in half a dozen combinations and was about to give up when she tried their wedding anniversary and the phone unlocked. She smiled, let out a soft squeal and clicked on the messages icon.

There were only two contacts on the phone, the first text exchange was with someone called "Pest Control".

> —*What kind of problem do you need help with?*
> —*I've got a rodent infestation in my house.*
> —*A large rodent like a raccoon or something small like a mouse?*
> —*Small like a mouse. How soon are you available to take care of my problem?*

The texts were familiar. Zoe held her breath, puffed up her cheeks and then blew it out. *I know I've seen these texts before.*

Slowly, bits of her memories started to connect in a more linear way. She clicked over to the other contact, "Wardrobe Consultant" and opened the most recent message. It had been sent that morning and hadn't yet been read. *That's why it was pinging. It was a new message alert.*

> —*Sr. Bello, what's going on? I've been waiting for a week to hear from you. Is she dead?*

Zoe grabbed for the bed to steady herself. When she regained her balance, she sat down and read the full chain of texts from the beginning.

> —*When I got furloughed from T and C I thought it would only be a few weeks. They announced this week that they're*

closing some of their stores. Rumor is they're going to file for bankruptcy. What am I supposed to do now?

—You're too good for that place. Trust me, it will all be over on Thursday.

Feeling sick, Zoe scrolled through the chain of texts until she got to the end.

—I can't wait to feel your body next to mine again.

Nauseous, she now knew her husband was behind everything. She didn't know exactly how but she knew why. She also knew she was the intended victim the masked woman was talking about that first day in the park, not the woman's husband.

She called Sean. "I don't have a lot of time," whispered Zoe. "This is deadly serious. I need you to come here and then go to the police for me."

"I'm at the restaurant," said Sean, wary now of anything Zoe said. "I can't play this game today. In fact, I don't think we should play detective anymore, ever. Things got way too real."

"We don't have to play anymore, but right now, I need your help. I found a burner phone in Conner's bag."

"So you did take his phone?"

"Conner is behind everything — the flower deliveryman, the Ambien overdose. He and the masked woman are in on it together," said Zoe sounding more frantic and hysterical. "Sean, Conner is Sr. Bello."

"Stop it, Zoe. I can't do this right now. We've got a full restaurant. Two of the servers came down with the virus, so I'm waiting tables. You've got to stop all this conspiracy stuff. You go too far. I don't want to do this. Maybe you *should* go to a therapist."

Stung by his words, Zoe held back her tears. "I know I sound completely nuts but I have proof and I need you to trust me this one last time. If I can just read you the texts."

There was a long silence on the phone. "It's a matter of life and death. Sean, are you still there?"

"I'm still here."

"Sean, listen to me. There may have been a few times where I got a little out of control but this time it's for real. If you can do this one last thing for me I promise, I'll never mention crime again. They're sending me off to the Cherry Ridge Mental Hospital in Mahopac for observation soon. You have to come here before they do, get Conner's phone and take it to Detective Williams."

There was silence on the phone. "Sean, are you there?"

CHAPTER FIFTY-ONE

At the 24th Precinct, Daryl and Heather briefed the Strangler task force on their latest intelligence. "We're back at square one, people. Oscar Jaworski, the man who attacked Zoe Brandt in her apartment, is not our Strangler," said Daryl. "Today is June 12th which means the real Strangler is most likely going to strike again in three days. Every man and woman on this team needs to live, eat and breathe this case, or another young woman is going to turn up dead."

When the meeting ended, the two detectives went back to their desks in the bullpen. "What's your take on Conner Brandt?" said Daryl.

"Arrogant asshole?" said Heather chewing on the end of a pen. "But he's no different from the rest of them. All the Feds behave like that when they interact with cops. They think they're so elite."

"I meant what do you think of Conner Brandt as a person. Something about him strikes me as off."

"As a couple, they don't go together. He's Mr. FBI Type A personality and she's two inches away from being a Unabomber."

"Come on, Zoe Brandt isn't dangerous."

"Maybe not, but she's got a few frayed connections."

"Maybe he found her eccentricities endearing at first but over time they grated on his FBI nerves," said Daryl. "Let's swing by Regency Hospital before we head home tonight."

* * *

At a little after 1 p.m., Conner entered his wife's hospital room.

"How are you feeling? You've got more color in your face, babe," said Conner, smiling as he moved towards her. A faint look of fear flashed in her eyes but he didn't notice.

"I saw your doctor when I signed your release forms," he continued as he moved closer. "They're going to move you tomorrow morning by hospital transport to the Cherry Ridge facility. I'll meet you up there."

"Don't come any closer," said Zoe backing up.

"What are you talking about?"

"It was you," she hissed. "All this time, it was always you. You tried to have me killed. You were behind the whole thing with that woman."

"Behind what whole thing?"

"I know everything, Conner. I know about the woman."

"What woman?"

"That Wardrobe Consultant person."

Conner remained poker-faced. "What are you talking about?"

"From Thayer and Company. You're having an affair with her. You both planned my murder."

"Here we go with Zoe's crazy conspiracy theories again. Everyone is always out to get Zoe. That's your problem, you make up something from nothing. You invent crazy things in your head. I never tried to kill you. How could you think such a terrible thing?"

"I know what I know," said Zoe emphatically.

"Just like you knew the attaché to the Canadian ambassador was running a slave ring and transporting young women to Vancouver?" said Conner shaking his head mockingly.

"Maybe I was mistaken about that, but you trying to kill me, that I am sure of."

"Like you were sure the Korean manicurist in our neighborhood was trying to recruit you to become a drug mule? Like then?" said Conner with the same tone in his voice. "She threatened to sue you for slander, remember? Another situation that ended badly."

"She asked me some very peculiar questions when I was getting my nails done," said Zoe. "But this time it's different."

"Okay, you got me," said Conner, putting his fists together in front of him as if to allow her to handcuff him. "I *was* trying to kill you."

"You're having an affair and you wanted to get rid of me," said Zoe as Conner smirked. "I saw that mask in your closet, Conner. It was the same mask I saw on the woman in the park."

"What woman in the park?"

"The masked woman on the bench in Central Park who was texting about killing someone. I read her texts with my binoculars from our window. She had on a mask with a shirt and tie on it. I found that same mask in your closet. It was FBI-issued."

"I work for the FBI. Why wouldn't I have an FBI-issued mask?"

"But she doesn't. How did she get the mask, Conner?"

"I don't know who you're talking about."

"I saw all the text messages. I know everything."

"I've had enough of your crazy accusations for one week. My whole life has been turned upside down by you. You're getting really tiresome. I'm going home now."

"You're not going to get away with this," she said.

"Get away with another delusional plot you cooked up from nothing right before you were admitted to a mental hospital?"

"It's not cooked up from nothing."

"Don't you get it," said Conner starting to lose his cool, "No one's going to believe anything you say. You've got a history of making up stories and nearly getting arrested. Even Sean's had enough and thinks you might be crazy. You tried to kill yourself and now you're accusing your husband, a decorated federal officer, of trying to murder you based on a fantasy. Can you spell paranoid?"

"I know the truth now, Conner."

"And, I know you're nuts," he said with a sneer as he walked to the door of her room. "See you tomorrow, babe. I'll meet you at the loony bin. Don't forget your toothbrush. You may be there a long while."

* * *

Instead of going straight home from the hospital, Conner took a long walk to burn off steam. Everything had gone wrong and he needed time to figure things out. It was a nice night and he eventually stopped at a deli and picked up a cold six-pack of beer and a bag of chips. Walking to a small, empty courtyard park, he sat down. He opened a beer, thinking only about finding his missing burner phone. *Where the hell did she put it? It's got to still be in the apartment.*

Without that phone, he had no way to contact Gabriela without compromising their identities. He didn't remember her number because he had programmed it into the missing phone. He couldn't call her iPhone or go to her home in person, that would be too risky and leave a trail. Taking another sip of beer he worried what Gabi might do when she didn't hear from him. Her hot temper was what drew him to her, but it was also something he had to manage to prevent a combustion. By the time he finished his third beer and had a nice long conversation with a man on a nearby bench who had just had a fight with his wife, nearly three hours had passed since he left Zoe in the hospital. He planned to go through his apartment again when he got home until he found that goddamned phone, even if it took all night.

As he walked up Central Park West near his building, a masked man and woman got out of a parked car.

"Conner Brandt," said the man in a booming voice holding up a badge, "you're under arrest for the attempted murder of Zoe Brandt. You have the right to remain silent . . ."

As Detective Williams read FBI Special Agent Conner Brandt his rights, Detective Kim snapped on a pair of handcuffs and led Conner to the back seat of a waiting car. While Conner was being transported, a police vehicle had been dispatched to pick up and arrest Gabriela García-Harmen at her apartment on the Lower East Side, right off 14th Street.

Conner was taken into the 24th Precinct and booked. While he waited to be processed, two police officers led a stunned Gabriela through a side door into the central booking room. When she and Conner saw each other, they stopped and stared, mouths open under their masks.

"What are you doing here?" said Conner to Gabriela.

"I hate to spoil the surprise, but given the circumstances, I'm afraid I must," said Daryl. "It seems Ms. García-Harmen had booked a lovely cozy getaway for the two of you. You were to fly to Key West the last weekend of October. It sounds like it would have been a wonderfully romantic trip. Ms. García-Harmen sent you some pictures and photos of the plane tickets and hotel reservation this afternoon along with a little love note. Since I had your burner phone, thanks to your wife and Mr. McAllister acting as her courier, we were able to identify Ms. García-Harmen . . . and you, Sr. Bello."

Conner looked over at Gabriela in disbelief.

"You said we'd be together in October," said Gabriela. "I thought it would be nice to get away then and relax."

Conner looked away and shook his head.

"Gabriela García-Harmen, you're under arrest for conspiracy for the attempted murder of Zoe Brandt," said Daryl.

"I did nothing," said an indignant Gabriela. "I don't know anything about a murder. If he planned something bad, he never told me. All he said was that his wife would be gone soon and we would be together. How was I to know he meant that?"

“Tell that to the district attorney,” said Daryl as another police officer took Gabriela by the arm and walked her out of the room.

“Don’t say anything else, Gabi. Do you hear me?” shouted Conner as they led him in the opposite direction.

CHAPTER FIFTY-TWO

Saturday — June 13, 2020

With time ticking towards the 15th of the month and the city bracing for another murder, Daryl and Heather climbed up the metal fire stairs to their floor after interviewing another possible witness. In the stairwell, Daryl received a call from the postal inspector and put it on speaker so his partner could hear.

"Sorry this took so long. What with Covid-19, our whole operation is a mess. That West Side postal route you asked about has had two different mail carriers over the past five years," said the postal inspector. "One is a woman and the other a man. Both are career postal employees who've come up through the ranks."

"Who has that route now?" asked Daryl.

"His name is Jonathan Arnold, been with USPS for eleven years, solid record, good reviews, no problems or complaints," said the postal inspector. "He started working for us in the Bronx and was there for five years. He moved to another route in Astoria for four. About two and a half years ago he picked up his current route in Manhattan."

"Can I get a copy of Arnold's previous routes?" said Daryl before he ended the call and looked at his partner.

"We'd better see if there were any unsolved murders of young women in the Bronx or Astoria. This guy may have been practicing his skills a long time ago and no one put two and two together."

After briefing their captain on their discovery, their superior placed a call to the police commissioner. Daryl and Heather were given the green light to assemble a team and stake out the area surrounding Jonathan Arnold's West 107th Street apartment building and take him down.

By 5:30, nineteen police officers including a SWAT team of eight were hidden at various points around Jonathan Arnold's block between Broadway and Amsterdam. Not wanting to create a scene in the USPS mail-sorting facility where Arnold worked, the police opted to arrest him at home for better containment and less chance of civilian exposure. The detectives monitored the entire operation from a vacant first-floor art studio across the street from Arnold's building.

A spokesperson from the postal service said that Arnold usually punched out and returned his mail vehicle between 5:30 and 5:45. With the police team in place well ahead of that time, everything would look normal when Arnold returned home. They hoped to make an arrest without incident.

At 6:30 p.m., after stopping at an Italian deli to pick up a meatball hero, Jonathan Arnold walked cheerfully down Broadway towards 107th Street. He was looking forward to eating his sandwich and doing what he did every night, a little *Jeopardy* on TV and playing Fortnite until two or three in the morning. That had been his daily schedule for years. Preferring the virtual world to the real one, the only time he enjoyed reality was when he was on one of his special "dates".

Approaching 107th Street, he daydreamed about his upcoming "date" in two days with Marisa Robinson, a dark-haired beauty who lived in one of his apartment buildings on 99th Street. She had recently gotten divorced and he figured she was no doubt lonely. In two days, he would help her get over her divorce.

About to cross the street onto his block, he saw something move on the roof of his building a quarter way down. His instincts told him not to turn and to keep going straight. Continuing downtown he bypassed 107th Street entirely and kept going. Two blocks further south, he turned left onto 105th, walked half a block east and pulled out his phone. A total geek and reasonably paranoid, Jonathan Arnold had installed hidden cameras within his apartment building's hallways. "You can never have too much security," he had often told himself. With this surveillance equipment in place he was able to see anything going on in, at or around his building.

Opening the app that activated his home security equipment, images of armed police officers were visible in the hallway on the floor above his apartment. Jonathan sighed. The game was over and it was time to get out of New York. He had known this day would come and he was prepared, though he hadn't expected it quite so soon.

CHAPTER FIFTY-THREE

Tuesday — June 30, 2020

Several weeks after Conner Brandt was arrested, Zoe went back to work at Villa d'Luna managing the outdoor afternoon and evening shifts. Miranda had been very supportive when she learned from Sean what Zoe had been through. Even cranky Juliet Pasternak, after she heard what had happened, apologized for everything and put her "mean girl" away. She even offered to fill in temporarily until Zoe was physically and emotionally ready to go back to work.

The outdoor restaurant seating was going well even though their business was less than half of what it had been. While Miranda had planned on closing for the winter, Sean did some research and had convinced her to invest in extra high-end efficient heat lamps that would enable them to keep the restaurant open on all but the most bitter cold days.

"Cafés in Paris stay open all winter," he said. "We can do the same."

Not long after Zoe returned to work at the restaurant she received a call from Detectives Williams and Kim asking for a meeting with her and Sean. Waiting for the detectives to arrive at Zoe's apartment that morning, the two friends speculated on what the meeting was all about.

"Maybe we're going to get a commendation?" said Sean.

"I doubt it," said Zoe. "I think they want to update us on the case."

The doorman buzzed from the lobby. When Zoe opened her front door for the two detectives, she could tell Daryl Williams was smiling at her even though he was wearing a mask. The detective truly admired the young woman's pluckiness and determination and was sorry he hadn't been able to stop all that had happened to her. Despite her own personal risk, Zoe had worked tirelessly to prevent the murder of a total stranger never realizing she was the actual target. In her efforts to do the right thing, Zoe Brandt had lost a lot and had almost been killed twice.

"Come in, detectives," said Zoe as she closed the front door. Waiting in the living room, Sean stood next to the picture window gazing out at Central Park.

The windows had been left wide open providing ample ventilation and the warm summer breeze filled the large space. Four dining-room chairs had been set up in front of the window six feet apart. Daryl cleared his throat. "We wanted to tie up some loose ends for you," he began, "and officially confirm what you already may know. I'm sure you've figured out by now that the intended victim of the murder plot you saw in the texts was not Ms. García-Harmen's husband, it was you. The man who attacked you in this apartment had been hired by your husband. That man as we previously told you was not the West Side Strangler."

Zoe nodded. "The serial killer is still out there."

"Unfortunately. But at least, your husband is not. From what they tell me, it looks like he'll be a guest of the State of New York for quite a long time," said Daryl.

"We've kept everything out of the press because the FBI wants to keep Conner's arrest quiet for a while," said Heather. "Your husband was the key person on a large FBI undercover operation. If the people he was investigating got wind that the FBI had infiltrated their organization it would blow the lid off the whole thing. The police commissioner got a call from the head of the Manhattan FBI field office. We've all agreed to keep Conner's arrest under wraps, at least for the time being. They'd like the same from the two of you as well."

Zoe bit her lip and nodded again as she took it all in. "Of course," she said.

"Won't say a word," said Sean.

"We wanted you to hear it from us," said Daryl. "You're safe now, Zoe. The DA thinks they have enough evidence to seek the maximum. Conner Brandt won't get out for a long time."

Zoe's body slumped in her chair. "None of it makes sense," she said getting teary. "I've gone over it in my head a million times. If Conner didn't want to be married to me and wanted to be with her so badly, why didn't he just get a divorce?"

"We've learned a fair amount about Conner and Ms. García-Harmen. She's quite an operator," said Heather. "We dug into her past and communicated with the Mexican police. Gabriela was well known to them in Mexico City. She worked the rich old man circuit trading sexual favors for cash and expensive jewelry. Apparently, she bilked one wealthy old man out of a great deal of money and then hit the road for New York."

"That's who Conner fell for?" said Zoe. "A grifter?"

"After she overstayed her visa in the US," said Daryl, "she seduced the husband of the family who employed her as a nanny. She took him for a fair amount too. When her employer lost his job at Blue Crest Financial—"

"Blue Crest Financial! That's where she got the white bag with the red letters," said Sean. "I knew there was a connection."

"When that man lost his job at Blue Crest," said Daryl, "he couldn't afford Gabriela and her extravagant tastes.

When the family terminated her employment, she married Greg Harmen as a stop-gap to get her green card and become legal in the United States."

Zoe and Sean turned and looked at each other.

"Greg Harmen is also a victim here," said Heather. "He knew nothing about any of this. Seems Gabriela's had her sights set on living the high life in New York City ever since she was a kid. After she got her green card and deportation was no longer an issue, she looked around for someone who could provide her with the more luxurious lifestyle she felt she deserved. That's when she met your husband."

"But Conner had no money," said Zoe.

"On the FBI's dime he looked like he did. Conner had gone to Thayer and Company to buy a whole new wardrobe for his undercover assignment," said Daryl. "When she saw him spending thousands on clothes without concern for price, she thought he had real potential. He wined and dined her using his expense account and regularly met her at his FBI-issued "cover apartment" on Park Avenue.

"That's when Gabriela started calling him Senor Bello," said Heather. "That was her pet name for him. They agreed never to use their real names when texting. He was always Sr. Bello and she was his Wardrobe Consultant."

"But it was all fake, Conner didn't make that kind of money," said Zoe. "He couldn't afford all those expensive clothes. We struggled to pay our bills at the end of every month. Eventually, she would have found that out."

"She did find out," said Heather. "He finally came clean and Ms. García-Harmen was all ready to move on."

"Why did she stay?" said Zoe.

Daryl glanced around the expansive living room and spread his arms. "For this place," said Daryl. "Conner brought Gabriela here once when you were away at a high-school reunion weekend and when she saw this apartment, that changed everything. From that day on, she was all in. You may think of this place as home, Zoe, but it's worth a lot of money — millions and millions.

"I know but . . ." said Zoe.

"When you saw the text about the murder, you — and we — assumed they were talking about killing a man, her husband, but the actual intended victim was always you. All of us got that wrong. Greg Harmen was never the target. She wanted Conner to get rid of you so the two of them could take possession of this apartment."

"I still don't understand," said Zoe.

"Because the apartment belonged to you before you got married, if you and Conner divorced, he'd have no claim to it. That didn't sit well with Gabi. She wanted your apartment, lock, stock and barrel. He wanted her and was willing to do whatever she asked."

"She's like that black widow spider that eats their mates," said Sean.

"We believe Gabi was the one who cooked up the whole idea and pushed your husband to do it. Regardless, he went along with it and arranged the whole thing. When you killed the man he hired to murder you, Conner had to take matters into his own hands or risk losing Gabriela. He wasn't willing to give her up so he spiked your drink and tried to make it look like a suicide. He made sure that both he and Gabriela had no communication and solid alibis for their whereabouts that day in case it ever came back to bite them. From our reports, it seems that Gabriela flirted with every shopkeeper in Manhattan that afternoon. Once you were out of the picture, they planned to marry and eventually, we think she would have gotten rid of Conner for someone with a bigger bank account. By then, she'd be the owner of your apartment on Central Park West."

"Why did Gabriela sit out there across the street?" said Sean looking out the window at the park bench. "Wasn't that a little risky sitting right near your murder victim's home?"

"We asked her that. Apparently, she wanted to get to know the neighborhood," said Heather. "According to police reports, ever since they cooked up the idea, she'd been sitting on that bench in the park for months. Whenever she had free time, she'd go there and dream about her new life in her multi-million-dollar apartment overlooking the park. Occasionally, she'd bring her husband Greg with her, a sick joke only she knew about. Poor guy had no clue he was being used. He was with her on the day you saw them with your binoculars."

"So, her husband was never in danger?" said Zoe.

"No. The text you saw that day was referring to the attack on you," said Daryl. "From what Ms. Harmen disclosed in her plea deal, she was going to divorce her husband. He had nothing of value. She already had her green card and figured she might get a little financial settlement if she divorced him. Once you were out of the way and Conner became the sole owner of this apartment, she would dump husband number one and marry husband number two and his luxury co-op."

"Let me ask you something," said Zoe later as she walked the detectives to the front door. "Did you believe me when I reported this whole thing or did you think I was crazy?"

"In the beginning there were a lot of holes in your story. I'll admit I had my doubts," said Daryl, "but there was an honesty about you that told me you were telling the truth."

"I owe you an apology. I thought you were completely nuts," said Heather. "Turns out I was wrong and I'm glad my partner had more faith in you than I did."

"If you ever need anything, call me," said Daryl just before he and Heather left. "And Zoe, stay away from crime scenes. You hear?"

Back in the living room, Zoe and Sean sat opposite each other by the window. "From now on, I have full veto power on any man you go out with," said Sean. "Clearly, you're a terrible judge of character."

"I won't be seeing anyone for a long time, maybe never. I'm swearing off men for a long while."

"And we're done playing detective. Those days are over, right?" said Sean staring at his friend. "This whole thing got way too dangerous."

"I agree, we're totally finished," said Zoe getting up and looking out the window. Reaching for the binoculars on a nearby table, she held them up to her eyes and looked down on the street below while fiddling with the focus controls. "It was definitely too real. After everything that happened I promise, I'm so over it. I will never ever do that . . . wait . . . what? Holy shit. Oh my God, Sean, you're *not* going to believe what I see right now. There's this hulking bald man in a blue sweatshirt. He looks German. He's walking a black poodle with a red collar. He's following this platinum blonde woman who is talking on her phone. She has no idea he's behind her. I think I see a knife sticking out of his sleeve and . . ."

EPILOGUE

THE NEW YORK ECHO — June 30, 2020
STRANGLER ELUDES COPS AGAIN
by Tommy Devlin

On the evening of June 13, a large-scale police operation assembled on West 107th Street to capture a fugitive — the man they believed to be the West Side Strangler. The SWAT team was in place, but the elusive Strangler never materialized. According to police, an examination of the contents of the man's apartment confirmed he was the right person. They have not released the name of the individual in question but believe he may have fled from New York and is now operating under an assumed name . . .

After dodging the cops, Jonathan Arnold sat down on a stoop several blocks away, pulled his mask down and unwrapped and ate his meatball hero. Contemplating his next move as he chewed, he finished his supper, pulled out a bottle of water from his jacket pocket and washed it all down. Wiping his mouth with his sleeve, he deposited the empty bag in a nearby garbage can. Jonathan Arnold killed, but he didn't litter — he considered that wrong.

At the nearest subway station, he took a train to Midtown. It was rush hour but because of the virus, the subways were empty. Getting off at 42nd Street, he moved calmly, even slowly, like a man who had nowhere in particular to go. Climbing up the subway stairs he changed trains and took another one out to Queens near his old mail route in Astoria. Out there, the trains were not underground but on elevated tracks where you could see the panorama of New York around you while you moved. When his subway arrived at his stop, he got off and sauntered down the metal stairs to the ground below.

Walking along the vacant Queens streets, he stopped to purchase another bottle of water and a bag of potato chips from a corner store. Munching and licking his fingers repeatedly, he walked further from the commercial district and into a more residential area. It had been a while since he had been out there but he knew the neighborhood like the back of his hand, his old mail route.

At nearly 8:30 p.m., it was getting dark and the streetlights turned on all at once. Ahead, he saw the intersection he was looking for and made a right turn. Half a block down on the left were several rows of locked garages. He had a key to one of them. He paid for it annually with cash and had been renting it under a fake name for years.

Using the flashlight on his phone to identify storage unit #17, he thrust his key into the lock. Opening the metal door, he reached in and turned on the overhead light. The room was musty and had an overwhelming stench of mildew. He found the odor comforting. His mother's house had always smelled like that.

A few pieces of old furniture acquired when his mother died were stacked on one side of the unit. There had been no room for her things at his place in Manhattan but he couldn't part with it so he had rented the unit for that purpose. She hadn't been a very good mother but was the only one he had.

After he developed a strong interest in some highly unlawful activities, the storage space took on new importance.

The little garage became his insurance policy in case things ever went awry and that day had come. He was there to pick up his "Get out of Dodge" bag, as he liked to call it.

Over in the far corner, sitting on top of an old dresser was a large duffle bag. Inside the bag was a week's worth of clothing, toiletries, a guidebook for Florida, a burner phone, a fake driver's license with a different name, maps, and several bus and train schedules. There was also a locked waterproof metal box that held a wallet filled with cash. Opening it, he let out a breath when he saw all the money was still there, and then put the wallet in his pocket.

Throwing the bag over his shoulder, he was about to walk out of the storage unit for what he expected would be the last time, when he stopped and turned around. Reaching inside a box, he retrieved his high-school yearbook. Next to the book was an old prom corsage wristband with the last remnants of a dead flower, once white, now beige and shriveled. He grabbed the corsage and the yearbook and placed them inside of his duffle bag. Locking the door, he walked back to the subway and took the train to the Port Authority Bus Terminal.

As soon as he got off the train at 42nd Street, he smashed his Android phone into several pieces and threw the bits in different garbage cans as he walked. Putting his pre-paid phone into his breast pocket, he purchased a one-way ticket to Oceanside, Florida and waited for his bus departure to be called.

For the next twenty-four hours the bus made its way south and the ride provided Jonathan with quiet time to reflect on his deeds. He remembered his first kill in the Bronx. That was followed by two girls in Astoria. But things didn't get really good until he moved to Manhattan, when he had his first date with Lisa Eng. *She was my favorite, and she had such pretty, long black hair.* Then, there were all the others — Carly, Nicole, Rosie, Michelle and Katie. He didn't include the teacher in Central Park. He had been itchy that night and had gone out for a late-night walk. Spotting the obviously intoxicated teacher quite by accident, he decided to go for it. The young woman was so inebriated he didn't enjoy the experience at all. She had collapsed in seconds and didn't put up a fight which took all the fun out of it. After that, he swore off "unplanned dates" preferring the carefully selected and vetted women on his route.

The next day, a bleary-eyed Jonathan Arnold stumbled off the bus steps in Oceanside, Florida. It was hot and humid there compared to the weather in New York. He opened the top two buttons of his shirt while he waited for the driver to remove his bag from the luggage compartment. With his duffle over his shoulder, Jonathan set out on foot for the long-term-stay motel room he had reserved.

Over the next three months, he made a concerted effort to alter his appearance. He changed his diet to vegan and lost twenty-seven pounds. Working out daily, he cut his long-ish curly black hair into a short, almost military style. He grew a beard that he kept closely cropped and got rid of his glasses in favor of contacts. Every day he scanned the online newspapers and job boards for work opportunities.

By September, looking dramatically different and significantly more fit, Jonathan was ready to apply for jobs using his new name, the one he had on all his fake IDs — Matthew Gennaro.

Florida's "season" as they called it, was during the winter months, November through April. That's when all the "snowbirds" from up north flew down for the winter for a vacation in "the warm". That was when all the hiring was done — usually.

2020 was like no other year. Nobody knew what to expect. The country was still at various levels of viral lockdown with disagreements on what restrictions were too much and what were too little. Some people never went out, some only went to the supermarket or the doctor's office and were completely masked and gloved. Others thought the whole thing was a joke, or even called it a hoax.

Given the state of the country, the job market was hard to predict. Jonathan wasn't worried. He had plenty of money and he didn't need much. Not only did he have his wallet full of cash, he had also long ago purchased cryptocurrency and had set up dozens of bank accounts in South Carolina, Georgia and Florida under different names. He even had one offshore account in the Cayman Islands.

Looking through the job listings one morning while drinking a Diet Coke, he searched for the advertisements that had been posted within the last week. One in particular caught his eye.

> *"Pink Flamingo Ice Creamery looking for drivers. Several ice-cream truck routes opening up in the Oceanside, Florida area starting October 1. No experience needed. Apply in person."*

Jonathan grinned. Ring-a-ding-ding. He liked ice cream and thought an ice-cream route would be almost as good as a mail route, maybe better. He didn't like kids that much but teenaged girls bought ice cream and he decided driving an ice-cream truck would be totally sweet.

That same day, Matt Gennaro went for an interview at the Pink Flamingo Ice Creamery. The following Monday with a dried, yellowed wrist corsage hanging from his rear-view mirror, Matt Gennaro rang the bells of his ice-cream truck. He was looking forward to making some new friends and hopefully soon, going on a few dates.

THE END

ACKNOWLEDGEMENTS

People have commented that this manuscript reminded them a little of the book *Harriet the Spy*. That book happened to be my favorite when I was a kid. I even had my own spy route with my neighborhood pal when I was ten. It hadn't occurred to me when I was writing it, but I must have channeled my inner Harriet when creating the character of Zoe Brandt.

A huge thanks to my always first readers Peter Black, Diane McGarvey and Marlene Pedersen. Their comments and observations helped this book take form. To get all my law enforcement facts straight, I consulted with NYC police officers as well as several federal agents. Their input was invaluable, especially when it came to the dark web. I'd also like to thank Tom Conners (retired police officer) and his brother, Patrick Conners (former US Postal Service Employee) for their help in keeping the police and postal sections authentic.

If you've enjoyed this book, please leave a review on Amazon or Goodreads as it helps so much. Thank you.

THE JOFFE BOOKS STORY

We began in 2014 when Jasper agreed to publish his mum's much-rejected romance novel and it became a bestseller.

Since then we've grown into the largest independent publisher in the UK. We're extremely proud to publish some of the very best writers in the world, including Joy Ellis, Faith Martin, Caro Ramsay, Helen Forrester, Simon Brett and Robert Goddard. Everyone at Joffe Books loves reading and we never forget that it all begins with the magic of an author telling a story.

We are proud to publish talented first-time authors, as well as established writers whose books we love introducing to a new generation of readers.

We have been shortlisted for Independent Publisher of the Year at the British Book Awards three times, in 2020, 2021 and 2022, and for the Diversity and Inclusivity Award at the Independent Publishing Awards in 2022.

We built this company with your help, and we love to hear from you, so please email us about absolutely anything bookish at feedback@joffebooks.com

If you want to receive free books every Friday and hear about all our new releases, join our mailing list: www.joffebooks.com/contact

And when you tell your friends about us, just remember: it's pronounced Joffe as in coffee or toffee!

ALSO BY MCGARVEY BLACK

STANDALONES

TRUST ONLY ME

THE FIRST HUSBAND

MY SISTER'S KILLER

THE WOMAN UPSTAIRS

Printed in Great Britain
by Amazon

57280663R00158